Mosaic Man

for all in the family, including friends

Mosaic Man

Ronald Sukenick

Normal

Published by FC2
with support given by the English Department
Unit for Contemporary Literature of
Illinois State University and the Illinois Arts Council.

Address all inquiries to:
FC2
Unit for Contemporary Literature
Illinois State University, Campus Box 4241
Normal, IL 61790-4241

ISBN: 1-57366-079-5

Library of Congress Cataloging-in-Publication Data
Sukenick, Ronald.
Mosaic man / Ronald Sukenick.
p. cm.
ISBN 1-57366-079-5 (alk. paper)
1. Jews—United States—Fiction. I. Title.
PS3569.U33M67   1999
813'.54--dc21   98-53043
CIP

Book Design: Martin Riker
Cover Design: Todd Michael Bushman
Cover Image: after a silk screen by Caroline Sury
Produced and Printed in the United States of America
Printed on recycled paper with soy ink

This program is partially sponsored by a grant from the Illinois Arts Council

Portions of this novel were originally published, in whole or in part, in
*After Yesterday's Crash: the Avant-Pop Anthology, Before Columbus Fiction
Anthology, Boulevard, Fiction, Fiction International, New Letters, O. Henry
Prize Stories, Rampike, The Southern California Anthology*, and *Witness*.

CONTENTS

I. TESTIMONY

II. WRITING

I. TESTIMONY

GENES

In the beginning was the WORD which is unspeakable, unreadable and unintelligible. Beyond human perception. Sublime. Writing not yet language. Dazzle. Pure information. Generative. Algorithmic. Digital, i.e. DNA. Digital Not Analog. Helical. The master code. Original. The first person. Iconoclastic. Always beginning.

Then the WORD says. It says language. It says analogy. A metaphor. A picture. RNA. Real Not Artificial. You. Mensch. Personal. Genetic. Chronic. Iconic. Scripture. A story. Worth thousands of words. All of them analogous. Guilt. Knowledge. Dream. The world, i.e. A mensch in the world. The WORD in the world. In the book of life. There but hidden. Finding it. In the story. As promised.

Inevitably the pictures are replicated. Multiplied. Viral. Simulacra, i.e. Facsimiles. Androids. Manikins. Gelded. Gilded. Scripted. Analogy becomes anality. A nullity. Idolatry. Sublimated. Assimilated. Dissimulated. Story becomes history. Becomes nightmare. Obsessive. Frozen. Dead data. Generic. Pillars of salt. Words in vain. Graven images finally. Imitation. Fake. Not you. Losing it. In the same world as you.

Where's the WORD?

What's the story?

9

*　*　*

1988. The Arab music sifts into the room over a narrow alley in working class Paris. It sifts like the morning light through the gauzy curtains swaying slightly against the long windows.

The alley is populated by French proletarians, Black and North Africans, East Indians, Orientals, Tamil Separatists, Moslem Fundamentalists, women wrapped in gorgeous patterned African cloth or covered face to foot in monotone robes, and kids of all ages and colors. At the end of the alley he hears men trilling at one another in some rhythmic African language, while out on the street, he knows, a knot of Arabs in the cafe called Djerba la Douce are jabbering in Arab, French housewives are gossiping in the bakery called La Duchesse Exquise, and down the block in El Palomar de los Taxistas the cabbies are arguing in Portuguese.

The woman upstairs is having another attack of logorrhea. She's crazy half the time. She's also half Jewish. Her mother's half. The half that counts. Several times a year she goes off the deep end, opens her windows and treats the neighbors to a monologue that morning noon and night can last three days.

During which time she periodically tosses the contents of the apartment into the court, cushions, towels, hats, brassieres, food, garbage, dishes, small articles of furniture, until you wonder how much could be left up there.

"One is chez soi. Eh! One is in one's own home. Why should they try to bother you? Eh! You don't interfere with me, I don't interfere with you. It's not your onions. Eh!"

Then singing: "Today is the day of paradise."

Then very loud: "Salaud! Bastard! Someone is going to put a knife in you. Eh! Cut you up. Eh! No, monsieur. I'm not a virgin. I've been a virgin more than once, but not this time. No, monsieur. I want to have a good time. Like anyone. That's normal. You think I live in some other world? No, monsieur. Never again. I live in the same world as you. Whether you like it or not. One is chez soi. Eh! You can't get rid of me just like that.

Eh! Like garbage. Eh! Not in my own apartment. In the same world as you. Unless you intend to kill me. You think just because you're stronger. Just because you can . . . Ah, no! That, no! One draws some lines. One puts one's foot down. They think they can do what they want with me. But I have friends. Important friends. Very important friends, monsieur, no matter what. Eh! Friends who will step in at just the right moment and turn the sky to blood. To blood, monsieur. You understand? This is France, after all. One is chez soi."

The Vietnamese across the way turns his Oriental music on. Loud.

Even the dogs are forced to be polyglot in this seething confusion of internationality. A patchwork of laundry hangs from the windows. At the alley entrance a fat lady holds her German Shepherd's leash as it shits on the curb-your-dog logo in the sidewalk. Residents at their windows observe one another across the cobblestones while avoiding one another's eyes.

Watching this scene from his desk through the long windows, it's clear to Ron that Europe, Africa, the East is where it all came from back in the States. The ingredients survive the melting pot.

That's probably why, when Ron picks up the phrase "les règles du jeu"—the rules of the game—from a conversation down below, he paranoidly puns it to mean "Jewish rules."

Even here, in this mongrel corner of cosmopolis.

Because for the first time here since the Petain regime under the Nazis, a clearly racist party has gained power and influence. It's as if there had been a break in the narrative during which time became meaningless, during which apocalyptic events occurred but had no reality, were not really registered in the collected conscious, and suddenly the story begins again.

"Saturday and Sunday," one member of the National Front is quoted as saying in today's paper, "between the Jews and the Arabs who invade the boulevards, you can no longer go out. We're invaded by a fauna that doesn't represent the true France. An old

11

Parisian of French stock can no longer be found in Paris."

Neo-fascist skinheads attack Blacks, Arabs and other "foreigners" in the metros of Paris and the streets of Brittany.

There's a movement afoot, echoed by one in Germany and led by a historian named Robert Faurisson, to deny the historical reality of the Holocaust.

Scholars are probing the Nazi sympathies of influential thinkers like Heidigger, and the behavior of intellectuals during the occupation.

The right wing parties are falling all over themselves to form a quick coalition with the extreme right National Front, led by a man named Jean-Marie Le Pen. Simone Weil, the most eminent Jewish politician in France, has tried to object cautiously to the deal some of her colleagues have made with Le Pen. The response from one presumably non-extremist politician: "The more she talks, the more she fosters anti-semitism in France."

In other words, Jews had better keep their mouths shut.

Le Pen is mightier than the word.

Raymond Barre, the ex-Prime Minister, has declared himself "troubled" by the coalition with the racists. He who remarked on the bombing of a synagogue that it killed a Jew and two innocent people.

The day during the German occupation when he was arrested by the Nazis, Maurice Cling said, had been a day when "I was very happy. Because the weather was nice, it was the month of May and it was my birthday in addition. I was very happy because I knew I was going to get the present of a pen. I was fifteen. I had been at school in the morning and I knew I was going to have a party. I had a new suit. I felt too well dressed because I didn't like wearing new clothes vis-à-vis my school comrades.

"They arrested me at school. Because the Nazis had forgotten me in their list. And it was my mother who asked that they come and get me at school. Because she thought that it was necessary to stay together in order to help one another.

"We didn't understand at all. Some weeks before, we had a cousin in Toulouse who had sent his young wife, who wasn't Jewish, with some false identity cards for my parents, which she hid in a skein of wool, with her baby in her arms, knitting. And inside the wool were the identity cards so that with them we could hide. A young woman, not Jewish, twenty or so years old, come from Toulouse to risk her life for some people she's never seen. And my mother said 'No,' because my older brother had to pass his high school degree in a week or two, and for them it was very important for Jews to pursue their studies, and that they should pass their baccalaureate, and she said, 'Afterwards, we'll see.' Which shows very well that we had no awareness of the danger.

"It was perhaps naive of them, but at the time it was absolutely unthinkable that a man like my father who had been decorated with the two most important medals France could award during World War One, with the glory, if you will, of Verdun, with these men that were considered as gods, the idea that one could take these men and massacre them without any apparent reason, now even, when you read the history, it's difficult to believe or understand.

"The image that I retain was that we didn't have enough to eat, we suffered from certain persecutions, there were restrictions as to schedules and stores, for the metro, for everything, that made life more and more difficult, with a menace that became more pronounced, always in mystery.

"We didn't know where people were sent. There was some information on the radio, I heard my parents talking about it between themselves but they hid it from us. We didn't really believe it because it was unbelievable. We believed it was probably propaganda. There were many rumors, also, in those conditions. So it was difficult among the crowd of rumors to know what was the truth.

"And besides, what was the truth was not plausible. You see?

"So we could more easily attach ourselves to lies which were credible. Normal people could not believe those things.

"Thus the shock of deportation, where I was plunged into the worst, that is, Auschwitz, the Nazi system of extermination, where they threw off their mask completely, the shock for me was proportional to this unreal world, this cocoon in which I lived and the school which carried on with its ideology—liberal, humanist, literary. You understand?"

"I did not say he was lying," said Supreme Court Justice Felix Frankfurter, on hearing about it from an eye witness. "I said that I don't believe him. There is a difference. My mind, my heart, they are made in such a way that I cannot conceive it."

But Felix Frankfurter should be able to say, "What's happening here is that something is happening that is not happening, you see. That is, of course it's happening but not for us. And perhaps it's not even happening to them, although of course it is, because they can't conceive it. Because this can't happen. This is impossible, impossible even though it's happening, if you follow me. So this means either it is real, or we are real, we can't have it both ways. And we know we are real. Because if we aren't real who are we? If we aren't real anything can be real. And if this can happen then anything can happen and when does it stop? Nothing follows from what came before, one thing has nothing to do with another. So it can't be happening and if it is I cannot conceive it, I have no explanation."

This is where Felix Frankfurter would lose it. His words would stop referring to anything.

Ignore what he just said.

Didier has never personally encountered anti-semitism, he explains at the beginning of dinner. His last name, he says, is not necessarily Jewish. He doesn't have many Jewish friends, he isn't especially Jewish. He isn't a Zionist. His family has been in France a long time.

"I know we were very lucky during the war because the family didn't lose anyone in the camps. In general I'd say that the French

Jews who had many, many problems, who were deported massively, who were denounced, tortured, massacred, etcetera, were mainly the foreign Jews. Those who were denounced by the French, it was always the immigrants, the others."

It's not a problem for his wife, being married to a Jew, nor is the marriage a problem for Didier, he says during the leg of lamb.

But it's a problem for her family.

Their relations with her are much less warm since her marriage. For her mother, unconsciously, he's different, not like the others.

"I who felt myself not Jewish," says Didier, "for the first time, I felt different. As soon as there's a little something, it comes up. From the exterior, everything's fine. But there's a false note. It's the first time I've run across this genre of anti-semitism. It's true that it poses some problems for us, for our well being."

"Oh yes?" says his wife. "You say that?"

"Pardon me, I hope it's not so. Because on occasion it springs out, something that's hidden. Because I feel this sort of bias that upsets me, that takes me by surprise because it's the first time that I've experienced that sort of behavior."

"It's a kind of behavior of the ordinary French person that's quite frequent," adds Didier over dessert. "Not overtly hostile, but always a little phrase, an allusion, that I feel because I can't do otherwise, and in fact it's a little disagreeable.

"Not that I lose sleep over it."

What's the story? Am I a Jew? Maybe the question is inside out. Because ours is a Jewish civilization at its root. Rx two tablets. Jewish rules. Holy moses, that was the deal. Remember? My world is your world. Maybe the problem is denial. Denying mine is denying yours.

How many of you have had the feeling that you're from another world, not this one? That you're someone else, not the person you're supposed to be?

That's sometimes Ron's feeling and sometimes events bear it out. That must be the way it feels to be Jewish, and even if you think you're not a Jew, if you've ever felt that way you may be Jewish too. Whether Christian, Moslem, if you go back far enough. Even if you think you're not.

> Scholars and Descendants Uncover
> Hidden Legacy of Jews in Southwest:
> After several centuries, scholars are
> uncovering the history of Spanish Jews
> who converted to Catholicism under
> threat of expulsion by Spain's monarchs
> in 1492 and then found refuge and
> obscurity in the mountains of New
> Mexico. Daniel Yocum, a twenty-three
> year old engineering student, suspected
> he had Jewish roots. Ramon Salas discov-
> ered he was related to Daniel Yocum after
> tracing his own lineage 17 generations.
> "Personally, whether someone is truly a
> Jew or not, only God can judge, and not
> mortals." (*New York Times*)

Personally, being Jewish is just an advanced case of being human, and being human may be a terminal disease that's run its course. Personally, maybe we're just beings, forget human, beings among other beings, some hairy, some furry, some feathery, some leathery, and some who possibly will soon arrive from other sectors of the universe.

Exiting Brooklyn as a kid Ron too is looking for something, though he doesn't know what it is.

But that's normal. If he knows what it is he wouldn't have to look for it. It comes as if from outer space and hovers in his mind like a forgotten word, a sign, a sanction, a symbol, a ghostly oscar, but not the glitzy oscar of Hollywood. A serious oscar, unreal, that makes everything else real.

Whatever it is, he thinks it may be rooted in Europe. He thinks maybe they'd left it there. Or brought it with them in the exodus and lost it en route. Or maybe Ron lost it when he was a kid. He doesn't know what it is but he knows he's going to have to trace the root.

Where's the story?
What's the word?
Are you a
Jew?
You.

EX/ODE

Annotated Family Annals
    Analog recorder—transcription and analysis
      Legend:

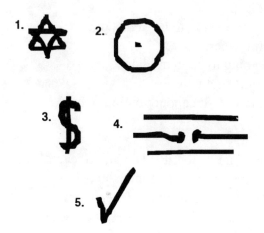

1. Jewish rules; 2. reality; 3. making it/losing it;
4. reel/unreal; 5. the true story, the word.

—>

Hello?

Hello?

Hello, mother?

Oh yeah, hello Ronnie, how are you?

Good, how are you?

Sort of lonesome.

You know, I'm coming next week.

You're coming next week?

Yeah, I'll be in New York next weekend.

Uh-huh. Oh I'll be so happy to see you. I feel so forsaken.

Well I'll be there soon.

Are you writing another book?

Yes, I'm writing another one. And you're going to be in it too, this one.

Huh?

You're going to be in this one. From the tapes we made. The recorder is on now.

I didn't hear.

I said you're going to be in this one.

I'm going where?

You're going to be in my book.

I don't quite get you.

I'm going to write about you in my book.

Oh. Really?

Yes.

Oh, that's interesting. I'll be glad to read it.

Yeah. I think it should be interesting.

It's so good to talk to you. I feel so forsaken.

Yes. Well I can understand that. But I'll see you soon, doesn't that cheer you up?

When are you coming in?

Next weekend.

You're coming next week?

Yeah.

Oh. Good. I'll be so happy to see you. I feel so forsaken.

Yeah.
I'll see you then.
Yeah, I'll see you soon then.
Okay, darling.
Lots of love.
Love.
Bye.
Bye.

—>

It's quite complicated.
It's not complicated, Dad.
Well, when you know how.
The only way you can erase it is by recording over it again.
Well, when you press that, does that press the two together?
Yeah. But you can press only one of them, too.
Now, what is this to press without the red, what is that for?
To play. To stop press stop.
This is to stop. And what's this?
Well, I'm gonna show you.
Now everything we say is being recorded?
Now everything we say is being recorded. Okay, now it's recording.
Now it's recording. Hello there! Now what are we looking for?
I'll know when I find it.
I didn't know we lost it.

—>

My father escaped from Russia because they wanted him

to serve in the army   he
ruined one of his eyes

He ruined one of his
eyes purposely? How

I don't know, he did
something, he stuck a pin or
his

eye so that they couldn't take him in the service.

They
wouldn't take him   right to this
country   the smartest thing he
    Your grandmother's   Bialystok,
  a cloth mill

where the house was.

—>

you both had fathers who made a lot of
  lost it
    Well my father lost a lot of   he had
partners who were crooks. But he made a lot   He was
considered the richest man in

    And my father   the sewing machine
business
                  invent   he
never had it patented. He was too busy goin out havin good
times.
    Singer Sewing Machines

they took it. When my father died,
he didn't have a dime

He spent money like a drunken sailor. If he would, you know,
buy a plant or a factory and then sell it, right away he used to
close the business and
go away

Saratoga, or to
Sharon Springs

$

—they in Bklyn kept sending false alarms i
knowing the dreaded phone call would come one
day he'd been sick—that morning when i almost
*died myself—though found the tapes—*transcribed
here—maybe this is where they lost it—$ = making
it = cars sex food America—making it is losing it—

He had a car, a
Chevrolet, with a bell
on the front of it, and
that was in Saratoga
Springs, and there were
very wealthy men there
that had Packards, Pierce Arrows, Cadillacs. So he'd say to one
of them, 'What kind of car you got?' The man would say, 'I got a
Pierce Arrow,' that was supposed to be one of the best, he'd say,
'That's also a good car.' He had a little Chevrolet.

A little Chevrolet.

That's also a good car.

mother, how she suffered.

hell on earth.

why don't you take your wife? He
said, 'I got enough for one.'

proud of his
children.

Oh yeah.

He said, 'This is my stock.'

My stock.

He used to call us 'my stock.'

to New
York.

Yeah.

a restaurant.

Shapiro's!

23

One of the best known

'Mr. Frey is here, Mr. Frey is here!' They all came running, we got attention like we were the King of England.

He used to spend a fortune there.

It's funny, it's true, when you mention that, both rich men all their lives.

But one was stingy and the other was a spendthrift, right?

Stingy. They never had a sled, they never had a roller skate. Nothing.

—the way it was—a fingerprint of reality—not $ but jewish rules—halakha the law *haggadah the story—the dreaded phone call at 5 a.m.—he fell down she called police and ambulance—the morning i found the tapes—stored above a radiator damaged—*

we were ten children and a mother and father. And when we used to have seders, all around the table, and it was really something that if you'd see it now it would be a phenomenon, to see all these children, all so devoted to their

your father religious?

temple not because he was religious, he was far from a religious man. But the women over there made such a fuss over him. He was a good looking man, he was six feet tall. He was six feet tall. And the women just

They practically threw themselves

But he was   If the girl forgot to put salt on the table, he wouldn't ask for it. He got up, he took his hat and coat, and he walked out. He was such a tyrant. Morris took right after

mean like Morris?

My father was so busy with himself

Morris was really the father

24

Her father   wine, women and song. He could do without the song, but he couldn't do without the wine and the

—>

Granma. You know, my mother never wanted to go visit Brooklyn   she was a fearful person anyway, she'd been through a pogrom in Bialystok or someplace like that.

But anyway, Granma Sukenick
always smiling, she was full of life, she was just like
Or like   your father was an outgoing guy
            like Isadore. Isadore you know
always had a dirty joke, a big cigar in his mouth.

                                    in
the first place, do you remember the house, what that was like? It must have been a mansion for some wealthy guy, because you'd walk in, and down in that ground level there was a stove as big as between those two walls, one of those coal stoves. And there was a big table. And no matter when you came, there were people eating there. Not family   it was a place
                              where they knew, if you
                              needed a meal, you
                              know, just off the boat,
                              whatever, come to the
                              Sukenick's house

—can't retrieve everything but this is the story—
not history but the word itself as spoken—before   she was always
my mad dash into Bklyn and into the past—and   cooking.
my near-fatal collision with it—*i hung up the
phone and threw on some clothes fighting out of
sleep out of dream running down to the car—to the
real not artificial not the received version—*   fell down

and had an accident, she died right after that.

I remember that they sat shiva in the driveway, it must have been the spring, and the old man, he was very agnostic, he didn't believe in anything, he had no truck with any of that stuff, and he wouldn't let them sit more than one or two days, that was all, that's enough, go home, just remember what she was like.

—>

we had a barn, if I could write a story about what happened in that barn . . . [laughter] Oh yeah.

You had a horse

I didn't do that with a horse. I might have done it with a cow, but not a horse . . . [laughter]

amongst a bunch of gentile girls. Myrtle Tinkle was one of them, I still remember the name, Myrtle Tinkle. She lived right next door to us, a gentile girl. They were all gentile girls. It was great. A lot of fun. One time I got a punch in the jaw because I

There were very few Jews, very few Jews. Irish and Swedish. And if you'd go to the synagogue on Rosh Hashonah and Yom Kippur, and you'd walk past the corner, they'd be standing on the corner, there were whatchacall saloons then, today you'd call them taverns, you used to walk past and they'd say, 'Sheeny! Dirty Jews!' They'd call you names, y'know and all. Terrible! The toughest. The toughest of the tough. I used to get into a fight every day of the week.

start doing his building there. Brooklyn was just about developing, you know.

farmers, we had cows all near us, we had our own horse in our back yard. We'd grow vegetables in our back yard. We'd grow tomatoes, radishes, cucumbers, lettuce. We had a great big grape arbor, we'd have grapes all the time, big black and white grapes, and when the sun was out we used to sit there in the shade and eat black grapes and play pinochle at the same time.

—>

I must have been about fifteen, because when I graduated high school, I cried for days because I wanted to go back to school. But who ever heard of a girl going back to school after high school, they never heard of such a thing. So I had to go to work.

Mr. James, who worked for   He was trying to make you too. He was a football player, but he worked for
I was afraid to be alone with him.

a big husky guy. Yeah, I remember him. Oh, what a great football player he was, woohoo! He played with a team called the Emeralds. They were the team that started all these fancy plays, like forward passes.

—>

The son married one of the most beautiful girls. You never met anyone so pretty in your whole life. Besides being pretty, the father was a judge, and he had so much money, and the mother had so much money. The son became a lawyer and he opened up an office, and his father-in-law, who's got a great deal of influence, got him in, and he's the assistant to a District Attorney.

And he's got three children.

Three beautiful children.

I haven't seen them but I'm told, in your life, you

—knowing death and fear the real thing at 5 a.m.
not the version with the $ behind it—jumped into
car still sleep eyed—**what are they talking about**
here she was ugly the kids brats the judge a swine—
haven't seen such three beautiful children.

Well he's good looking and his wife is beautiful. Beautiful. She's gorgeous. Absolutely gorgeous.

They were millionaires. Do you know that with a chauffeured limousine? They had five in help. Sadie's in-laws had five in help. They had a cook, they had a waitress, they had a nurse, and they had five in help. They lived in an apartment in New York that was considered one of the finest apartments.

—>

Do you remember Three Finger Brown?
Sure I do.
Where did you meet him?
Sophie Katz had a home on the same block that he did near Long Beach.
And he said, 'Good morning, how are you this morning?'
All the gangsters used to congregate there.
We met him. So cordial.
Three Finger Brown was a former baseball pitcher for the Chicago Cubs, he only had three fingers. And this fellow had two fingers shot off by the gangsters. A different man. But he was executed.
He was so cordial.
Where was he shot?
I don't know whether it was in his head or his . . .
No, I mean what part of New York?
Where he lived. A very

28

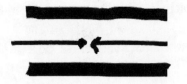

nice man.
So pleasant.
But. If you crossed him
the next morning you
were gonna die.
And he was so cordial.

—as long as you're wealthy—the legend unreels what's the story here, the word, the gospel?—i speed down to the Bklyn-Battery Tunnel tires screeching around battery on fdr drive not yet realizing it was a deathtrap—me going into Bklyn bumping into what was coming out—

around here too

the house next to the Long Island Railroad cut
there.

That was where the legendary Murder, Inc.

used to
pay off the cops too.

Sal's barber
shop?
Yup.
So I grew up having my hair cut
This whole neighborhood was nothing but gang leaders. And don't worry, they did me out of plenty of money. If I'd do a job for them and they owed me, say, three hundred dollars, they'd pay me a hundred and say that's all they're gonna pay me. Who could argue with them?
Once I had to fix a bridge for one
'fix the hole or you're in the hole, you get
bumped,' that's the way they talked.
and he never showed up, and I threw it away finally, I melted it for the gold.
next day who walks into the office
'if you come back later I'll give it you.'
'Either you give it to me or I give it to you.'
Well a month elapsed and he never showed up. But after

29

that they found him in the East River, with his head battered in, his body all tied up in chains

—>

Remember Ernie Fall?
I remember him.   The aviator.
What happened to him?
He died. He was a booze artist.

                                        he was chasing
around with a lot of women too.
          a very handsome guy.

He was, yeah. And he was a fighter. Boy.

                                        But he
was drinking too much.
          You know, when the war started, he was the pilot
                    in Atlanta, Georgia,
          all over the country y'know in that big plane
                    they used to sometimes land in Floyd
Bennett Field. And when he landed at Floyd Bennett Field he
used to say, 'Come on over to Floyd Bennett Field, I'll take you
up in a plane.' But I wouldn't go up with him, you know why?
He used to do tricks in the plane, somersaults, and I would never
take a chance with im.
          But he was some guy, he was quite a guy. Then he was dis-
gusted with being around the United States, he wanted to go out
to some other country. He went to India, I think. And he used to
fly a plane over the Himalaya Mountains. But he was a booze
artist, he used to drink—he took about ten cures and nothing
helped him
                    I wanted to be an aviator.

—so this is the story?—the story of losing it? *jewish rules?—i go speeding into the tunnel entrance—out of the sentimental fantasy i could do something about the situation—*

You know, my mother, I'll never forget it as long as I live. She says, 'If I have to die, I want to die in my own home. I don't want to go to a nursing home.' She pleaded. And Uncle Morris and Aunt Dora said, 'What do you mean she said she can't go to a nursing home. It's the only place for her.' I said, 'She wants to be at home, she wants to stay in her own bed. Leave her here. I'm here, you're not here. I live downstairs. Get a nurse. I'll see that she's all right.' And they said to me, I still remember the words as though it were yesterday. Uncle Morris says to me, 'Either you put up or shut up.' Either put up all the money for everything or shut up and mind your own business.

Her oldest brother was so cold-hearted. Oh!

And I remember, when I went to that home, and my mother was crying, it was about a week before she died. I'll carry that to my grave with me.

—>

Grandpa lived in a little brown stone house in Coney Island. As I remember, he was actually living with a woman out there. Oh no. But he had a lot of women in his life.

I know that. It's a family trait.

And they were all really very unfair about that, by the way.

Why were they unfair about it?

Oh, you know, your mother and the sisters. Oh I could

31

understand it. What I remember about him he was alone, and he was old. And my father used to take me on Sunday morning, we'd come up these two steps and he'd be sitting on the porch all by himself. And he was such a handsome man.

Everybody said that.

He was so handsome, I can't tell you. He was really such a good-looking man. And he'd sit there alone, and I used to feel sorry for him because he was always so alone. He'd rock on that chair.

His wife had died already?

Rebecca? No.

So why were they living separately?

They threw him out. The children and she all got together and they threw him out.

The story I'd heard was that he'd gone away to live with some woman in Coney Island.

This was Coney Island. If there was a woman there I didn't see her. He sat alone.

—>

I think we ought to have some more wine.

Let's get a half a carafe.

What's that? I don't know what I'm eating.

That's veal parmesan. You've had veal parmesan lots of times. Don't you know what that is?

Ronnie, you want string beans?

Veal parmesan. Taste it. You want some spaghetti?

Maybe later, not now.

Mother, would you like some chicken?

No.

I can't eat all this.

No, you can have it.

I'm not hungry, Gloria.

Here take it.
Just a little.
Who would like some fish? Would you like some fish?
How is it?
It's good, you want to taste it? Want some, Dad?
What is it?
How's yours?
Ooo, good. Taste a piece.
What is it?
Veal parmesan. Did you want some spaghetti?
Not right now, thanks. Don't forget to eat your string beans.
Me?
Getting him to eat vegetables. He wouldn't eat a vegetable if you sit on your ear.
That's good isn't it, Dad?
The string beans are very good.
He likes the way they're cooked, they have garlic.
Yeah, they got garlic in them.
I'll make them that way at home. With olive oil?
Any kind of oil is okay.
You want some spaghetti?

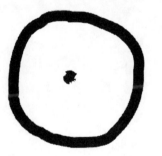

—reality at last—*headlights cars coming at me*—

No thanks.
It's good.
I'm sure it is.
You don't like spaghetti?
I like spaghetti, but I don't want any now.
Taste a piece of this veal.
I have some fish.

That's all right.
Don't you like it?
Yeah.
The string beans are good, aren't they good?

What did you order?

Fish.

Is it good?

Want some?

Why don't you just taste it to see if you like it?

I'll trade you some veal for some fish. How about that? Make a trade?

Yeah.

Here's the fish.

Who wants some veal parmesan? It's good.

You like the fish, Dad?

Huh?

You like that fish?

This is not fish.

That's fish, what you're eating now. This is fish that you just cut.

No, this is veal parmesan.

—the law is honor thy father and mother—the reality is eating—trying to get back—the family— but there's something fishy here—pathos or farce of the lost supper—one will betray us—me—

But what you're eating right now is fish.

Oh, no, it isn't. I can tell the difference between veal parmesan and fish.

How?

By taste.

You didn't taste it yet. Taste that.

It is fish. Who put it there?

A little genie.

That is fish.

Nobody want any veal parmesan?

Mother, would you like a little more veal? Ronnie's full.

Here's a piece of veal parmesan.

No, I don't want any, I'm trying to get rid of mine.

I thought you had fish.

You just gave me some veal parmesan before. You gave me half of what you had on your plate.

Why don't you order lobster?
What?
They have wonderful lobster and clams.
Have some spaghetti.
There's more there.
Eat some spaghetti, it's so good for you.
There's more there.
You want a little bit of chicken now?

—>

He fell.
You fell. Where did you fall?
I didn't hurt myself.
Where did you fall?

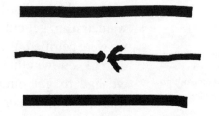

—i was careening down the wrong lane of the tunnel—two lanes of cars heading right at me i was going to die—glimpse of traffic cop his hand over his eyes me jerking the wheel—

On the floor.
Well, how come?
I heard a thud, and I ran in.
I saw your mother's beautiful figure and I fainted.
I see. What did you do, trip on something?

Where did you trip? What happened?
Outside of the bathroom.
What happened that you fell?
I was tryin to do an acrobatic stunt.

You know, during the night I wake up, I can't find him. He's not in bed, he's not anywhere. I jump out of bed and I found him in the bathroom.

Well I'm allowed to go to the bathroom during the night.
I thought something happened to him.

What do you think about the lawyer?

He's very good, you got the best lawyer possible for this kind of case.

But I mean, what do you think is going to happen, do you know?

Nothing's gonna happen. You're gonna keep the apartment, and that's that.

I don't believe a word that this landlord says. How did you make out with the lawyer? Did he think there's any hope for us?

Yeah, you don't have to worry about anything. You don't have to worry about the apartment.

Do you like the lawyer?

—wheels screamed car tipped reversed direction—
—you can't cross the same river twice—you pay
your toll the waters part you're out—you can't go
back—it backfires the lawyer's deal ends in
betrayal my fault—they invent their own story
innocent and pathetic—but the reel is unreal—they
lost it—for the true story go to the teller not the
tale—the writer not the writ—hand writing mind
dreaming—

Yes, he's a very nice man.

When the landlord wanted us to get out, we were petrified. We didn't know whether we had to get out. Dad was working on a patient, all of a sudden the phone rings, and I thought he was busy and the nurse didn't come in yet, so I jumped out of bed and I answered the phone. 'By tomorrow morning,' over night, 'I want to see your furniture, I want to see your dental office, out on the sidewalk.'

We're accustomed to the apartment, I like the apartment.

You know, Ronnie, I hesitate to make any drastic move with him. You know, it frightens me.

—>

You know what, I still believe, Ronnie, a loaf of bread, a jug of wine and thou. Right?

You still believe that.

A groan.

What's the matter?

I'm sleepy.

You know, when you sit home with him all day with no place to go, it's a terrible feeling. And especially Thanksgiving, Christmas, these holidays, and all my friends have either moved away, or they're gone. And it's a lonely feeling.

—>

This is a beautiful apartment. Do you think Dad could see it?

Probably.

Yes, I'm sure he can, Mom.

Tomorrow I'll wake up thinking I dreamed this all.

Actually, Mother, this is a dream. I didn't want to tell you this.

Mother, are you having fun?

Am I ever. Tomorrow I'll think it was a dream, I won't believe it.

Gloria says it is a dream.

It's a dream.

I keep sitting here and wishing Dad were here.

Me too.

What is that?

A tape recorder. In case you don't remember you were here, we can play you the tape.

We can prove it. We want to make sure we have evidence you were here.

I just looked in the mirror and saw myself so grey!

—>

It must have been very hard on you to have your closest sister, Sadie, die young.

I never got over it. I feel so forsaken. So uprooted. So meaningless. I think it was all a dream. Do you know that the night she died, and this is the gospel truth, she woke up that night, and she says, 'Now I see the story.' And she died an hour later.

—maybe it is a dream—otherwise how does it happen that i can look out the window of this very same apartment and see the tunnel entrance where i almost died except for quick reflexes—that's too coincidental to be real— Bklyn still coming at me but me now safely above it?—as i listen to the end of my mother's story—which she thinks is a dream—the tape recorder doesn't prove anything—i could have dreamed it all up—but aren't dreams real too?— a way of getting at the truth?—the final story?—

the only gospel
the hand writing

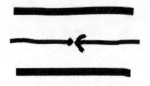

UMBILICUS

He looked for Benny down in the basement, where he often worked with his tools. He wanted to tell Benny about his two dreams. One was the one he had when he was awake about taking off with Captain Midnight in the Flying Wing. The other was the one he kept having when he was asleep about being thrown into this completely dark box where, paralyzed, he couldn't breathe.

But when Benny came down he said he only had time to read him a comic strip because the family was coming over, which one did he want him to read. So Ronnie picked "Terry and the Pirates," and Benny opened the paper and started reading.

"'Why so soft-hearted, Terry?' asks Hu Shee," sez Benny. "'We'll hang if that dolt reports our stealing his boat,' she says."

"Who's Hu Shee?"

"Yer not supposed to know."

"What's a 'dolt'? A grown-up?"

"Sometimes I tink so," sez My Uncle Benny. "But yer tinkin of 'adult.' That ain't the same ting. A 'dolt's a dope. Not all adults are dopes, ainit?"

"You ain't."

"I dunno about that. Anyways, they're rowin down the river in this boat, see, an Terry sez to her, 'I may be soft—but I know how I'd feel in that native's place!' and Hu Shee sez, 'I do not see how you people ever win a war.'"

"Watsat mean?"

"It means if yuh wanna win yuh gotta be mean."

"Izzat true?" I ask.

"Maybe it depends on what you wanna win, ainit? It depends on yer dream."

"What dream?"

"Everybody's got a dream."

"So where were you when I sold it?" The Uncles were saying as Ronnie came upstairs. The Uncles were there. They were all eating something, nuts, bananas, chicken fat on matzo, chopped chicken liver, noshes that his grandmother set out. The Uncles ate all the time whatever they were doing and they were all fat, as if they believed in the survival of the fattest. They were all smoking big cigars and the room was filled with smoke.

"You were supposed to wait for us," complained The Uncles.

"Where were you?" asked The Uncles.

"We were on the road, where did you think we were?" answered The Uncles.

"I don't care where you were, you weren't there. So I set the price, what did you expect?"

"We expect some money."

"I told you, there was no more money. You got what you got and that's it."

"Impossible, you couldn't let it go for that."

"Take it or leave it."

"Son of a bitch."

"Who you calling son of a bitch?"

"You, you son of a bitch."

"Wait a minute, wait a minute," said The Uncles. "Forget it. He can make it up next time. You can make it up next time, right?"

"Like hell I will," said The Uncles.

"Listen, listen, brothers shouldn't fight, ainit?" said My Uncle Benny.

"What do you know about it," said The Uncles.

"It's only money, ainit, it's only money."

The Uncles looked at one another and burst into loud laughter, slapping their legs and holding their fat bellies.

"It's only money," The Uncles repeated, still laughing.

"I don't understand why people are mean to one another," said My Uncle Benny.

"That's because you're an idiot," said The Uncles.

"Not an idiot, just a little retarded."

"Not retarded, just a little slow."

"Just a little backward."

"A little bashful."

The Uncles belched.

"When's he gonna grow up?" asked The Uncles.

"Like the rabbi said before the briss, it won't be long now," answered The Uncles.

"Let's play cards," said The Uncles.

"Yeah, a little pinochle," The Uncles said. "Benny, get the cards."

They were supposed to meet Captain Midnight at Floyd Bennett Field. My Uncle Benny knew Ronnie's dream. That's why he used to take him to Floyd Bennett Field, its Fiorello LaGuardia Art Deco hangars, to watch the airplanes before it became a Naval Air Station with Marine guards at the gates and Vought Corsairs and Brewster Buffaloes and Grumman Wildcats in long rows with their wings folded up as if they were on aircraft carriers. So Ronnie knew Floyd Bennett Field, and he knew that long, low shadow at the far end that nobody was allowed to get close to.

Captain Midnight, of course, was the pilot and Ronnie was the co-pilot. The other Secret Squadron members assigned to this mission were Happy Landis and Sgt. Leibowitz. Happy Landis was the radio operator and gunner. She was one of the few pre-teenage girls allowed to participate in a secret mission.

41

Sgt. Leibowitz was the bombardier/navigator. Sgt. Leibowitz was dead, Ronnie had just found out about him in the *Brooklyn Eagle* that day because they were putting up a memorial window for him in the Ocean Parkway Jewish Center. The Ocean Parkway Jewish Center was where Ronnie would be bar mitzvahed, and Sgt. Leibowitz came from E. 4th St. near where Ronnie lived. He died in the Army Air Corps over England. He had enlisted just after high school. He was the newest member of their crew.

Ronnie was very young when he saw Howard Hughes land at Floyd Bennett Field after his record breaking round-the-world flight and he thought his name was Howard Huge because he was so tall, not to mention rich and powerful. It was Ronnie's opinion that Captain Midnight was actually Howard Huge in disguise.

Some people went by the house cheering and yelling. All he could hear was the word "dead."

"Hey, Hitluhs dead," he said.

"What do you mean?"

"I jus hoidim yellininna street."

"Heard," she said. "There was something in the paper."

She picked up the *Daily News* and turned the pages. "'Foreign Secretary Anthony Eden was asked in Commons whether he could confirm a report that Hitler had been assassinated,'" she read, "'but he brushed it aside.'"

Suddenly he heard more cheering and the name "Roosevelt." She heard it too.

"Turn on the radio," she said.

He turned on the radio, but all he could get was the soap operas. But it was getting noisier outside and this time they heard it clearly. "He's dead! Yay! Roosevelt's dead!"

"Ahm gone outside," he said.

"You stay in here!"

"A-a-a-h."

"Stay home. I don't want you out there."

But when she went in the other room he sneaked out anyway.

There were people running around the streets cheering and waving copies of the *Journal American* with a big headline on the front page: "ROOSEVELT DEAD!"

Uncle Met was not one of The Uncles even though they called him Uncle Met. Not only was he not one of The Uncles he was not like one of The Uncles. He was simply married to one of The Sisters. Uncle Met was as different from The Uncles as My Uncle Benny was from them even though they were his brothers. But they were not different in the same way. So though it seemed logical that Benny should be working for Uncle Met in his drug store, it was not working. It was not working because Benny couldn't stand waiting on the customers.

"He's a little bashful," said The Uncles.

"He's a little withdrawn."

"A little slow."

"A little slow? A little backward."

"A little backward! A little retarded."

"Retarded! He's a moron."

"He's an idiot," concluded The Uncles.

"But it's not his fault," said The Uncles.

"Then whose fault is it?" asked The Uncles.

"Maybe it's Met's fault."

"It's not Met's fault," said My Uncle Benny. "It's my fault because I'm an idiot."

"You could be an idiot and it could still be his fault," said The Uncles.

"Well it ain't," said Benny.

"Well it ain't my fault," said The Uncles. "And if it ain't my fault and it ain't your fault it must be his fault."

"What's my fault?" asked Met.

"I forget," said The Uncles.

"What I think," said Met, "is that Benny is not any kind of dope at all, what I think is that Benny is a special person. Maybe special persons shouldn't work in drug stores." Uncle Met said this though he was a special person and he worked in a drug store. But what was special about Met was that he read a lot of books and he read them in a lot of different languages. Ronnie doubted that The Uncles ever read any books in any language.

"What's so special?" asked The Uncles.

"He's a dreamer."

"So?"

"We need dreamers. We don't have too many."

"What do we need em for?"

"We need em to dream things up. That's what Benny is doing when he's not waiting on customers. He's dreaming things up."

"No, no, lemme explain," said My Uncle Benny. "I'm not an educated man like Met and it ain't easy for me to explain things, yeah? You think I'm a dreamer. Maybe you even think I'm an idealist. But I'm just a very simple person and everything I think is very simple. I know it seems idiotic when I try to explain, ainit."

Benny's fingers fluttered through the air as if they were trying to describe a shape and his hands were trembling.

"What I mean is I know I have lots of troubles and I'm lots of trouble for other people looking out for me, yeah? But what's the difference? How can anyone really be unhappy? What do my troubles count if anyone can be happy, ainit. If you can get above it all. I can't understand how you can pass by a tree and not be happy just seeing it. Sometimes I think there are so many beautiful things you see at every step you take, even the most idiotic person has to see they're beautiful, ainit. When you look at a child, when you look at a sunset or even at the grass. When you look into the eyes of another person and you see that under everything else he wants to love you and be loved by you, how can you be mean to anybody? We're all one person, including animals. It's so simple, yeah? And yet I can't put it into words."

Benny's hands dropped to his sides and he shrugged, looking depressed. "I wish I was as smart as the rest of you."

The Uncles stared at him as if he were some kind of bug.

"An idiot!" they said, exasperated.

"He's living in another world," they said.

"He should have been a rabbi," said Met.

"It's the only thing to do with people like that. At least a rabbi can make a living," said The Uncles.

"A living!" scoffed The Uncles. "A rabbi, you call that a living? How much could he make?"

"If he wants to make a living let him start a business," said The Uncles.

"Let him work for me," said The Uncles.

"For you!" exclaimed The Uncles. "God forbid. At sweatshop wages yet."

"So, I'll make him an executive, he's my brother," said The Uncles.

"An executive you'll make him, but you'll pay him slave labor."

"In America there is no slave labor," said The Uncles. "American values are like Jewish values. The American dream is our dream, that's why we do so well here."

"While they die in Europe," said Met.

"It's just the Polish Jews. The others he wouldn't touch," said The Uncles.

"Keep dreaming," said Met.

His father brought most of the papers home in the evening, but there was nothing yet about President Roosevelt. You had to listen to the radio to find out he had a cerebral hemmorhage.

In the papers the war news was good. The page one summary in the *Times* said that American tanks were sixty-three miles from Berlin and one hundred and sixteen miles from the Russians coming from the east. Goebbels said it won't be long now it said on the front page of the *Post*. On the front page of the *Tribune* it said that Germans in Hannover were fighting one another in a frenzy to loot stores in the city as it was occupied by American troops, and that a man in London predicted that it would be the style for men to carry handbags after the war. On page three it said that five million Jews had been killed at an extermination camp called Oswiecim. It said the same thing on page six of the *Times*. It said they were gassed without finding out whether they were guilty of anything. He asked his mother about it but she said it couldn't be true.

None of it could be true because it was impossible. Cheering Roosevelt's death was impossible. Ronnie killing Christ was impossible. The Nuns telling kids not to play with him was impossible.

What was true was a secret mission with Captain Midnight to help rescue prisoners in concentration camps. Take off tonight. People knew about the concentration camps but few people believed that almost everyone in the camps had already been killed. It couldn't be true.

He remembered almost nothing of the trip to Floyd Bennett Field. He remembered going to sleep. Then he remembered being thrown into a blind black box and he couldn't breathe. They had said nothing was going to happen to him but when he awoke he was strapped nude on a table facing a cabinet filled with sharp, gleaming knives. He knew they were going to cut his throat. He knew there was no sense struggling, his only chance was Jew Jitsu. In Jew Jitsu you use whatever you have as a weapon, and since he was strapped hand and foot naked there was only one weapon he had. When the young nurse's aide came in to wash and shave him, he asked her to unstrap his hands.

"Why?" she asked. "It won't be long now."

"I have to make a phone call," he said.

"I'll make it," she answered.

"You don't have the number."

"Give it to me."

"I'd like to."

"Why?"

"Because I love you."

Since he didn't have any clothes on she could see he was

46

telling the truth. He was thirteen, after all.

"You're very sincere," she said. "I respect sincerity. I'm sincere too."

She turned her hospital badge over and on the other side there was a Secret Squadron decoder badge. She undid his straps and handed him his parachute, a jump suit, leather boots, fleece lined leather jacket, and helmet and goggles.

"Contact," she said.

"Contact," he said. "What's your name?"

"Happy. Happy Landis. I have a message from The Judge."

"What Judge?"

"Kenesaw Mountain Landis. He says to tell you 'finders keepers, losers weepers.'"

"I see. Well we better get on it. I'm out of here."

When they arrived at Floyd Bennett, Captain Midnight was already at the controls and Sgt. Leibowitz was waiting for them in the hatch of the Flying Wing. "Thumbs up!" said Sgt. Leibowitz, thrusting up his thumbs. Then he looked at his watch and said, "We have a fighter escort till o one hundred. Lockheed P-38 Lightnings. Then we're on our own."

One of the things that worried Ronnie about the Flying Wing was that just before they took off they had a visit from his father and Dr. Lubitz. Dr. Lubitz was a colonel and he was giving everyone on board a medical. He didn't have to bother with Sgt. Leibowitz because he was dead, or with Happy Landis because she wasn't real. Captain Midnight was on the radio and didn't get sick. But when Dr. Lubitz took Ronnie's temperature he looked serious.

"It's going up," he said.

"You think it's infantile paralysis?" asked Ronnie's father.

"Since he was exposed it could be. If it's appendix we'll have to cut. We'll have to wait till the morning."

"But the March of Dimes . . . ?"

"That's the dream. The reality is something else."

47

* * *

Captain Midnight pushed the throttle gently forward and the plane started to taxi down the runway. Just then the radio crackled. "Do you read me?" said a voice over the radio.

"Master code five," said Captain Midnight. "25, 22, 18, 6, 25." Captain Midnight spoke in numbers! He had memorized the entire secret code on the decoder badge! Decoded, that meant, ROGER.

"This is Judge Kenesaw Mountain Landis," said the radio. It sounded a little like Red Barber broadcasting the Dodger games. "I want you to remember as you begin this momentous secret mission that there is nothing to fear but fear itself. This is our finest hour in a day that will live in infamy. The hand that held the dagger has plunged it into the back of its neighbor. We will fight them on the beaches, we will fight them on the farms. If necessary we will wait till next year. I have called Branch Rickey and told him that Leo Durocher is not a nice guy. I have told him that Dixie Walker is a nice guy but that he doesn't win pennants. Also he doesn't like Negroes. Branch Rickey tells me that he is thinking of raiding the Negro League for players because he can get them for a song. I have told Branch Rickey that the colored ballplayers have their own league, let them stay in their own league. Don't forget that my word is law by the authority of God and the reserve clause. Never forget that we are saving the world for democracy in a death struggle with the axis powers. We are also saving paper, tin foil, fat and scrap metal. So don't despair, use your head, save your hair, buy Fitch Shampoo. And a special word for my young niece, Happy Landis. Remember, we don't play with little jewboys. Now, on behalf of America, godspeed." His thin, cracked Cracker voice crackled over the radio as he started to cackle, "Off we go, into the wide blue yonder, flying high, into the sun. Geronimo! Over and out."

Captain Midnight pulled his joystick and the nose wheel lifted off the runway, the experimental Northrop XB-35 tilting, the four engines roaring, and then they were in the air. Down below, Father Coughlin was praising Hitler's treatment of Jews and the circulation of his newspaper had reached six million. German-American Bund storm-troopers were parading in Yorkville. America First was vilifying Roosevelt for selling America to Communists, foreigners, and Jews. Gerald L. K. Smith with his message about the international Jewish conspiracy was ranting to the 1944 Republican Presidential platform committee. The Klu Klux Klan was conspiring against Jews and Negroes.

But up where Ronnie was now, the sky was blue. The relations among the crew were almost familial. As the Flying Wing climbed over Riis Park, over Belle Harbor, over Rockaway, over Far Rockaway, over the Five Towns, over Long Beach and Jones Beach and out over the Atlantic Ocean, it gradually came to Ronnie that he was free. Nothing could touch him. And Captain Midnight and his crew were going to rectify the situation with the Flying Wing and its mysterious bombs of silver, with the invisible noise of its roaring engines in the night sky, with its occult machine guns, with its silent bullets over Poland, with its body filled with secret fuel that would carry them, afterwards, all the way to the Himalayas where they would pick up an escort of shark-nosed Curtiss P-40s and rendezvous with the Flying Tigers and General Claire Chenault.

So what if the Flying Wing was slow, unstable and dangerous to fly? So what if, despite—or because of—its experimental design it was a sure loser in combat? It would find the enemy. It may be that it takes a loser to be a finder. It may be that only losers can break free of this world's invisible rulers. Find your keepers, lose your weepers.

Just as they were about to leave sight of land, the radio crackled again and it was Miss Maloney. Miss Maloney was the Principal of P.S. 121 and she always had everyone salute and say the Pledge of Allegiance on every possible occasion. That's what she wanted now, as her voice crackled over the radio, she wanted them to salute and say the Pledge of Allegiance. Ronnie wondered how she got permission to call them on a secret mission but he figured she probably knew Judge Kenesaw Mountain Landis or something. Miss Maloney was wearing a mink coat and a lot of rouge and lipstick, Ronnie couldn't see her but that's what she always wore. Her perfume was so heavy you could almost see it.

The kids called Miss Maloney Miss Baloney. They said she wasn't really American but came from a place called Tizovthee. As in my country 'tis of thee. "As you go off on this very important secret mission," said Miss Maloney in her very fussy voice, "I want you to remember that America is a country for everybody, even immigrants who aren't Americans. I want you never to forget that it won't be long now before you belong here as much as I do. I want you to always remember that soon it won't be long now. It won't be long when you belong. And now, I shall lead you in the Pledge of Allegiance. Please stand and put your hand over your heart."

They all stood up and saluted with their hands over their hearts, Ronnie, Happy Landis and Sgt. Leibowitz. "I pledge allegiance," they said, "to the flag, of the United States of America . . ." But just at that moment Captain Midnight held up a pencilled sign that said, "master code 4: 25, 9, 8, 26, 6, 10, 7." Decoded, that meant BALONEY. Then Captain Midnight switched the radio off and passed around a box of chocolate Malomars.

In the cockpit Sgt. Leibowitz told him they were carrying a load of special top-secret silver germ bombs containing the new anti-body called halom that, with the help of their top-secret Norden bomb sight, they were going to drop on the vital centers of the Third Reich in a carefully planned foray of precision bombing. And nobody had the slightest idea how halom was going to behave on a long flight. It had never been used before. It had never even been tested in a tactical situation.

The cockpit kept making Ronnie think of the cellar door, the slanted wooden door that led down dark stairs into the cellar of his house. Going through the cellar door was like going through the hatch into the darkened cockpit. The cellar made him feel suffocated and liberated at different times, or sometimes at the same times. He didn't know how to explain it to himself except that either way it made him feel like he was going to shit in his pants. Sometimes he played down there in his own dream world and he was happy. Sometimes he felt like he was trapped in a black box and he couldn't get himself to get out.

Often his grandfather was down in the cellar working in his workshop. Little white beard, tall and thin with spats and cravat and a diamond stickpin. In his workshop were a lot of bottles for when his grandfather was thirsty. He was frequently thirsty. When he was frequently thirsty he often said things that Ronnie didn't understand. Ronnie always assumed the things his grandfather said that he didn't understand he didn't understand because they were Yiddish. His grandfather was fumbling around looking for something. He mumbled something that sounded like "vessel." That sounded like Yiddish.

"Find the box," his grandfather said. He smelled like he'd just had a rubdown.

"What box?"

"The old box."

"What old box?"

"The box with nothing in it."

"Where do I look?"

"The empty book. Benny has it."

"Where did he put it?"

"It's in the empty room."

There was no empty room in the cellar so Ronnie didn't know what to do.

Later he asked My Uncle Benny about it. "I don't have it," said Benny.

51

"What is it?" Ronnie asked.

Benny thought a minute. "It's a dream," he said. "Try and remember it."

They say that halom was discovered by Fleming at the same time he discovered penicillin, but that he thought it was a useless strain of the same anti-body and put it aside. That's what My Uncle Benny said and he was a licensed pharmacist. It was Benny who told him about halom. He said it was a dream vaccine. He said if you were vaccinated with it you would have a lot of dreams. This was Benny's way of explaining to Ronnie why he was having so many dreams. He said he'd been vaccinated with halom and that meant all his dreams would be good, even his bad dreams would be good. So Ronnie stopped worrying about his dreams, even his bad dreams. He didn't exactly understand what it meant to be vaccinated with halom, but he didn't exactly understand what it meant to be vaccinated with a victrola needle either, which is what grown ups usually told him he'd been vaccinated with.

As soon as Captain Midnight let Ronnie know he didn't need to keep an eye on the instrument panel, Ronnie turned to Sgt. Leibowitz. Sgt. Leibowitz was supposed to be the bombardier.

"What happens when we drop the silver bombs on the Third Reich?" he asked Sgt. Leibowitz. "What do they do?"

"Do?" answered Sgt. Leibowitz. "What do you think they do? They make the water undrinkable. They ruin the crops. They make the weather turn bad. Everybody's skin breaks out. The frogs crawl out of the water and die and stink and are eaten by rats that spread lice that cause disease and people get sick and die. The Germans that will be left won't be Nazis anymore. This is denazification. Germ warfare. American germs against German germs. Anti-bodies against bodies. Once the anti-bodies do away with their bodies they choose to go on to another world. A world of dreams where there are no Nazis."

"What about the Jews? Aren't you afraid of hitting the Jews?"

"Jews? In Germany?" Sgt. Leibowitz laughed a bitter laugh.

"The Jews are already chosen. They're chosen to live in the other world."

When he turned around again Ronnie saw that Captain Midnight had put the airplane on automatic pilot and was reading the paper. It was the *New York Post*, and the headline read: "9th ACROSS ELBE." Just above it was another headline: "'Won't Be Long Now'—Goebbels."

When Ronnie looked out the cockpit window and saw a chicken on the wing he was at first surprised. Then he realized it was a chicken he recognized. The chicken waddling toward him on the wing of the Wing, comb and wattles waving in the wind, was a large white and grey cock, pin-striped like mattress ticking. Its feathers were blowing in the slipstream but it seemed to have no trouble keeping its balance on the gently yawing wing.

This was My Uncle Benny's famous trained chicken that he brought into Granma's apartment upstairs when it was a chick. Nobody knew where he got it, maybe next door where they raised chickens and rabbits in cages in the back yard. Naturally Granma told him to get rid of it. But he hid it somewhere in the house, and before you knew it the chick had turned into a chicken and his mother's attitude had changed from rejection to grudging tolerance. Maybe it was because what happened was that the chick as it grew got very attached to her. It would follow her around the house and, when old enough, learned to flutter up off the floor and sit on her knee. When My Uncle Benny understood that the chick was getting attached to his mother, he started training it to become her special pet.

My Uncle Benny was very good with animals. He felt comfortable with them. With children and with animals. He had a way of talking to animals without speaking that was very special. He could train them to do anything. He trained the chicken to run to the stairs and welcome his mother when she came in the door. Then he trained it to walk on a leash so that she could take it outside. She ended up getting very fond of the bird. Finally Benny trained it to go down to Cohen's candy store a block away and bring the newspaper home in its beak. That was the talk of the neighborhood for a while.

When the chicken reached the cock pit Ronnie rubbed his eyes and it disappeared. In the cock's place stood My Uncle Benny, who opened the hatch and climbed down into the cock pit.

"How did you get up here?" Ronnie asked.

"I'm a luftmensch. I can soar above the clouds."

"Why did you come?"

"I have a dream. It isn't mine and I don't know what it means. You're supposed to tell me."

"Whose is it?"

"I'm not allowed to tell."

"Why me?"

"You're it."

"How do you know?"

"Because the cork fell out and you stink."

"Maybe I do. Let me hear the dream."

"This is the dream as it was told to me by a judge. 'A doctor friend and I went to see a frog whose head and right front leg had been cut off. They were needed for something. It was said the frog was doing remarkably well. Sure enough, the frog was managing to get along. You had to give it credit. The only treatment it was getting for its wounds was a toothpick through each one, maybe to seal a vein. The doctor was impressed. However, it was having some trouble eating. It would keep butting the open stump of its neck against its food without getting any results. We were a little worried it would starve to death.

'On the way to lunch we came across an accident, and my doctor friend got out of the car to help a man in pain on the ground. It looked like he had a broken leg at least. But his girlfriend made a big fuss. "Nobody is going to touch him unless I'm convinced he's a man of culture," she kept insisting. We finally left and called the hospital for an ambulance.'"

"This is the Judge's dream, but it doesn't belong to him,"

said Ronnie. "I know, because it's a dream I myself have had in the past. The interpretation doesn't depend on the dream but on the dreamer. Tell the Judge that no matter how much you jiggle and dance, the last few drops go down your pants. That's the meaning of the dream for him. Because he's not a man of culture."

"What's the meaning of the dream for persons of culture?"

"For persons of culture the meaning is, ladies and gentlemen, take my advice, pull down your pants and slide on the ice."

"I see. And what's the meaning for you?"

"The meaning for me is, it won't be long now. It won't be long because I don't belong. But I'll get along. As long as I have you."

"So," said My Uncle Benny. "So, so long." My Uncle Benny metamorphosed into a chicken again and meandered toward the back of the cockpit, head tipping from side to side and cockscomb flopping. Then he disappeared.

Happy Landis unbuckled her seat belt and came over to where Ronnie was sitting. She unzipped her leather jacket exposing her tan cashmere sweater with the nascent breasts thrusting against the soft material. She pushed the sweater against his cheek and rubbed from side to side. "I didn't know little Jewish boys knew about dreams," she said.

"Master code one," said Captain Midnight. "8, 15, 10, 21, 23." Decoded that meant *shule*. Decoded from Yiddish it meant *school*. Did Captain Midnight know Yiddish? And if so, what was he talking about? But wait. Of course. Just because Ronnie was on a secret mission, it didn't mean he could skip his Hebrew lesson. If he missed his Hebrew lessons he wouldn't get bar mitzvahed, and if he didn't get bar mitzvahed he wouldn't get any bar mitzvah presents. He was already looking forward to it. It won't be long now, he thought. He was already making up his bar mitzvah speech. "Today I am a fountain pen. Today I am a fifty dollar war bond. Today I am a victrola and a baseball bat and a bicycle and a portable radio and a wrist watch . . ." Ronnie needed all those things to be a real American. That's why he had to be bar mitzvahed.

Unexpectedly, Mister Marter appeared in the cockpit. He took out his yarmulke and put it on, then handed one to Ronnie. Mister Marter was a refugee. It was said he was very poor and lived alone with a heart condition. He was some indefinite middling age and spoke with an unfamiliar accent. Ronnie wondered what the condition of his heart was and why he lived alone. He had an atmosphere of suffering about him that was visible in his expression, his manner of moving as if ready to fend off blows, his oppressed meekness, his willingness to put up with Ronnie's smart-aleck inattention. As a teacher, he was not the ideal role model, you might say. But between Ronnie's parents there seemed to be an unspoken compact about him, as if he had been the victim of something unspeakable.

"The translation for today," said Mister Marter, "is Genesis 1.31. What is your translation?"

"'And God saw all that he had made, and found it very good.'"

"And what does it mean?"

"It means what it says."

"And what does it say?"

"It says that everything is good."

"And is that true?"

"No."

"Then that couldn't be what it says. What it says is that everything is good, including evil. This is writ."

"Where does it say evil?"

"Where it says good it says evil. Because it's talking about everything, and if it's talking about everything it includes evil. It is written. But, it is asked, how can evil be called good? The answer is that evil may produce good. One school says that evil may even be necessary to produce good. When the Lord says to Cain, 'Your brother's blood cries out,' is He not aware of the evil? Yet the sage says that it is not the singular but the plural that is used: 'your brother's bloods.' And why the plural? The reason is it is not only Abel but his unborn children who are killed, and all his posterity. The meaning is that if a man kills a single person it is as if he has killed many persons and eventually as if he has killed a whole world. But the good is that if he saves a single person it is as if he has saved a whole world."

"You mean like the Allies are saving the world for democracy?"

A pained look crossed Mister Marter's face. "Let's go on," he said.

In the end Ronnie learned the Hebrew part of his bar mitzvah spiel by rote, not by writ.

"We better have something to eat," said Happy Landis.

She came back with a package of Malomars, another of Fig Newtons and another of social teas. While they had cookies and milk, Happy Landis brought Captain Midnight, up at the controls, a tray of schmaltz herring and Uneeda biscuits. "It's good for you," she said.

"A small fish sometimes kills on the seventh, seventeenth and twenty-seventh day of the month," the herring objected. "And some say also on the twenty-third day," it added.

"Who asked you?" said Happy Landis.

"If it has been well roasted there is no objection," said the herring. "But whoever eats black cumin, his heart will be torn out. For the heart, eat the broth of the beet left on the stove till it says tuk tuk. This is also good for fever. Read the Talmud. For chronic fever take a black hen, slit it open, shave the crown of the patient, place the hen over his head and leave it there until it sticks."

"Ugh! you're disgusting," said Happy Landis. "And you smell bad and you're stingy and clannish and pushy."

"You don't like herring?" asked the herring.

"It's not that I don't like herring, I don't like pushy herring."

"You don't like pushy herring try Coney Island Whitefish. You know what's Coney Island Whitefish?"

57

"No."

"You should ask your young friends there."

Happy Landis went to the back of the cabin where Ronnie and Sgt. Leibowitz were gorging themselves with Fig Newtons and chocolate Malomars. She picked up a social tea and asked them what a Coney Island Whitefish is. They both turned red, choked, and sprayed one another with bits of marshmallow and fig pulp.

"Are you asking for it?" asked Sgt. Leibowitz.

Happy Landis repeated Jane Russell's famous line from *The Outlaw*. "Yes," she said.

Ronnie knew that Howard Huge produced *The Outlaw* and even engineered a special brassiere for Jane Russell in it, so he suddenly got jealous. If Captain Midnight was Howard Huge there was nothing he could do about it because Howard Huge was bigger than him. Not until he was a fountain pen. He'd have to wait. It won't be long now.

Ronnie never got to explain to Happy Landis that Coney Island Whitefish were what they called the used scum bags floating in the bay off Brooklyn. Because all of a sudden the Wing started rocking and pitching and bumping up and down and they were thrown from one side of the cabin to the other. Ronnie grabbed a pole and wondered whether to pull the emergency cord. Happy was hanging on to a strap as the shrill, screechy sounds of metal on metal pierced their eardrums and made him want to stick his fingers in his ears. For some reason at that instant he noticed that the girl in the Miss Rheingold ad looked just like Happy Landis.

Then they stopped with a jolt and the doors opened. The sign on the platform said "Avenue I." They walked out on the platform and the doors closed behind them. The train rumbled slowly away down the track toward Coney Island, the Gravesend Local. Over the roof of the El station you could see fleets of pigeons flapping over Flatbush as they followed flags flung back and forth by fellows on the roofs of tenements. Near the stairs on the opposite platform was a sign that said, "To City." In the direction the train had come from, you could see the spires and pinnacles of Manhattan's skyline. The flat, watery sky of Brooklyn seemed dull dishwater compared to the tower pierced blue over Manhattan.

Manhattan was the apple of Ronnie's eye. Someday he would live on the other side of the bridge if he had anything to say about it. Meanwhile he identified with Avenue I. He was I. When he got over the bridge finally he would be someone else.

The mail came at dawn, special delivery, the letter carrier saying there was a letter for Ronnie. "I'm the Post Man," he said, "so don't open till Xxxmass." Ronnie was going to open it anyway but Captain Midnight beckoned to him from the pilot's seat. "Master code six," he said. "10, 1, 26, 26, 20, 18, 16, 2." Decoded that meant CALLHOME.

Ronnie fished a nickel out of his pocket and went to the phone booth in the back of the cabin. He dialed CLoverdale 8-2182. The phone rang a couple of times and his father answered. "Dr. Sukenick's office."

"Hello, this is Ronnie."

"What is it?"

"I'm calling from an experimental airplane high over the North Atlantic off Iceland."

"Oh. I thought you were in the bathroom."

"No. I'm on a secret mission."

"Is this a collect call?"

"Don't worry, they allow us free calls."

"Well what is it? I'm working on a patient."

"I just wanted to tell you not to worry. I'm on a dangerous top security bomber flight to a high-risk target."

"All right. I won't tell your mother."

"Also don't tell her that my girlfriend up here isn't Jewish."

"Wait a minute, I'll put her on the phone."

Pause.

"Hello, Ronnie? She's not Jewish?"

"Don't tell Granma."

"Wait a minute, she's right here. She wants to know if you have two sets of dishes up there."

"You know we don't use two sets of dishes anymore. Besides, we have paper plates."

"She wants to know if you keep kosher, at least."

"You know we don't keep kosher anymore."

"She wants to know if you're still going to temple on the holidays."

"You know I never go to temple unless you make me."

"Your Granma wants to know if you'll be down by the sabbath."

"I'll still be flying on the sabbath."

"You don't keep the sabbath, you don't go to temple any more, you've stopped keeping kosher and you're going with a shiksa. Ronnie, your Granma is very disturbed. She wants me to ask you, just tell your Granma so she wouldn't worry, are you still circumcised?"

"Mother, listen, there's a war on. I have to hang up now."

"Your Granma says as long as you're healthy. Don't hurt yourself."

"I won't."

"Yes you will."

"Don't worry I won't."

"You will."

"I won't."

His father got back on the phone. "Do what your mother tells you," he said.

"Please deposit another nickel," said the operator.

"I don't have another nickel," said Ronnie.

"That's no excuse," said his father, but the next thing Ronnie heard was a dial tone, so he hung up.

* * *

On the way back to the crew's quarters Ronnie passed Happy Landis on her way up to the front of the cockpit with a bottle of Haig and Haig and a shot glass on a tray.

"Someone having a snort?" Ronnie asked.

"Captain Midnight," she said. "It's breakfast. Haig and Haig. Pinch Bottle. That's what he always has. A pinch of Pinch."

Ronnie followed her with his eyes as she climbed up to the pilot's section of the flight deck, slim haunches swaying as she balanced the tray against the slight roll of the Wing. Mounting the steps the top half of her body disappeared and he could see her only waist down as she stopped next to the pilot's seat. And he could see her standing still there as Captain Midnight's big hand reached back behind his seat to cup one of her little buttocks and squeeze hard. He could see her standing there as he patted, palped, shook and pinched it while she remained perfectly still. A pinch of pinch. It made Ronnie feel dirty. Then the hand disappeared and Happy came back down the stairs balancing the tray with the shot glass and no bottle.

What was going on here? Ronnie wondered. How did Happy Landis know Captain Midnight's breakfast habits so well? How come she stands still for his crude caresses? Was Captain Midnight fucking Happy? Because if Captain Midnight was fucking Happy Ronnie guessed that he himself would never be fucking Happy. The fuck with it. Ronnie instantaneously decided that he didn't care if he was fucking Happy.

He closed the door to the bathroom, took off his clothes and turned on the shower. Just as he was washing the soap off Happy burst through the door shouting "May Day! May Day!" Ronnie leaped dripping out of the shower to see Happy with her skirt hiked up bending over exposing her ass while looking back at him with a mischievous smile. "I maidja look, I maidja look, I maidja buy a penny book," said Happy.

Ronnie grabbed a towel to cover his growing erection. "Would you like me to dry you off?" asked Happy. She tried to

61

grab the towel from him and they had a small tug of war as she made little swipes toward the bulge of towel. Then she turned around and pressed her now skirted ass against it and did a little dance. Ronnie passed out.

When Ronnie came to, Sgt. Leibowitz was forcing some Haig and Haig down his throat, asking, "What happened to you? Did Happy try to dry you off? She dried me off. She dries everyone off. That's part of her Secret Squadron mission. The emission test. Everybody's got to get the emission test."

Ronnie felt like a failure. He felt that he failed the emission test.

Sgt. Leibowitz decided it was time for some R & R, so he pulled down the movie screen in the crew's quarters and got out the projector. "This is Howard Hughes' *The Outlaw*, with Jane Russell," he said. It's censored in the theaters but we got a copy through channels."

Sgt. Leibowitz didn't have time to rewind the reel so he just started the movie in the middle. "Will you keep your eyes open?" Billy the Kid was saying.

"Yes," said Jane Russell. They were in her bedroom.

"Will you look right at me while I do it?" said Billy the Kid.

She looked right at him.

He did it.

Sgt. Leibowitz suddenly hauled off and hit Ronnie on the arm. "You flinched," he said.

"No I didn't," said Ronnie. He punched Sgt. Leibowitz on the arm. "You flinched," Ronnie said.

"No I didn't," said Sgt. Leibowitz. He gave Ronnie a real hard shot on the arm but Ronnie didn't move. Instead he hit Sgt. Leibowitz on the arm as hard as he could but Sgt. Leibowitz just stood there. Then he hit Ronnie on the arm and this time Ronnie staggered and took a few steps to keep his balance. Then Ronnie really wound up and hit Sgt. Leibowitz's arm so hard Sgt. Liebowitz almost fell down. Then Sgt. Leibowitz gave Ronnie a hit that sent him bouncing off the bulkhead. Ronnie could hardly lift his arm anymore but nobody was going to make him flinch. He came back with a running start and hit him one on the arm so hard that Sgt. Leibowitz crashed into the galley and all the pots and pans fell on his head. "You flinched," screamed Ronnie, "you flinched."

"Like hell I did," yelled Sgt. Leibowitz as he came reeling back across the crew's quarters. "You flinched."

"The hell I did," said Ronnie. "You flinched."

"Oh yeah, who says I flinched?"

"I says. What's it to you?"

"I didn't flinch. Nobody says I flinch."

"I say you flinch."

"Say that again and I'll let you have it."

"You flinch."

Just as they were about to let one another have it, Ronnie's puzzling friend Paisan appeared in the crew's quarters. "Nobody flinch," said Paisan.

Paisan was the strangest kid on the block. Ronnie wasn't sure that Paisan was born in this country. Maybe he was but he didn't act like someone who was born in this country. Paisan didn't like to get into fights and for some reason the kids didn't think he was yellow for not liking to get into fights. He also didn't like other people to get into fights.

"Take it easy," said Paisan. "Nobody flinch. Nobody got to flinch. Why anybody got to flinch?"

"Nobody's got to flinch?" asked Sgt. Leibowitz. "I always thought somebody had to flinch."

"Nah," said Paisan. "What's the difference?"

"What's the difference," repeated Ronnie. "Hey, I never thought of that."

"Are you sure?" asked Sgt. Leibowitz.

"Sure," said Paisan. "Better play stick ball. Catchaflyersup." He bounced a spawldeen and gave it a whack with a broom stick, but he hit a grounder. Sgt. Leibowitz fielded it and Paisan put the stick down and waited. Sgt. Leibowitz rolled it in fast and it hit

63

the stick and bounced way up and to one side but Paisan was thinking about something else and didn't try to catch it.

"I'm up," said Sgt. Leibowitz.

"Yeah, you're up," said Paisan. "I'm down. Who cares who's up who's down?" He turned around and walked away looking like he was thinking about something, leaving Ronnie and Sgt. Leibowitz completely mystified.

All of a sudden one of their outboard engines sputtered and lost power.

"What now?" asked Ronnie.

"I don't know," said Sgt. Leibowitz. "It's mysterious. We should have a mechanic on board."

Ronnie went to the phone booth and called My Uncle Benny. Everybody said Benny had magic fingers and could fix anything. In practically no time Benny showed up with his tool box, his cracked, blackened fingernails and with his hand over his missing front teeth, awed to be up there and painfully humble as he was introduced to Captain Midnight and the crew.

Then he walked down the passageway to the outboard motor and opened the access hatch. He sniffed carefully at the engine, opened his toolbox and selected an old collapsible top hat which sprang into shape when he struck it. He held the hat over the engine and groped around in it with his other hand. Suddenly he became still, and slowly pulled a matzo ball out of the hat. He handed it to Ronnie and plunged his hand back into the hat. In a minute he pulled out a schmaltz herring. The engine started to sputter but didn't catch. He frowned, wiped his hands on a towel, stuck his head through the hatch and put his ear to the engine. Little whiney sounds could be heard as the engine wheezed and coughed.

Benny took a thermometer out of his toolkit and shook it down, looked at the mercury, then plunged it somewhere into the hatch. In a minute he took it out, wiped it, held it up to the light, and whistled. "It's got a very high fever," he said. "I need to have a consultation." He pulled a card out of his pocket and gave it to Happy. "Call this number," he said.

Before long Dr. Lubitz appeared with his black bag. He took out his stethoscope and held it against the motor, moving it from time to time and listening intently. "It's congested," he said finally. "Nothing to do. But wait. Call me in the morning."

Before he left he took Benny aside and whispered something in his ear. Ronnie could hear the words "cut," "delirium," "permanent damage."

"But the March of Dimes . . . ?"

"That's the dream we all have. The reality is a nightmare we try to forget."

Then Dr. Lubitz left and Benny looked very grave. He went back to the hatch and rolled up his sleeves. He hadn't rolled up his sleeves before. Now Ronnie knew he was really serious.

Benny picked up the top hat and turned it upside down to make sure it was empty. Then he put it back on the motor and went in with both hands. "There's something blocking the system," he said. After a while he said, "Ah!" and came up holding by its ears a chocolate Easter bunny wrapped in gold foil. "The golden calf," he said, handing it to Happy. "Enjoy it," he added. "But it's not for you," he said to Ronnie. "That's gilt. You're allergic to gilt."

The engine hiccuped once, twice, caught for a few seconds, then burped and went silent.

Happy asked Benny if she could peel the bunny, but he said, "Wait. There's something else."

He thrust back in and probed around. Soon they heard small yowling sounds. Benny came back up with three long-haired black kittens, so tiny he could hold them all in one hand. Their eyes were still closed and they were clinging to one another with all their paws. Suddenly the engine caught and roared to life.

"This is for you," he said to Ronnie. "They crawled in there for warmth. You have to keep them warm." He handed them to Ronnie.

"God, no wonder the engine wasn't working," said Ronnie, "with all this stuff in it."

Benny rolled down his sleeves, wiped his hands, and packed the toolbox. Ronnie wanted to thank him but Benny just took his toolbox, smiled his timid smile, turned sideways and disappeared.

Suddenly the Wing shuddered as if traumatized and Captain Midnight banked sharply to the right. They had taken a hit.

"May Day! May Day!" yelled Sgt. Leibowitz from the bubble over the rear turret. "Bandits everywhere! This is it!"

From up above an inverted gull-winged Stuka was heading right at them in a screaming dive. Ronnie reached for the upper-wing turret controls and said, "Eh-eh-eh-eh-eh-eh-eh-eh." The Stuka shivered, a plume of smoke appeared from its engine and as it tried to pull out of its dive a wing broke off. Ronnie could see the pilot slumped over the controls as the Stuka fluttered down past them. "I got one, I got one!" he yelled.

Out the front-wing window Ronnie saw a Messerschmitt 109 coming in at twelve o'clock. In the same glance he saw the jagged coast of the British Isles probably somewhere near the border between Scotland and England. Just when Ronnie expected to see the 109's wings and prop hub flashing with its three twenty-millimeter cannon and two machine guns, it pulled up and veered. Then he noticed a Hawker Hurricane coming at the 109, its eight Colt Browning machine guns blazing.

They were over the Channel approaching Dunkerque when the war started for real. First they heard a few dull cracks of flak as they joined up with a formation of B-17 Flying Fortresses on a run into Germany. Then the ME-109s attacked en masse. They spread out and dove into the formation the Wing had joined, and dodged through lines of tracer bullets to pluck flowers of flame from the wings and motors of the ponderous Forts.

Suddenly black blossoms of flak started exploding all around them. The Wing rocked from some close misses and one of the Forts near them lost a wing tip and went into a shallow dive.

Ronnie watched it go down and saw the white blooms of two parachutes snap into the air. At the same time Ronnie saw two massive Republic P-47 Thunderbolts pursuing a couple of Messerschmitts that were trying to make evasive dives.

The sky around them was now filled with so many criss-crossing planes it looked like a fish tank alarmed by a marauding cat. What puzzled him was when a Grumman Wildcat flew by piloted by Ted Williams, unmistakably the Splendid Splinter himself squinting into the sun, until he remembered that Williams had left the Boston outfield for the Navy Air Corp and had become a World War Two ace. He couldn't figure it out when he saw Cookie Lavagetto zoom by in a Vought Corsair waving his Dodger hat. But when Ronnie saw Howie Schultz fly by in an old bi-wing Sopwith Camel, he knew he must be dreaming. Especially when the next thing was a British Spad piloted by Dolph Camilli chasing after a German Fokker D-VII from von Richtoffen's Flying Circus squadron. I mean, who needs two first basemen?

Just then, the Wing peeled off and dropped out of the Flying Fortress armada to pursue its own, and in some ways more dangerous mission.

By now they were over Germany itself, having crossed the Rhine near Koblenz. Ronnie went back to the rear of the cabin to check everything out. There was a whistling noise coming from the rear turret. When he got back there he found the glass bubble fractured by a line of machine-gun bullets and Sgt. Leibowitz hanging from his seat harness with one side of his head turned into raw hamburger. Sgt. Leibowitz was dead again. His mouth was gaping and his eyes bugged, as if he were surprised at this development. The whole left side of his skull was missing. When Ronnie looked at the back of the turret he found it, on the bulkhead. He bent over and vomited uncontrollably for a while, which only added to the mess. Then he went and told Happy Landis. "Don't go back there," he said.

Ronnie went up to the cockpit and told Captain Midnight about Sgt. Leibowitz. Captain Midnight was impassive, maybe because they were getting close to their target now and he was concentrating. His whole face was covered up by his leather helmet, his oxygen mask and his goggles. Only his forehead was exposed, and it kept breaking into wrinkles that looked like letters of an unfamiliar alphabet. Captain Midnight always looked like he was concentrating, he was like Charles Lindbergh that way. Ronnie noticed that the bottle of Haig & Haig on the console was now three quarters empty.

In fact they were not too much more than an hour away. They would pass to the north of Frankfurt, then south of Dresden, what was left of it, arrive in Poland from over Czechoslovakia somewhere between Katowice and Czestochowa and then they were about there.

The mood had changed, and they were all quiet and meditative as they approached their rendezvous with the nightmare of history that might write the final chapter to their own dreams.

"I have a premonition," Ronnie told Happy Landis. "I have the feeling that I'm not going to come out of this. Or at least not the way I was before. I have the feeling that none of us are going to come out of this the way we were before."

"You mean you think we're going to die?"

"I don't know if we're going to die, but I don't know if we're going to be alive either."

"What do you mean by that?"

"I don't know. Maybe we'll be alive but not human."

"That's silly. We have to be human."

"I don't know. Maybe not human but something else."

"What else is there?"

"Maybe we can't know yet. But I want to make certain the black box is working so we can be sure of what happened. Then maybe we'll be able to figure it out."

Ronnie went up to the cockpit to check out the black box.

When he got up there he saw that the bottle of Haig & Haig was empty, and Captain Midnight looked like he was really concentrating hard.

Ronnie noticed that the Wing was losing altitude and gaining speed, and at the same time it began circling uncertainly over Oscweicim. He looked down and could see why. From this height it was impossible to distinguish the camp from the industrial complex almost next door. Both had neatly laid out buildings, orderly rail and road networks and tall smokestacks pouring out black smoke. The only difference was that one of the installations had been bombed by the Allies. It turned out to have been the industrial complex. To the camp, nothing had been done.

Ronnie knew that the flight plan called for making the first bomb run here, because every minute counted, then circling back to drop the rest of their load over the heart of the Third Reich. But now Captain Midnight looked at Ronnie and said tersely, "Master code two. 22, 9, 9, 7, 8, 22, 19." Then he banked the Wing, still gaining speed, and headed back toward Germany.

Ronnie figured now or never, he'd better open the letter the Post Man had delivered. Maybe this is Xxxmass, he thought. He ripped the letter open and a photocopy fell out. It was from a biography of General Eisenhower by Peter Lyon, about an army V.I.P. visit made to a town named Ohrdruf when the truth about the camps started to emerge.

> The routine stink of death emanating
> from three thousand corpses that lay,
> some buried in shallow graves, some
> exposed, lice crawling over them,
> scabbed black where they had been
> gutted to provide a meal for famished
> survivors. Bradley was revolted. Patton
> withdrew to vomit in a corner.
> Eisenhower, his face frozen white,
> forced himself to examine every last
> corner of the camp.

This was on April 12. Bradley was revolted. Patton puked. Eisenhower looked. And on that same day Roosevelt dropped dead.

Ronnie got his Secret Squadron badge out and turned to master code two as fast as he could. But before Ronnie could decode Captain Midnight's message, something surprising happened. Captain Midnight suddenly let go of the joystick, fell off his seat, and toppled to the floor. Ronnie jumped down and quickly loosened Captain Midnight's uniform, removing his helmet. Captain Midnight was completely inert. He smelled as if he had been rubbed with rubbing alcohol. And they were losing altitude. The Wing was going faster and faster. They were quickly approaching mach one.

Ronnie had to do something fast. The whole mission now depended on him. He got into the pilot's seat, grabbed the joystick and pulled. The Wing just went faster. He pulled again, the Wing went faster still. He kept pulling and pulling but every time he pulled the Wing went faster and faster, closer and closer to the sound barrier. Everything was vibrating and rattling and groaning. The big ship felt like she was going to tear herself apart. She was yawing and fishtailing and trying to roll as the airstream screamed and it felt like she wanted to get away from him. Ronnie hung on. The Wing was now on the very verge and there was nothing he could do to stop her. Then, as if trapped in a spasm, he felt the huge shudder and release as the Wing went through the sound barrier.

Happy Landis was smiling at him from the co-pilot's seat. "I liked the way you did that," she said.

Happy went to the cabin to get the Malomars but came back with the box of kittens. They were mewing and crawling over one another.

"Poor little things," said Happy.

She picked one up by the nape of its neck and twisted its head till it went limp. Happy was not herself. He wondered who she was. She picked up the second kitten and taking a knife brought from the galley sawed it in two.

"Solomon's solution," she said. "That's what Jews do to Christian babies."

The third kitten she covered with lighter fluid and lit, holding it by its tail as it frantically squirmed and screamed. He saw that it was actually a small child. She held it by its leg until the flames reached her fingers, which were already bloody. Then she let it go. It dropped and hit the metal floor with a nauseating little thud.

"This is not anti-semitism," said Ronnie. "This is something else. Something worse."

But Ronnie didn't have time for speculation. The plane was going into a shallow dive and was approaching mach two. It felt as if they were in a freight car, going over bumpy tracks, faster and faster. The lights went out. He smelled gas.

Ronnie grabbed a flashlight and got down on the floor where Captain Midnight was lying. He pulled off Captain Midnight's oxygen mask and started slapping his face to wake him up. He heard a groan and shined the light into Captain Midnight's uncovered face. My god! It wasn't Howard Huge. It was his father's pilot friend, Ernie Fall. And they were falling.

The lights in the cockpit went on again. Hoping for landing instructions, Ronnie got his Secret Squadron badge out and decoded the last message from Captain Midnight. It said, TOOLATE.

Air speed was now approaching mach three. Ronnie was losing it. He felt dirty. He felt like he was covered with germs. He felt like he should undress and take a shower. He felt like his immune system was breaking down and he was being invaded by some virus. Above all he felt he couldn't stand it if the lights went off again. The cockpit with the lights off was like a black suffocation box with the walls coming closer and closer and the oxygen being withdrawn.

Then the lights went off again.

In the dark he knew he wasn't going to be able to hold out much longer. The dark assumed shapes that rushed at him, menacing, crushing, rushing blocks of death, unstoppable. He knew he was going to go crazy. He knew he was going to go over some edge.

71

He went over it.

The lights went on again. They were now at mach four. The Wing was screaming down toward Europe. Ever since Happy had killed the kittens Happy was no longer Happy and Ronnie was no longer himself. He dived at her and caught her by a leg, wrestled her down, ripped her clothes off, bit her neck and tasted blood. The lights went off again.

When they went on he was strapped naked to a table. He was in the hospital because he was infected. He was not innoculated. He had not gotten his halom injection. The serum had been lost. He had a disease with no symptoms, no diagnosis and no treatment. The only possible cure was sterilization. There was a doctor wearing an oxygen mask holding a gleaming scalpel. The lights went off again. He was in a black box. The lights went on. He couldn't move. They were putting him in an iron lung. The lights went off. Huge black shapes were racing at him. On. Something over his mouth and nose he couldn't breathe paralyzed. Off. He lost consciousness. On. He woke up he was vomiting and there was nothing but history, dissimulation and words in vain.

$

NUMBERS

1. The Old Country

Losing It

He goes to Europe to find it, but that's where he loses it completely.

It's thirteen years after the end of World War II, the Germans are still crazed. When Ron tells a German kid he meets hitchhiking that Ron doesn't speak German very well, the kid says, "That's because you want German culture to disappear from the face of the earth." Another boy he meets in a youth hostel hates Americans because his family was killed in the fire bombing of Dresden.

Maybe that's when Ron starts losing it. It's hard to know whether these people would have preferred that Hitler won the war and proceeded to annihilate ever larger segments of the human race, as planned.

Of course, nobody in Germany ever liked Hitler. But one guy Ron meets says he was in the SS, and when he discovers Ron is Jewish says it was only to disguise the fact that he too is Jewish. Ron can't figure out whether he's lying or crazy or, even worse, telling the truth.

In Heidelberg, Ron falls in with some students who are members of a korporation, which is something like a fraternity that takes itself seriously. Too seriously, still eager for saber scars.

Ron gets along with these students quite well. They aren't stupid. They aren't insensitive. But they yearn for joy, for freedom, for something greater than themselves.

Ron understands it all quite well. He feels the same way.

Ron goes with them up to a ruined stadium on a hill overlooking the famous university town. There they get drunk on beer and sing student songs. Ron gets drunk and sings with them. "Mach frei!" Ron yells in his pidgin Deutsch, waving his beer mug around.

"Be frei!" responds someone in his pidgin English, and chugs one down.

As they drink, one of the students in a fit of camaraderie, tells him that this is where the Nazis used to hold their torchlight rallies. That's why it's been abandoned since the war, he says. At night, under the stars, he says, it must have been fantastic.

What's the story here? Ron begins to wonder.

One night Ron is eating at a table outside some kind of student restaurant. Two young men sit down with their plates and introduce themselves. One is German. The other is Maltese. Before he knows it the Maltese is talking about the war.

"The one thing about Hitler," the Maltese says in a friendly, confidential way, "is that it's too bad he didn't kill the rest of them. The Jews."

Maybe this is when Ron loses it.

They Wanted to Break My Face

"Did I ever tell you the story," asks Adek, "how, when I was twenty-four, I knew a girl with whom I was very much in love? When I was in the army. During the year I was in the army I was in love with a girl who worked with me in the army. And this girl is the sister of Faurisson, the one who wrote on the concentration camps, who said they never existed. At that period he was writing on Rimbaud and Lautréamont. And I was the lover of his sister for a year.

74

"And it was interesting in connection with being Jewish, because I had some big problems with her brothers. Because they were very anti-semitic. We were going to get married even. He was the oldest brother. I met him twice at the time. He was the least aggressive, but the other brothers were very, very aggressive, they wanted to break my face because I was with their sister. They were politically completely on the extreme right.

And he even had some problems at the time, the revisionist, Robert Faurisson, for being in the extreme right during the Algerian war. He was defended by Breton at his trial because he had written the book on Rimbaud. Which is not exactly ordinary because Breton is on the left. And for his book on the concentration camps, he was defended by the whole ultra-left, including Cohn-Bendit's brother and a group of anarchists of the extreme-left. In fact, Claire was in it. You remember that girl Claire?"

"The pretty little blond? Very sympa?"

"Yes, absolutely. She was in that ultra-left group that defended Faurisson. Their reasoning was very complicated."

"I don't doubt it."

"Their reasoning was that the Nazi camps and the gas chambers had been overemphasized, and because of that the Russian Gulag has always been ignored. Thus, if the gas chambers existed, it's very inconvenient."

Absences

In Warsaw a distinguished poet tells Ron that anti-semitism continues in Poland, even though all its Jews have been annihilated, "like sensation in a severed arm."

A Rough Campaign Closes in Poland. The campaign also saw a return of anti-Semitism, which assumed a noisy role in the margins of politics after years of being dormant in the 1980's. The Mazowiecki campaign found in interviews that some of those opposed to the

75

Prime Minister based their views on a belief that he was of Jewish origin. Mr. Mazowiecki is a Catholic.

Mr. Walesa was routinely urged at election rallies to sweep the Jewish cabal out of the Warsaw Government. (*New York Times*)

Anti-semitism without Jews. What a wonderful, what a Polish, idea. Which must mean that anti-semitism is not anti-semitism.

What, then, is it?

Being a Nazi

"I don't feel that it was the Jews who suffered the Holocaust," says Adek. "I think there were beings who made others suffer in an unbelievable way, who above all denied that others could exist as human beings. I mean that's what strikes me, you see, it's not who was Jewish or not Jewish. It's that on one hand you had people who were defined as victims, and on the other, necessarily, since you had victims you had executioners.

It's that this situation is now in our heads as something possible, you see. That's the problem. It's that you have to know, when you walk through the streets, that at any glance you may be seeing someone who possibly could do the same thing. Or else, in another, there's the possibility of accepting such a situation. You understand? I mean, that's what I find so unsettling. It's that the man in the street has revealed himself in that manner in that epoch, you see.

"And it seems to me that the distrust I have in people now dates from the Holocaust. I always expect the worst, and I find it fabulous when it happens that people show themselves as generous, I'm always surprised that people can express generosity or goodness. Because one is not full of that kind of impulse, or in any case, one harbors many things that can make one a Nazi, you see. One can become things that are quite frightening."

2. First Kinks

Blue Nudes

1958. Ecole des Beaux Arts. Ron, along with Adek and about twenty other young men of Adek's atelier, is stripped down to his underpants and along with the others, painting himself blue.

The Ecole des Beaux Arts is divided into a series of ateliers, each with its own character, something like a fraternity.

The character of Adek's atelier, to be frank at the start, is bad. It seems to consist largely of right-wingers and anti-semites. Today the students in Adek's atelier would certainly be supporters of the neofascist National Front of Jean-Marie Le Pen. Yet Adek, obviously a Jew, and whose father died at Auschwitz, is clearly a part of the atelier's macho camaraderie.

"At eighteen I lived in the concentration camps through my imagination," Adek, who is an artist, is quoted as saying in a recent interview. "I fantasized a lot about the pair of the victim and the executioner and I found a sort of confusion between the two. It's the theme of my current paintings, the victims can become the executioners by a change of costume."

Adek's current paintings are dominated by cloth, cloth on canvas, you might say. But it's cloth that has the quality of a primal stuff out of which figures emerge and into which they merge, in this case figures of SS killers and concentration camp victims, the one turning into the other through the medium of cloth, the stripes of the prisoners continuous with the uniforms of the SS.

And the use of cloth is a brilliant stroke, because the typical profession of impoverished pre-war immigrant Jews here in France was tailor. Why? Because all you needed was a needle and a spool of thread.

Adek reminds Ron of the Polish side of his heritage, brooding, self-effacing, masochistic, traits which Adek can enact with precision and brilliance. Like certain other Jews, he's attracted to the position of victim and has learned how to use it to moral advantage.

But the victim becomes the executioner. Jews have a chameleon history, and Adek, scintillating and incurably gregarious, knows instinctively how to take on the color of his environment.

Tonight the color is blue.

John Paul Sartre

The *Bal des Quat'z Arts* is an event that doesn't happen any more, you'll see why.

Toward evening, Ron, Adek and the rest, naked or almost, plus a fat pig of an artist's model named Lulu, charge out into the streets. It's the hour when people are still drinking their aperitifs or demis on the open terraces of the cafés, and others are beginning to fill the restaurants.

Shouting and chanting, the students hit the cafes on Rue Bonaparte and Rue de Seine, and on out to Saint Germain des Près. Arriving at a café, they shout, sing, bang the tables and bother the customers as much as possible. Soon the chant begins: "A! Boire! A! Boire! A! Boire!"

Lulu gets up on a table and does an obscene little dance, allowing the customers the privilege of looking at her fat ass. It isn't long before the management provides the requested drink, if only to get rid of the students and minimize impending property damage. There's no question of cops. This is a tradition. Medieval, Ron is told. Incorrectly.

Meanwhile, maybe twenty other ateliers, each painted its own color, are out doing the same thing, so this may be the twentieth time the café has been through this during the evening.

At one of the cafés in St. Germain des Près, probably the Deux Magots, or maybe it's the Brasserie Lipp, the atelier runs into Jean Paul Sartre sitting at a table, I think with de Beauvoir.

For the young fascists in the atelier, this is a golden opportunity. To bump into the country's leading leftist intellectual in a situation where all is permitted is something that doesn't happen every day.

One of these guys, let's call him Pierre, because that couldn't

78

have been his name, is habitually more aggressive than the others and is one of the few people in the atelier who openly harrasses Adek about being Jewish. Later, Adek finds out—am I making this up?—anyway, as I remember, that this kid is himself Jewish, but is hiding the fact from everybody.

The victim becomes the executioner.

This is the kid who starts banging on Sartre's table, chanting, "A! Boire! A bas la gauche! A! Boire! A bas la gauche!" a chant which the others immediately take up.

Sartre and his friend don't like this at all obviously, but what they like even less is what happens next.

What happens next is that the students sic Lulu on them. Lulu, of course, is not part of the atelier. There are very few women in the Ecole des Beaux Arts at the time. Those who are have to pretty much submit to becoming the sexual slaves of the leaders of the particular atelier. So at the time it's very hard for women to get through the Ecole des Beaux Arts.

Lulu is a life model for the atelier, as well as a sexual convenience, and hangs around because she seems to like the ambience. Much later Ron will discover that she seems also to like right wingers.

You can almost see Pierre's eyes light up with inspiration as he suddenly changes the chant, immediately followed by the others: "Lu! lu! Lu! lu! Lu! lu! Lu! lu!"

Lulu is a ferocious exhibitionist. This is an invitation for her to do her thing. Her thing is basically to expose herself in public on every possible occasion. She has her own particular version of the Can-can reminiscent of the Toulouse Lautrec cabaret scene when the police would come around to ascertain whether the performers were wearing their underpants. Lulu isn't.

This is a dance Lulu performs without music, and basically without dance either.

Ron's always wondered what the West's greatest post-war philosopher thought about when Lulu got up on a table and regaled him with a view of her *cul*.

"There's one end of capitalism," Ron is sure he hears him quip. But his French is shaky at the time. Could it be translated as, "There's capitalism at its end"? or maybe as, "There's the goal of capitalism"? or possibly, "There's capitalism at its extreme"? or maybe, "There's capitalism sulking"? or even, "There's capitalism in the mud"? or else, "There's capitalism's inner tube"? or even, imaginably, "Capitalism's a blood sausage"? or "a bloody sausage"?

In any case, he said something.

Was this perhaps the moment Sartre became sufficiently disillusioned with Western culture to turn down, some years later, the Nobel Prize? If so, it renders completely understandable a gesture which has puzzled many people.

In any case, what Ron has taken up to now at the level of student pranks, is beginning to seem a little rowdier than he's anticipated. But it's only when someone picks up Sartre's drink and drinks it that the waiters begin closing in.

Evidently, there are limits that the French instinctively recognize. At this point the kids in the atelier drain the beers the management has handed out, call Lulu to heel, and leave the café.

They're now in the intellectual's quarter, and at the next café toward Carrefour Odeon a young woman, one who looks like someone Ron would like to go out with, yells a mocking taunt at the group of blues. "If you guys knew how to screw," she says so everyone in the café can hear, "you wouldn't need to run around with your dicks hanging out."

This gets a big laugh from the tables. "Sale Juive," is the brilliant come-back of the student next to Ron. "Dirty Jew."

And suddenly a voice in Ron's head says, "Hey, wait a minute."

But on to Montparnasse, the atelier drinking its way from one café to the next, and pretty soon Ron is beyond such subtleties of analysis.

Take Norman Mailer

The night is getting chilly, especially if you're dressed only in the color blue. But there are many cafés with beer and wine to warm you between the Latin Quarter and Montparnasse. By the time they get to Montparnasse things are getting blurry for Ron.

It's at La Coupole in Montparnasse where the notorious encounter between Ron and Professor Vigée takes place.

I call it notorious because though Ron, drunk as a bat, forgets about it the very moment it happens, people keep reminding him of it afterward through the years. Just the other day, thirty years later, a friend of his, Serge Doubrovsky, who is, like Vigée, a writer and a French professor, reminds him again with a sly smile.

Maybe the encounter is notorious because Professor Vigée is a rather well-placed French-Jewish writer. Or maybe it's notorious because Professor Vigée is directly responsible for saving the fellowship that sent Ron to France when it was almost torpedoed by a scathing letter of reference from Ron's former French professor, a lady who was also Ron's disgruntled ex-lover.

It's Ron who suddenly sees Professor Vigée at a table on the terrasse of the Coupole and, forgetting that practically naked and painted blue he doesn't look much like his tweedy academic avatar, immediately goes over and greets him.

As I remember, what Ron had in mind was to thank the Professor for his fellowship and present himself as if to say, You see, here I am! In the thick of things!

But the Professor, from what I gather by all accounts, first of all doesn't recognize Ron and, seeing this apparition approaching emitting slurred, drunken sounds that bear some puzzling relation to a retarded version of the French language, is first of all startled and also a little alarmed.

When it dawns on the Professor who this is, he's astonished and maybe a bit appalled. Ron is supposed to be here hoarding knowledge, not joining the barbarian horde. This does not accord with *les règles du jeu*—"Jewish rules." Good Jewish boys don't behave like swine.

However, when they do, they seem to become objects of fascination. Take Norman Mailer.

Thanks to Professor Vigée, Ron's in Paris to do research on the influence of French culture on the great but obscure American poet, Wallace Stevens.

In the course of his work, the eminent French philosophe, Jean Wahl, tells Ron that he's sure he met Stevens in France with the wife—he's very specific about her name—of one of Stevens' friends, a friend to whom one of his major poems is dedicated. Ron is puzzled because Stevens had always claimed he had never set foot in Europe, and he knew that such information might blow the standard view of the great poet sky high.

Like the news, after his death, that stolid Wordsworth whelped a French daughter in his revolutionary youth.

Ron's ensuing confusion has thrown his project into doubt, and given him a bad case of writer's block, which leaves him ample time to squander on affairs like the *Bal des Quat'z Arts.*

To tell the truth, I don't have the vaguest memory of what next transpired between the Professor and Ron, so why make it up? Either Ron offered the Professor a drink, or swiped his drink, or made obscene advances to his female companion, I've heard several versions, often with the implication that there's much left unsaid.

It will have to remain unsaid.

He Hears Her Scream Once

The next thing Ron does remember, they're in some huge hall. There's a stage set up on one end, whose use is not yet obvious, and a dance floor.

Each atelier seems to be allotted its own territory in the hall where its members camp and guard its women, who are generally kept in various states of undress, sometimes nude. The ateliers are very fussy about letting outsiders fuck their women, Ron discovers, unless they're invited to fuck them.

Actually, Ron isn't too clear about the status of the women

before the fact. He knows the ateliers are supposed to bring women, but he's not sure what happens next. Though he's hoping.

A lot of the female guests look like foreign girls. It turns out that most French girls stay away from the *Bal* because they know what's going to happen to them if they attend. According to the guys in the atelier, it used to be, not many years ago, that lower class girls in Paris were flattered to get it on with the nice young men of wealth and breeding who mostly compose the student body of the Ecole des Beaux Arts. They grumble over the way things are degenerating.

Adek, of course, is totally proletarian and poor as a mouse. He's not only poor, he believes in being poor. In fact it's only by being poor that he can justify hanging around with these rich reactionaries. He exercises bad taste as a matter of solidarity with the proletariat. He persists in drinking only the cheapest wine available, about the quality of what the clochards get high on at night on the quai under the bridges of the Seine.

"Once," says Adek, "my grocer gave me a bottle of really good wine by accident, and I drank it by mistake. The effect compared to what I usually drink was practically psychedelic."

I think in those days Adek would have killed so as not to betray the community of victims—the poor, the Jews, the deprived—to which he was fiercely committed. Even then, when the rest of the atelier went to their right wing rallies, he would resolutely head for some demonstration by the left.

Once the ateliers herd all their women into the hall, they lock the doors. For the night. No one can get out till the morning and no one else can get in, including the forces of law and order.

For a while the *Bal* proceeds like any other giant party, lots of music, lots of dancing. Then Ron finds out what the stage is for.

Each atelier in succession presents its women to the crowd. A poil. Nude.

Some women, drunk, or exhibitionists, or just plain whores hired for the occasion, walk out onto the stage willingly, or semi-willingly, or reluctantly, and display themselves on commands from the wings or to shouts from the crowd.

Others are not so willing. They are shoved or dragged onto the stage. Sometimes they appear minus an article of clothing and then run off stage, only to be shoved back on a moment later, minus another article of clothing, until they're totally nude. Often these girls are in tears. Ron distinctly hears one girl sob, "I didn't know."

At this point Ron, who up to now has participated like a tourist in an entertaining example of foreign customs, has the sudden sense that nobody has the right to do this sort of thing to anybody.

The bestiality is contagious. A kind of brutish hysteria takes over. Everybody is drunk and chanting: A! Poil! A! Poil! A! Poil! A! Poil!" Ron now of course realizes that he's somehow got involved in what he would later call a swine event.

One girl, a tall zaftig American, who totally refuses to submit, punching and scratching and biting each time she's pushed out onto the stage, is finally held by three or four guys while her clothes are ripped off in front of the crowd. Still struggling, she's passed down naked to the grasping hands of the mob.

Ron sees a green hand clutching her thigh, a yellow one squeezing her breast, a black one pulling an arm, and feels an irresistible flash of lust as he reaches for her with the rest.

Then, smeared with the colors of the ateliers contending for her possession, she's raised and fumbled over the heads of the crowd like a loose foot ball until a squabbling party of oranges and blacks manages to run off with her now limp figure.

He can't tell what happens to her. He hears her scream once.

Esthetic of Evil

Revolting. Ron has a huge erection. Immobilized between lust and disgust, he suddenly feels awful. He feels queasy and weak, as if he's fighting off an infection.

Maybe it's all the drinking. But for some reason he can't understand, he feels like he's been raped too. That's not the way he puts it to himself at the time. But at the time Ron doesn't understand anything much, especially his own feelings. Adek, at least, who later would be mortified by his participation in the *Bal*, in recent years has come to understand more about his own.

"Any form of power is insupportable to me," says Adek in his recently published interview. "I always distrust myself when I'm in a privileged position. I'm afraid of being among those who are privileged because I don't know how I'll react myself, maybe I'll abuse it, or have pleasure in exercising it, and I don't want to take that risk."

These days Adek is more conscious of the possiblity of his having emotions, as he puts it to Ron not long ago, "that I refuse to have."

Many years after the *Bal*, just a few months ago, Adek tells Ron that at that time Lulu was a close friend of Le Pen, who had been a politically active student and, young though he was, had already been elected to the National Assembly.

Le Pen, according to Adek, has always, from the beginning, been able to articulate feelings that people normally refuse to have.

"He dares to say things," says Adek. "And he dares to say them through something, you see, on the order of sexual fantasies. He always has things that turn on sexuality, Le Pen, yes, there are always those implications, you see, he talks about how if you open France to foreigners you open your women to them. And very, very often when it's not something like that it's, well, something like, 'I've shown my drawers and I'm waiting for Chirac to show his.'

"But it's always sort of at the level of underwear, of this very French banter where you talk about everything that's troubling. You see? It's not so much that he's a skilful politician, it's that he represents a way of thinking people have. His effect has been that everything that seemed forbidden before no longer seems so.

"I find it a very, very unhealthy phenomenon. He trails something unhealthy after him. He's very astonishing, Le Pen, because there's a lot of scandal around him—his financial inheritance was suspect, his wife getting mad at him and showing her ass in the French *Playboy* wearing a maid costume, producing a record of Nazi songs—and the more he wallows in it, the more votes he wins. As if he carries on his shoulders everybody's mediocrity. You see? He's mediocre, and he permits everyone to be mediocre. He talks garbage, and he permits everyone to talk garbage. That's it."

"People like it that he's a little corrupt."

"Completely. I'm convinced, because when he's corrupt they can identify with him. Yes, because someone who's excessively moral, if you want, they can't identify with him, he'll make them feel guilty for having those thoughts. Le Pen gives them complete liberty to have the filthiest thoughts—he out-does them."

"He's a little like an artist," Ron suggests.

"I think less an artist than a believer. Because he's always had this line. Me, I've known Le Pen since the Beaux Arts, when he was a big friend of Lulu's.

"On the other hand he feels free to say no matter what. He's a libertine, he represents a Beaux Arts type, he's very, very Beaux Arts. In his triviality, his attitude toward women, toward gluttony. There's a Rabelaisian side to him, but not a healthy one."

"Like Goering."

"There you are. He's a libertine."

Later, reeling home in the empty hour before dawn, fragments of Wallace Stevens' "Esthetique du Mal," on which he has been working intensively, swim through Ron's head. *The death of Satan was a tragedy for the imagination. . . . We are not at the center of a diamond. . . . Life is a bitter aspic.* A wild vision invades him as he staggers, naked and shivering, through the livid streets.

Suppose that Stevens had a secret life in Paris that explained why Jean Wahl encountered him there? In Paris, and in New York and Key West where he liked to go when he was away from the insurance company of which he became Vice President. It was logical that there would be some libertine equivalent of the sensuousness of the poetry, beyond the asceticism of the public life. The secretive character of his poetic career as he pursued business success, the alienation from his wife, the trips to Key West with the boys, the peculiar fist fight with Hemingway, the rumor about a "homosexual clique" in his insurance company relayed to Ron by a professor at Cornell, the occasional literary encounter with esthetic foreign young men, the remark to Ron by Phillip Rahv, who knew him and published some of his poetry in *Partisan Review*, that his never having been to Europe was "bullshit."

No wonder that, as Ron reels through the streets this early A.M. in his drunken delirium, he has a vision of Stevens on a red Matisse couch, huge and fat and nude, colored blue, surrounded by equally colorful and nude boys and girls, drinking an enormous martini. An avuncular voluptuary who could have been cut from Stevens' own erotic poem, "Le Monocle de Mon Oncle."

Ron knows, of course, that this is merely the projection of his own nature, split between thinky and kinky. But there is much about the great poet that echoes divisions within himself. And then there is the Modernist elitism that allowed for Stevens' frigid poetic abstraction, his reputed admiration for Mussolini, so that at times Ron finds the poetry itself "a bitter aspic"—hard to swallow.

On one side Stevens had forged a faith of skepticism, ambiguity and complexity that was almost Jewish. On the other, he had indulged a blood and earth paganism that was almost fascist. Ron thinks of the pronouncement of the scholar Adorno that after Auschwitz poetry is no longer possible. It's possible, Ron thinks, but maybe schizophrenic. Because words no longer correspond with data.

Ron can only appeal for help in the poet's own words, which he does aloud to the bored surprise of the yawning concierge as he wobbles home through his courtyard: "Oh! Rabbi, rabbi, fend my soul for me, / And true savant of this dark nature be."

3. The Virus

An Attack

The first time Ron realizes he's having an attack of the virus is the first time he's living alone in Paris, and it's communicated to him by the books of the French novelist Céline.

Ron is very attracted to Céline's books because, though bitter, they're funny and have their own kind of charm. And Ron is charmed, he's enthralled, and as sometimes happens when an artist casts a spell on him like that, he drops everything, including eating and even sleeping, to read through some of his books.

However, Céline, though Ron is not in a position to know this at the time, is definitely a carrier, brutal, anti-semitic and fascist. And so without being aware of it, Ron opens himself to an attack of the virus.

Soon he finds himself being very mean to the girl he's going out with, he doesn't even know why. She's a young, innocent girl from Brooklyn who trusts him a lot, maybe because they have similar backgrounds. But Ron doesn't want to be trusted a lot, it seems to infuriate him to be trusted a lot, though obviously he doesn't tell the girl.

Her name is Ronda. It's her junior year abroad and she's all excited about being in Paris. Just a nice, middle class girl, all vulnerability and baby fat. A nice Jewish girl from Brooklyn who in fact has much in common with Ron and even went to the same high school he did, Midwood, though of course some years later.

Ron's relation with Ronda is odd because it's so double-edged. He doesn't pretend to understand it. When it becomes obvious that she's attracted to him he tries to shoo her away. He doesn't want to be going out with a girl from his old high school here in Paris, he wants to be going out with a French woman, a grownup with lots of experience and character laced, possibly, with vicious tendencies to be defined.

Nevertheless he does go out with her, if only because his vicious French woman has yet to show up in his life.

Ronda is a virgin. Ron doesn't know that at first. What she wants is a man considerably older than herself, Ron will do, who has had a certain amount of experience with what she thinks of as vice, though Ron doesn't know this either. What she thinks of as vice is making love, she's just out of Brooklyn, what does she know.

Ron has the odd experience with her of being nasty without any reason for being nasty, and even without wanting to be nasty. That's how he figures, in retrospect, that Céline had communicated the virus to him.

So the first time Ronda comes to Ron's little room in his hotel in the then existentialist quarter of Paris, Rue Jacob, Ron doesn't beat around any bushes, he just abruptly proposes that they make love. As if to say, in Paris, if you come to a man's room, you have to make love.

It isn't a very nice way to seduce a girl, but Ron's idea is that since she probably will refuse to make love, it will be an easy way to get rid of her. It's not that Ron doesn't like Ronda, he doesn't know what it is that makes him want to get rid of her. Maybe it's that she's too nice. She's what they'd call in Brooklyn "a lovely girl." Ron doesn't want any truck with lovely girls. Don't ask him why. Let's say it's because of Céline.

But when Ron asks Ronda to make love with him she outflanks him by answering neither yes nor no. Instead she tells Ron she's a virgin. For some reason this puts Ron into a cold rage.

"So why did you come here if you're a virgin? Is it my business that you're a virgin? What are you telling me this for?"

Ronda just shrugs and looks embarrassed. Ron knows he's being irrational but there doesn't seem to be anything he can do about it. Since she doesn't make any move to leave, Ron starts to undress her. He knows he's being a pig, in fact he doesn't even feel like making love, what he feels like is being a pig. He's angry that she's such a nice girl. Nice girls always make him extremely uncomfortable. The only solution is to fix her so she's not so nice.

Instead of resisting being undressed Ronda helps him a little until she's naked. Ron pushes her back on the bed and gets a condom out, unzips his pants and unrolls it down his cock. He's really not being very nice and he knows it, but he goes to work on her anyway.

When he hits her hymen he knows it's going to be a job, it feels like the gate of the castle and there's nothing to do but use his cock like a battering ram. He figures he must be hurting her but she doesn't make a sound. Finally he breaks through and comes just like that. Not very nice. She doesn't even move. Finally she asks, "Is that it?"

"I'm afraid that's it," says Ron.

"Thanks," she says. Then adds, "Well, I guess I should go now."

"Let me get my cock out of you first," says Ron.

"I didn't mean . . ."

"Shit, how do you get blood off a bedspread?"

"Oh god, I'm sorry," she says. "Let me fix it." She gets some water and rubs it on the spread, then gets dressed.

Leaving, she stands by the door waiting for a goodbye kiss she's not going to get.

"I guess I'll see you," she says.

There are tears on her cheeks, so as a concession Ron says, "Yeah, I'll call you up."

Which he doesn't. After she leaves he feels horrible. He doesn't know why he's being such a swine.

Chicken

The very next day Ron gets violently sick, fever, diarrhea, the whole thing. It's the virus for sure, it must have been incubating for a while because for some days Ron's felt strange.

The hellish thing is that the toilet is down three flights of a steep, precarious spiral staircase, across the court, and up two flights on the other side. It's almost always out of the squares of torn newspaper they use for toilet paper and it stinks. The worst thing is that when Ron gets an attack, which can be as often as

90

every twenty minutes, it's a toss up as to whether, tripping and sliding down the spiral staircase and falling up the stairs, he can get over there in time.

And if somebody is in there, forget it.

Ron has no medication, he can't afford a doctor, so he figures the best thing he can do is stop eating. So he doesn't eat anything for a day or two and just lies there sleeping and reading Céline. After a few days he manages to crawl out to a local Chinese restaurant and order a bowl of rice and some tea once a day.

The management of the restaurant treats him as if he's some kind of large cockroach, but at least they don't throw him out.

The owner of the hotel eyes him as if he's thinking of calling the police, or maybe the Humane Society or even local pest control.

What Ron doesn't realize, because he has no mirror, is not only has he not shaved or gotten out of his clothes for almost a week now, but he's covered with chicken feathers. The whole room is gradually being covered with chicken feathers.

What it is is that the hotel stuffs its own pillows and quilts with feathers, which the owner's wife chops up every day in the courtyard. Evidently she doesn't stuff them too well, because they have a way of leaking feathers all the time, and since Ron is doing nothing but sleeping and reading Céline in bed there's almost nothing left in his pillows or quilt and there are feathers all over the place.

Ron is wearing woolens to keep warm and the feathers adhere to his clothes, not to mention his hair and growing beard, and he looks like something that's crawled out of an aviary at the zoo.

One day there's a knock on the door and it's Ronda. When she walks in and sees him standing there like that she puts her hand to her mouth, supressing a little scream.

In retrospect, Ron realizes she probably thought he'd undergone a metamorphosis into a large chicken.

"What's wrong?" Ron asks her.

"Nothing, nothing," she says. "Are you all right?"

"Of course I'm all right, don't I look all right?" Then, irrationally thinking she's shocked to see him because he's been so mean to her, he starts apologizing profusely for screwing her.

"No, no, not at all," she insists. "You were very nice. It was a very good experience for me."

This gets him totally irritated with her again. "What do you mean nice, don't try to humor me because I'm sick. Who do you think you're talking to, to some schmuck from Brooklyn?"

"No, really. I mean it. You did a good job."

"Look, just get out of here, will you? Just leave me alone."

"All right, I'm going. I don't want to upset you."

And she leaves, just like that. But for the next several days he finds things to eat and drink outside his door, which he wolfs.

Soon he finds he's regaining his strength. He realizes he's been starving himself, and probably also overtaxing his mind by reading too much Céline. So along with his change of diet, he decides to read some trash novels he's found in the room. They're full of violence and soft porn, implying values that might inspire a Storm Trooper and, in fact, one of them is about the exploits of a Storm Trooper.

After the bracing bitterness of Céline he finds that this kind of sloppy sleaze makes him sick. It panders to a scattershot spectrum of all too human neuroses. As soon as he starts reading the trash books he has a violent relapse. It seems he's lost his appetite for trash.

Ron goes back to Céline. It's like drinking a cup of espresso. Bracingly inhumane.

Only then does Ron realize what's going on between him and the poisonous texts of the great novelist. Ron's being immunized.

White Slave?

Once Ron has recovered, he starts going to the café where he hangs out at the time. La Palette is near the Ecole des Beaux Arts, and he often meets people he knows there, including Strop Banally. Strop is a kind of rake with no evident income, and seems to live off women, in fact Ron sometimes wonders whether he isn't a downright pimp. Or worse.

But Strop is unfailingly jaunty and impertinent. Ron finds him tonic, as in gin and.

After a while Ronda starts showing up at the café every day to sit at Ron's table, irritating him and spoiling his aperitif. One day Ron has an inspiration.

"You know that fifty francs I owe you?" he says to Strop.

"Yeah?"

"Well I'm still broke."

"Big news."

"Well, but suppose instead of the fifty I introduce you to this really sexy woman, and not only sexy but some one who'll be like putty in your hands, you'll be able to do with her as you will."

"I don't need women, Ron."

"I know you don't, but I think you'll find Ronda just your meat."

"Well, forget the fifty francs anyway. But I'll meet her if you want."

Just as Ron predicts, Strop turns out to be attracted to Ronda for wholly unwholesome reasons. And when he introduces them she immediately relates to Strop like a puppy to her owner, or a slave to her master, there's something disgusting and masochistic about it. But at least Ron expects he'll take her out of circulation for a while, if not permanently.

As a matter of fact, Ron doesn't see either of them around for a while. He wonders where she's hanging out. Sometimes he actually wants to see Ronda. As if he'd gotten fond of her.

Still, it's a relief to be able to sip his demi peacefully again in the afternoons at La Palette.

Then he gets worried. What if Strop really does something mean to her? What if he's corrupting her in some weird way? What if he sells her into the white slave trade or something? Why is Ron such a bastard with pathetic Ronda?

Ron senses that his difficulty with Ronda, and probably hers with him, is that they're too much alike. Despite all appearances they are both afflicted with a certain innocence, an unworldliness in the way they deal with the world, almost as if the world doesn't really exist.

In what strange realm do they live, you have to wonder.

Even their vices have an air of artifice, as if they are something learned from books. The similarity is almost familial.

At some level they are both aware of this unworldliness and despise it. Life seems to be a disease they yearn to catch.

In Ron this results in a pursuit of vulgarity. Ronda on the other hand craves the intrusion of the alien, a penetration by the banal. Her desire for violation is much deeper than masochism.

The consequence of this syndrome for Ronda seems to be a tendency to compromising situations. As with Strop.

But one day Ronda shows up at the café looking surprisingly womanly and well. When she sits down at his table Ron immediately wants to take her to bed again.

"Where've you been?" he asks.

"I'm in love," she announces.

"Oh yeah? Who with?"

"Strop."

"Strop? How can you hang out with a swine like Strop?" Ron has an unexpected pang of jealousy. And of anger. "A nice Jewish girl like you," he adds mockingly.

"Why not?"

"Why, he's . . . insincere." Ron hadn't expected to say that.

"So? Morals are fine but they don't make life worth living."

The innocent sweep of her remark makes a response inappropriate, Ron feels. If not impossible.

He wonders whether she's found it.

4. The Golden Calf

Art

Einstein once said that "the intellectual decline brought on by a shallow materialism is a far greater menace to the survival of Jewry than numerous external foes who threaten its existence with violence." This was in 1936, and of course Einstein was wrong.

Or was he?

If you had told Ron in 1958 that his Paris acquaintance, Art, would be a literary sensation in ten years, he would have assumed you were not somebody worth talking to. If you had told him in 1958 that Art, with his libidinously ambitious idea of success, would come to be taken seriously, he would have thought you were kidding. Art behaves as if there's no difference between worldly success and artistic success. Ron can't believe it.

But maybe that's only because Ron's story is not his story. Maybe Ron should have more sympathy for shallow materialism.

Ron meets Art through Strop. Art is a blond kid with freckles. He doesn't look. When he sits in a cafe with Strop the two of them project the image of the American upper crust, off on a carefree junket around Europe before going back to learn how to run General Motors or the State Department.

But Art still hasn't cut the umbilicus. He's still a member of the tribe by virtue of an acute case of victim identification syndrome. As soon as he becomes aware of a victim, a victim of anything, he substitutes himself. But only, of course, to the extent of usurping the victim's moral advantage. He's not a masochist, or if he is he's only a sentimental masochist.

Ten years later, Art's story about a Lubovitcher who runs for President is celebrated as the vanguard of the new "Jewish novel," written in a style of "black humor" influenced by the comedian Lenny Bruce. But Art's reputation as a literary clown collapses with his next book, which is about himself, and makes it obvious he takes himself seriously and has absolutely no intention of being funny.

Nevertheless, Art's pen has inadvertently led him to tap a profound Jewish craving for a shallow materialism leading to recognition and acceptance. As a result he goes on to dazzling commercial success, confirming his opinion of himself as a great writer.

And don't Jews crave a shallow materialism like anyone else? The fact that Art has become a great writer despite his literary pretensions simply proves that the pen is mightier than the pigs who feed in it.

The Second Commandment

But as a matter of fact, Ron at the time does not merit literary company any better than Art's. These are the days when Ron thinks of himself as a novelist, or at least as a future novelist. Just like Art. So why shouldn't Art judge Ron's writing by Art's standards?

It's not till Ron starts writing his first novel, *Up*, that he realizes he doesn't want to be a novelist. It's then that he realizes he finds the whole idea of what's called a novel boring. He realizes that he simply doesn't like the idea of making things up. It's a children's game. If he wants to make things up, he can go to work in Hollywood, preferably for Walt Disney.

But it's not till this very second, as I write these words, that Ron realizes his dislike for making things up is deeply connected with Jewish rules. The Jewish tradition has a long history of struggle against imitation, Ron remembers. Imitation is not the real thing. It's made up. It leads to the graven image. Which leads to the Golden Calf.

Graven images give you the liberty to make things up. It doesn't help if you call it Art, it's a false liberty, Ron believes. It's libertine.

Once you start making things up you start indulging yourself. You erect idols that are wish fantasies. But idols are always cheap imitations of treacherous gods. This is what Art has come to in our tradition, Ron thinks.

God's injunction against graven images is His second

commandment to the Jews, Ron reminds himself, right after declaring Himself God. And before the commandments against murder, stealing, coveting, false witness, honoring your parents and all the rest.

And in *Deuteronomy* God rages on and on about the dire consequences of graven images, graven images of anything, nearly destroying the Jews because of their worship of the Golden Calf.

Do people think that God was kidding?

There are many Jews today who worship the Golden Calf, Ron knows. But they know they shouldn't. Just as Ron knows he shouldn't be writing novels.

The Golden Calf is for the barbarian horde. If that's what they want. Just as imitation is for those who don't want the real thing.

Of course it has to be said that every time Ron looks over his shoulder at a book he's written, he finds it's turned into a novel. Behind his back.

5. Book of Daisy

The Assholes

1958. If you want to see what America is like, go to Paris.

Paris is like a petri dish for Americans, it isolates the germ and lets it grow. You take a few Americans fresh from the States, drop them into the medium of the dish and wait a few months, sometimes just a few weeks, then examine the resulting growth.

When Ron first drops into that petri dish he's living in a series of fleabags on Rue Monsieur le Prince. The Beats, already famous and with whom he has incidental contact, are living in the Beat Hotel on Rue Gît-le-coeur.

One night Ron sneaks a woman into his room on Monsieur le Prince, a good looking girl named Daisy Shane, just out of Sarah Lawrence, because she gives every indication of wanting to get it on. But when they get into bed—and it's a tiny single bed too—she tells Ron she doesn't do that kind of thing with boys.

She isn't kidding either. Daisy is American as apple pie, and that's what apple pie is like in those days. Frozen.

Ron is frozen himself. But he's frozen stiff and she's just frozen. Stiff or not, Ron finally realizes he's not going to get anywhere.

By three A.M. Ron is so pissed and frustrated and sleepless that he kicks her out.

"But where am I going to go?" whines Daisy.

"Your problem, sweetheart."

But for days afterward Ron worries, where *did* she go, a young, inexperienced girl with no French in a strange, tough city?

Even more though, Ron is worried about himself, like that wasn't a nice thing to do. Because at the time Ron's thing is being a nice guy. Is it possible, he wonders, that he's not really a nice guy?

The fertile isolation of the petri dish is already having its effect. The germ is germinating.

Next time Ron sees Daisy she's with Gregory Corso. They're all sitting around a table on the terrasse Aux Deux Magots. Those days you can still go to the Deux Magots with a straight face, though it's already starting to fill with American tourists inflamed with the romance of Existentialism, who refer to it as "the Aux Deux Magots."

Corso or no, Daisy is as frozen as ever. She says she's staying with Corso in the Beat Hotel. She confides to Ron that the toilet is so filthy in the Beat Hotel she cries every time she goes to the john.

There are many Americans who come to Paris planning to stay till their money runs out and then when it runs out decide they don't want to go back to the States. Young men and women with no careers, they usually blunder around a few months on a few emergency checks from home and then they go back anyway. Those who stick with it settle into a lazy, pleasant, marginal life which is either admittedly aimless or which they often call something like "painting" or "writing." Now and then it actually is.

They develop a variety of petty hustles to beat the impossibility of getting a work permit, and the women always have an additional option as a last resort.

A few months after meeting Daisy with Corso, Ron sees her sitting in a cheap café on Carrefour d'Odeon with Art and Strop. He sits down and says hello to Daisy. She's got a long pony tail that emphasizes her youth, and wears one of those yellow t-shirts that says *Herald Tribune.*

Art is dressed in full establishment Ivy with tie and tweed jacket, khaki slacks and white bucks. Strop is wearing a leather jacket and dark glasses and seems to be assuming the role of a rebel, which of course is a traditional American way of working into the establishment. He refers to middle class American tourists generically as "the assholes."

As in, "Why don't we go over to St. Germain des Près and watch the assholes."

Daisy is going on about her financial difficulties and how she doesn't know where her next franc is coming from.

"I'm living on the money for my ticket home," she says. "Now I don't know what to do."

"I thought you were hustling money from one of the assholes," says Strop.

"He wasn't an asshole, he was my boyfriend."

"That doesn't mean he wasn't an asshole," says Art.

"Who are the assholes?" Ron asks innocently.

"Who are the assholes," repeats Art. "You know who the assholes are."

But it's a question Ron continues to ask himself.

"I don't know where to turn," Daisy says.

"Maybe it's time to use that number I gave you," says Strop.

Daisy bursts into tears.

Ron suddenly has an appointment and leaves. He knows what the number is. It's the number Strop gives women when they're down to their last asset.

Some months later Ron bumps into Daisy at Shakespeare &

Co., mingling with the middle class derelicts attending a poetry reading. He didn't know she liked poetry but he knows she's interested in Art, who is reading some Ogden Nash style doggerel.

The bookstore is not the same Shakespeare & Co. that was a center for literary exiles of the Lost Generation, but what the hell, it's something else. The indescribable miscellany of strays who hang out there look like the center of the Lost and Found Generation.

Daisy is upset. She just left a guy she was going out with.

"I'm just, I don't know, shook up."

"How long were you going out with him?"

"Three days."

"Three days, so what's the big deal?"

"We had a bad fight. Actually, I thought he was going to beat me up."

"How come?"

"Well I told him I'd go to Geneva with him, but I didn't tell him I'd stay there. When I asked for some money I guess he thought I was going to go shopping or something. After he found out I was taking the train back to Paris he got furious. I mean what does he want, I just met him."

"Anyone I know?"

"No, he's a much older man."

One thing you have to hand to Daisy, in the Paris wars she's an intrepid soldier. She's got guts and somehow she sticks it out in the sometimes somber City of Light.

Pigs in Shit

Many months later Ron meets Daisy again at a big American party in the seizième, in a quartier that's sort of the equivalent of Park Avenue, and she doesn't look any the worse for wear.

This is a party involving the early *Paris Review* gang. Through Art, Ron has acquired a passing friendship with a Rockefeller scion who invites him. They go over together on the Metro. The trip is confusing because the pretty Radcliffe grad his friend is with keeps rubbing up against Ron like she wants to get it on. Ron would have willingly obliged since he doesn't have a girl at the time and is horny to the point of death. But as soon as they get to this bash they all immediately lose themselves in the mob and the martinis and Ron never sees either of them again.

When after several hours of martinis Ron comes out the other side of the tobacco smoke and alcohol fumes, he's for some reason leaving the party with Art, Daisy and several drunk and raucous young American guys of a kind with which he does not normally hang out. They all wear jackets and ties, now rather askew, and seem to be having something like a prep school reunion. Aside from being stinking drunk, they show all the signs of good breeding.

Much as Ron dislikes this type he finds something attractive about them. They seem happy. Happy-go-lucky. Why shouldn't they be? Golden children of the Golden Calf. Carefree Canaanites. The ring leader, Guy Lobe, is from New Canaan, Conn.

Lobe is slightly older and works in Paris. They head for his apartment on the Ile St. Louis, where there is the promise of yet more booze and possibly other, unspecified goodies.

They end up in Lobe's apartment, which is well furnished with oriental rugs, antiques and whisky, and he even has a little pot, which is very exciting in those days. I mean, you could blow some pot and it was like so far out you could tell yourself that all your inhibitions were off on a walk around the block.

Not counting Lobe there are three of these guys besides Art and Ron. They're on their summer vacations from various business and law schools. After a while it becomes obvious that Daisy has been to bed with Lobe, and maybe also with Art. She doesn't even bother denying the heavy-handed innuendos of these two.

Daisy's new sexual license makes Ron a little jealous, but it's not too surprising at this stage of her growth in the petri dish. And really he's less jealous than envious of these guys who had whatever it took to make her acquiesce.

But now maybe because of these vibes a joke starts where they begin saying since she's already got it on with two of them she might as well make it with the others. Daisy just laughs at them and tells them to stop being jerks.

Ron figures she might be a little uneasy by this time, the only woman with all these drunks, and he offers to leave with her. But the other guys boo and hiss and accuse him of trying to hog her for himself, and Daisy just tells Ron to stop being a jerk.

They joke and badger her for a while about sex but naturally they don't get anywhere though she's reasonably good natured about it.

Finally Lobe says, jokingly Ron presumes, "All right, we'll pay you."

"I don't do that kind of thing," says Daisy with a smug little smile.

"Bull shit," says Art. He puts his hand on her ass and says, "Twenty-five bucks." She knocks his hand away.

"Each," he adds.

Daisy sort of giggles. She's as drunk as the rest of them and her laugh sounds slightly hysterical now.

"What the shit, make it fifty," says another guy as he starts pawing her.

"Cut the crap," she snaps. The guys are more focussed now and she's treating it less like a joke. "And get your dirty hands off."

The place goes quiet for about a minute.

Then Guy Lobe says, "How much do you want?"

She gives him a long, hard look and then she just shrugs her shoulders.

"All right," says Lobe. "A hundred." He looks around. "Is that okay with everyone? A hundred a piece."

"I don't have any money," Ron says.

"He doesn't have any money," someone repeats.

"Fuck him. He can watch," says Art.

Daisy's eyes are beginning to look glazed, like she's about to go catatonic. "Let's see the money," she says.

"A hundred bucks. One shot a piece," says Lobe.

They start pulling out their wallets, Art goes around collecting the bills.

"Going once, going twice," he says. "Okay." Art puts the money on the table, big bills, Ron sees at least two hundreds, some fifties.

Lobe starts unzipping her dress. She doesn't resist. They hoot as he takes her clothes off, applauding and whistling as Lobe drops each item to the floor.

Ron already knows she has a beautiful body but he doesn't realize how beautiful. She's got a body worth a million bucks and Ron can understand why she's decided to cash in on it. The guys can see they're going to get their money's worth. It shuts them up for a minute anyway.

"Shit, a hundred bucks a piece," says one of them finally with a forced laugh. "Which piece is mine?"

"I want a breast," snickers another.

"Interesting what money can buy," says Lobe.

"Or what you can sell for it," says Art.

What they do is get her on her hands and knees on the table and play with her for a while. Ron gets a look at her face and she's staring into space. The best way Ron can describe her expression to himself is she looks like she's taking a shit.

The guys around the table are still laughing some but it doesn't sound like laughter anymore. It sounds like their throats have gone dry, like Ron's. The sounds that come out are like the coughing of an old drunk stumbling along an empty street on a winter night.

Finally they put her on her back with her legs off the edge of the table. Art takes out his cock, grabs her ass and goes in. The others watch like animals watching a stud mounting the female in heat. "Hung like a stallion!" one of them says with unconvincing bravado.

It doesn't take very long, it seems like maybe thirty seconds before Art groans, twitches and flops out.

For Ron what's going on is a certain loss of innocence, even though he's just watching. If I ever thought I was a nice guy, forget it, he thinks. All he wishes is that he had a hundred bucks.

The third guy comes in her mouth. After that they give her a bottle of whisky and she takes a long drink.

Lobe goes last. He turns her over and penetrates her from behind, then pulls out and carefully separates her cheeks to expose her asshole. With a look on his face that might best be described as devout, he bends down and starts licking her ass hole, working his tongue all around and then in. You can actually see the point of his tongue flicking in and out of her hole. After a short time the tip of his tongue starts turning yellow-brown, she's probably been eating in those student restaurants.

"Good god," says one of the guys. "Holy shit," says another. *Treyf*, Ron thinks, and is immediately surprised at thinking it.

Lobe straightens up and starts drilling his cock up her ass. "Wait," she says, "that's not . . ." She gives a little cry and then takes it.

Soon Lobe is up to the hilt and moving like a piston. He comes with a loud yell that could be of triumph or despair, Ron can't tell which. After he pulls out he takes a mouthful of whisky, swishes it around, and spits it on the Persian rug.

When he's done with it they offer her the bottle. She shakes her head. "The money," she says numbly.

"The money," Art repeats. He picks it up and counts it out in front of her nose. Then he rolls the bills lengthwise in a tight cone. "Hold her," he says.

But it's not necessary. She just lays there as he carefully works the cone into her ass. She starts wriggling to accomodate his thrust, the first sign of animation she's shown. With one last, hard push the bills disappear.

At that moment her body stiffens, she screams and her head rolls so Ron can see her face, eyes closed, mouth gaping, bearing an expression that could be pain or bliss.

"Yeck," says one of the guys.

Now evidently disgusted with her, and maybe with themselves, they get her dress on quickly, hustle her out the door and down to the street. "Oink, oink, oink," says Art as she stumbles out the courtyard door.

Ron follows quickly after her, but must have turned in the opposite direction. She seems to have disappeared in the dark streets. At this point her ass is literally worth five hundred dollars.

It's two A.M. and everything is closed, including of course the Metro. Ron can't find a taxi, he hopes she can. If not he figures she's going to have to walk carefully because they didn't even give her time to get her underwear on.

When Ron remembers this episode it gives laundered money a new meaning.

6. How To Be Jewish

Cryptic Interlude

All of the above is true, and Ron doesn't like it. One can become things that are quite frightening.

But Ron is a fundamentalist of the book. He believes that books should be literally true. It is only the literally true that is fundamentally mysterious.

Ron is currently doing research for a project whose title is *Wholly Book*. It is a book he keeps trying to summon up through fast and prayer. Actually there isn't much fasting involved except when he's drinking to help with the praying. But there is a sort of prayer involved, a kind of praying that resembles a kind of wishing that resembles a kind of dreaming.

This book Ron is dreaming up would be a book containing what he calls the collected conscious.

His quixotic idea is that the collected conscious as the antibody to the virus should be collected in a book that is wholly a book and not partly an illusion.

The collected conscious cannot be collected even partly in a book that is part illusion that is partial to being something it literally is not.

The collected conscious is too fundamental to manifest itself in a partial book.

What we yearn for Ron obscurely believes is a book that is true beyond illusion and this book could only be a fundamental book that does not pretend to be something it literally is not (doven).

This book would be the book that is wholly book (doven).

This would be a book that Ron believes in wholly (doven).

This would be and is the wholly book of books.

Amen.

The Doctor

Ron thinks it began with the infamous swine flu vaccine fiasco, but at a certain point Americans changed. Not long after World War II, as if America had been invaded by some germ. It was not worse than before, but different.

And possibly worse. It remains to be seen.

Maybe the germ was transmitted after the defeat of Germany, when all those Nazi Germans, led by Werner von Braun & Co., were unleashed on our shores by secret government agencies hell-bent on our protection from foreign infection.

Maybe the virus evolved in the camps via the experiments of Dr. Mengele. Or developed as a result of some biogenetic mutation from the A-bomb.

Ron is of the opinion that though the virus may have come from Europe, if not Hiroshima, it was probably spread in America by air conditioning. He thinks it's a phenomenon parallel to Legionnaire's Disease, whose virus is spread by large cooling systems.

He thinks this virus is carried by individual cooling units. He points to the boom in room-size air conditioners just after World War Two. He believes it is more than coincidence that the trend to individual air conditioners with their intrinsic environmental selfishness took hold at the same time as the degeneration of political morality during the McCarthy era. This was when civic philosophy, sickening, fell victim to epidemic self-interest.

But for some years Ron has been a certified Doctor of Philosophy. What is he waiting for? It must be good for something.

No doubt about it, the air conditioners are the carriers. There is even an air conditioner called the Carrier.

Ron believes that even if none of this is literally true, it is none-the-less symbolically true.

Be Frei

Ron in Paris gets a letter from home, it's from Bea Frey. It reads:

>Dear Ronnie,
>
>I know I should call you Dr. but I remember you as little Ronnie Uncle Ben's best friend. Thank you for the book Up. I can't believe you would start being a writer with the small typewriter Uncle Ben and I bought you for your I believe 6th birthday. Do you remember Uncle Ben bringing a bag of small potatoes to Grandma on Saturdays. Grandma would call the whole family together to have boiled potatoes and butter. Sometimes I regret moving from the house. But certain circumstances forced us to. Ben had a hard life working for the family. But when he and I came to Florida, he lived the life he should have had all the time. He was a completely different person. Hope this finds you happy and well for a happy Passover.
>
>Love Aunt Bea

Now I see the story, thinks Ron. It's never too late. To change. To become a completely different person.

AUTONOMY

Is It Good For The Jews?

The family comes from Bialystok, but he knows that any traces there are gone. In 1941 there were 50,000 Jews in Bialystok. In 1945 1,085 remained, some actually from neighboring towns. That means at least 48,915 were killed, among whom no doubt all the Sukenicks. Figure it out.

On top of that there were pogroms and pervasive anti-semitism in Poland even after 1945, and later, in 1968, a government campaign drove almost all remaining Jews out of the country. After the war there were 250,000 Jews of the original 3,000,000 who survived or returned. Today, in a nation of 39,000,000, there are 4,000 Jews, 46,000 less than there were in Bialystok alone before the war.

So why bother going back to Bialystok, or anywhere in Poland for that matter? There's nothing to go back to. No, his destination is the Sukiennice, the huge Medieval cloth hall in the center of Kracow. Because he's searching not for his origins, but for Ronald Sukenick himself. I mean, given Jewish grandparents from Poland, he's always suspected a Polish component of his personality absent to his consciousness.

His family, you see, had owned a cloth mill in Bialystok. And then there is the name, a lexicographer in Warsaw works it out for him. *Sukno* is a kind of fine, woolen cloth used for overcoats.

And a *sukiennik* is one who makes it. So destination Sukiennice, simple as that. Sukenick seeks sukiennik.

Ron is there to give readings from his fiction. This is just after Jaruzelski's military takeover that crushed Solidarity until it rose again to triumph years later.

He starts in Warsaw. There his hotel is filled with Arab terrorists. Warsaw's where they come for R & R he's reliably informed. At breakfast a man in a red checkered kefiyah and a heavy black moustache tries to sell him a small golden hand, charm bracelet size, and a tiny archaic calf statuette, also golden. Claims he "got" them from a Jew. Ativistic warnings activate in primal circuit boards. Bloody Canaanite idols? Pre-abramic oedipal butchery? Moloch offal? Human burnt offerings? Allah suicide assassin? Jesus cannibal sacrifice? Ron has the feeling these gilt symbols, symbols of get and got, grasp and greed, are part of an impenetrable ancient code, read in steaming entrails by priests hostaged to death. Gilt for guilt. Fascist death cult nihilism. Bondage and libertinage licensed by potent chthonic gods rising from mud, blood and shit. Maybe it's only his imagination, but he turns his back and walks away, the PLO type still dangling his charms.

Now he's in Lublin, the focus of his professional trip whose underlying purpose is to give what intellectual and moral support he can to the increasingly oppressed but quixotic intelligentsia. Solidarity. With this country and its new death camp saint whose Auschwitz cell is the only one decorated with fresh flowers. It's another Jew who mentions that the martyr priest, Kolbe, had sacrificed himself for another Pole in the camp and had run an anti-semitic periodical before the war. When Ron complains about the viciously anti-semitic caricatures in a Wajda film, his closest Polish associate informs him it's not anti-semitic, that's just how Jews are. But the status of Jews has improved recently since the regime tried to persecute them as the instigators of Solidarity, because everybody knows there are almost none left.

In Lublin the patrons of the restaurant Ron is eating in are toasting Brezhnev's death just that day, while on the campus of the university, students walk around sullenly under the eyes of the brutish ZOMO security police, which is in process of suppressing uprisings in other cities—Gdansk, Warsaw, Katowice and Nowa Huta, adjacent to Kracow. The only news about the strikes and demonstrations is coming through on BBC, Radio Free Europe and Voice of America, when they aren't jammed. But it's clear that the Polish cavalry on its horses, waving its swords, is still charging the enemy tanks.

Considering ZOMO surveillance, frankly, Ron is for once glad to have the Embassy's International Communications Agency staff on his case. But is the ICA also the CIA? Do they also covet the Golden Calf? Or are they part of a CIA international anti-Moloch SWAT team? Moloch, after all, is the lord of the flies. Whose side is who on? Who's on his? Anti-semite Walesa patriots? Voice of America freedom mongers? CIA liberation spies? What code scans here?

Surveillance is heavy-handed. Every time you make a phone call the ring signal is punctuated by a message that says the call is being recorded. But most people ignore it. The kids are defiant.

"I took a trip to Czechoslovakia," says a student, "and people there are very nervous about police spies. We have them here too, but we don't care."

Ron and these rebellious students have no trouble with rapport. Ron understands very well that you can get to a point beyond which you don't care. He thinks of the Jewish ghetto fighters in Poland's cities, fighting an impossible battle till they're wiped out. But for Ron something is missing. The students have no sense of the contradictions involved in quixotic rebellion against a society of which you need above all to be part. The desire to live a life you haven't been able to live deprives you of some of the the joys of suicide. The students' situation seems difficult, but not impossible. The impossibility of the Jewish situation in Poland, is now, Ron supposes, clear.

A young Jewish intellectual tells Ron a story about how, during the government's post-war purge of the remaining Jews in the country, an old Jewish revolutionary walked into a Party meeting and was confronted by a misbegotten anti-Zionist banner declaring, "JEWS BACK TO SIAM." No doubt a Polish joke, confusing Sion with Siam. But in fact Ron is a Siamist, if not a Zionist. He's haunted by the absence of Siam. The absence of an impossible promise to meet the impossibility of the situation.

According to Ron's snapshots, the weather of the Sukiennice is damp, grey fog condensing on grey stone. The old cloth hall is very large, its facade a graceful arcade on whose slender pillars the weight of the massive structure seems to rest. It's set in an immense plaza with the Baroque tower of the old town hall on one side and a small Byzantine church on the other, so ancient it is partly sunk into the ground. The people hurrying across this great space are hunched over and have their hands in their pockets. Inside the Sukiennice cloth is still sold in the stone stalls where, Ron feels sure, his grandfather sold his in the 1870's.

And there outside the Sukiennice Ron finds the absent Ronald Sukenick. It's not simply that she has his father's green eyes, a trait common to many Poles. Though she is emphatically Slavic and Ron anything but, he feels he's found his Siamese twin.

They meet by appointment in front of the monumental statue of Adam Mickiewicz, Poland's liberation hero-poet, off to one side of the Sukiennice. She had told Ron that she wanted to meet in a public place because that was the only way to be private.

Ron doesn't know how he's going to recognize her but in fact there's no problem. He's been told that she would approach him very openly, that that would be the key. So when a stunning green-eyed blond appears before him, and when she immediately says in a resonant voice, "Bona knabino malfermi," Ron is not at a loss for words. As a Doctor of Philosophy in a literary discipline he recognizes Esperanto when he hears it, and of course knows that Esperanto was invented by a Jew from Bialystok.

With his training in languages Ron is able to decipher her greeting almost instantaneously and compose an appropriate reply. What she has said to him translates roughly as, 'Good open girl.'

"Malbona knabo fermi," responds Ron. 'Bad closed boy.'

Her taut face relaxes and she smiles. They lapse into English, their resources of Esperanto having been exhausted.

Marta is a writer and translator. She's one of the few writers publishing in the underground press under her own name. She hardly speaks at first, staring dully at the ground as they walk around the square. The adjective that occurs to Ron is morose.

Ron knows that Marta had been interned for many weeks after the military coup and when released had been fired from her job as a journalist. She then found her current job as a writer for an obscure veterinary magazine which has suddenly developed an allegorical level in the manner of George Orwell, along with a new audience.

Ron supposes that, like many of her compatriots, she's suffering a profound depression because of the political situation, but he's wrong. As soon as she starts talking about that situation she becomes energized, animated, almost gay. Her tactics, she says, are different from those of many Solidarity people. The underground must not hide itself, she says. That's why she uses her real name in underground publications, and why she wants the underground press and magazine she's helped start to be openly defiant.

"We are not subversives," she says. "We are fighting a war for our own country. It belongs to us."

"Many think it's a war you can't win."

"Of course we can't win. Not now. Maybe not ever."

"Then why fight?"

"Because we're stupid. Stupidity is our means of survival. It is what you call a Polish joke. I have heard people say that Walesa is stupid. Maybe he is. But sometimes it takes some really stupid people to change a situation the smart people know is hopeless."

When she starts talking about stupidity Ron suddenly feels right at home, back in Siam, so to speak, impossible promise. He's always disliked those smart people who know what it's all

113

about, the wise guys born to succeed, who are realistic and cynical and forget about Siam to run after their golden calves. Now he knows why. It's because he's stupid. He's stupid because he wants to be stupid, obstinately stupid like his friend in the Sukiennice.

So here's to you, Marta, and to stupid people everywhere. Marta is a sukiennik. When you want something really dumb, a Siam of any sort, you need a sukiennik to make it. Out of whole cloth.

With Marta's help Ron buys a piece of cloth in one of the stone stalls of the Sukiennice. Later, whenever he looked at it, he would think, a *sukiennik* is one who makes it.

That evening Marta takes Ron home with her. For dinner. And she wants him to meet her husband. The husband, a small, dark young man with mud colored eyes, is some sort of intellectual, it's not clear to Ron exactly how he makes a living. He seems in-grown, driven into himself. Ron wonders if he's Jewish or part Jewish, in the long tradition of Jews who have disappeared into a given national culture. Anyway, Ron immediately identifies with him too. As well as with Marta.

Marta has gone to some trouble to make a dinner. Maybe it's because Ron's expressed an interest in traditional cooking. The first course is a delicious, sweet soup, which turns out to be prune soup. After they eat it Marta shows Ron the recipe:

> Wash and soak 800 g prunes overnight.
> Cook them in 2 litres of water until they
> are soft, sieve or liquidize, add 200 g
> sugar and bring back to the boil. Slowly
> add 0.20 litres smetana or milk. Serve
> hot with potatoes or without smetana or
> milk if a meat dish is to follow.

"What do you think?" Marta asks.

"I think it's very good," says Ron, wondering what smetana is and about the meat or milk dish proviso.

Much of the dinner table talk is about the political situation, especially about the recent appointment of Glemp by the Polish Pope to replace himself as Cardinal of Poland. Glemp. The sound of a gob of spit hawked up in the throat of a brutish peasant. Every Polish intellectual Ron has met has clutched his head and groaned at the very sound of the name. Ron keeps wanting to ask the political question that pervaded his childhood: Is it good for the Jews? But he stops himself. What Jews?

The next course is a sort of dumpling stuffed with liver. When they're done Marta again shows Ron the recipe:

> Wash 400 g beef liver, drain and grill. When cool put through a mincer and mix with 300 g onion, chopped and fried, a chopped hard-boiled egg and salt and pepper. Make a dough from an egg, 300 g flour and water. Roll out thinly and cut into 3 cm squares. Place a portion of the filling on each square. Wet the edges and fold over, seal well. Drop into gently boiling water, and simmer for about 15 mins. Take out with a perforated spoon, drain and fry in hot oil on both sides. Serve as a hot hors d'oeuvre or to accompany a main dish.

This is obviously some Polish version of kreplach, Ron realizes. For the next dish, she gives Ron the recipe ahead of time:

> Rinse 200 g beans and soak overnight in cold boiledwater. Rinse 2 kg beef, cut into large cubes, sprinkle with salt, pepper, paprika and garlic to taste. Heat 100 g oil in a casserole and fry the meat with 200 g chopped onion. Add the beans, cover with water and simmer for about 2 hours. Now add 200 g buckwheat kasha, cover the casserole and leave in a low oven until ready to serve.

When the dish is served Ron realizes he's eating cholent, there can't be any doubt about it. Marta looks at him inquisitively as he tastes it.

"Is it right?" she asks.

Ron is no cholent expert, but he nods in wonderment. "Is it cholent?" he asks.

"I hope so," she says.

But when she serves him carrot and apple tzimmes for dessert, Ron finally understands she's trying to cook him a Jewish meal.

"People our age have never known many Jews here," she explains. "We want to know what Jews were like. What their culture was, what they ate. How they thought."

After dinner the three of them sit on the couch and drink vodka. Soon it becomes obvious to Ron that the way Marta keeps touching his thigh is not accidental. He starts getting turned on. Ron prefers his triangles with two women but he's not doctrinaire. The husband, though, seems a little tense.

Ron has the impression this is something they've done before, or more likely something Marta's done before and wants to try again. She's told him she's travelled in the States and who knows what bad habits she's picked up there.

Marta lets her hand rest on Ron's knee and looks into his eyes. "They say Jews have more fun," she says. "Is it true?"

"It's true," says Ron, "but is it fun?"

"Malbono knabino malfermi," says Marta, sort of wriggling as she says it. 'Bad open girl.'

The husband seems still more tense, sitting rigid with his hands in his lap, stiff as a puppet. Is it fun? Or is it something else?

As a Doctor of Philosophy, Ron can perceive someone's wife coming on to him. He can also apprehend when the husband gives tacit permission. He even understands when the husband wants to get into the act. But as a Doctor of Philosophy he also comprehends that the way such things happen is they either happen or they don't happen and either way it's because of factors out of your control.

Here, Ron guesses, the factor out of control is that though the husband wants to be sensually free he isn't free and as a Polish or even European Jew, if that's what he is, he'll never be free.

116

What would it take to bring such a puppet to life, the life of the world? Short of electroshock? Short of amnesia? There's something fishy here. For everything you pay, the more you know the less you play. That's Jewish rules. Here clay remains clay, no spark. Here joy is guilt, freedom is Moloch. Here earthiness ends beneath the earth. Here death makes you free, sensuous life never.

And maybe it shouldn't. Is it good for the Jews?

What Jews?

In any case Ron has to get to sleep early tonight. Tomorrow at dawn he leaves Kracow. He's with great difficulty altered his morning's intinerary to go to Auschwitz.

Ron gets up, finally, and says he has to go to sleep.

"Good closed boy," says Marta, drily.

Jerusalem

The landscape around Jerusalem is very minimal. You have the oasis of the town dense with trees and perfumed by flowers, with its glistening domes and architecture of pink stone, the labyrinth of the walled Old City enveloped by the complicated elaborations of its post-medieval growth, the emerging layers of its ancient and continuing destiny as incubator of civilizations in the pervasive archaeological digs, then rocky green hills then trees to the west and to the east beyond meandering but sharply defined limits, the desert—brown earth, dry rock, erosion, geologic rubble.

Nevertheless, it's from this dead landscape that the living water flows.

His unforeseen attachment to this arid country, its fabricated Jewish state and its fabricated language, is totally irrational. And why shouldn't it be?

Maybe it's because he likes the fate of being Jewish—it makes everything else seem so low key.

He came up from Tel Aviv, soft, oceanic, cosmopolitan metropolis. On the airplane this morning the Texan peered out a port hole and said, "Hot damn! It looks like Miami Beach."

The plane was cradling them down with a slight roll, wing tips seesawing slowly over the coast at Tel Aviv. The Texan twisted his soft neck toward the port hole, then back toward Ron. His plaid jacket, his knit tie, his pale haberdasher face. The kind of face that makes you feel you've seen it before and you probably have.

"Suppose we wanted to destabilize the situation completely." The Texan. "This is the plot. First we blow up El Aqsa and the Dome of the Rock, clearing the Temple Mount. Then we help the Jews build the Third Temple, see. Which brings on World War Three, Armageddon, the Second Coming, the end of the world and redemption. Hoo-hee!"

The Texan's voice is blurred with jet lag and Jack Daniels.

"Very intelligent," Ron remarks.

"It is if you're coming from the faith. But even to me it

could make sense and I'm coming from the intelligence."

The Texan blinks at him through his contact lenses. No doubt he wonders how literally Ron takes that. Whether he hasn't been too loose with somebody he hasn't seen before. Trying to recall what else he's said. Suspended in the airliner intimacy of alcohol, time-slip, and the certainty you'll never meet again.

The Texan probably thinks, Oh well, we'll never meet again, as he turns back to the airscape of sea, cloud fragments and white miamesque beach structures out the port hole.

But Israel is a small country.

Ron came up from Tel Aviv this morning, soft, oceanic, cosmopolitan metropolis. "The whore," remarked the black coated, black bearded, black hatted, earlocked religious in the Mercedes limo as it climbed away from the hazy, lazy Mediterrenean. Who asked him?

Ron used to take the sherut from Jerusalem to Tel Aviv and back all the time, it's a familiar drive now. But the first time still sticks in his mind. So he's more than surprised when he takes in the occupants of the sherut this morning.

The first time it was passengers from the plane, among whom the earlocked religious, a blond American woman, a professor from Giv'at Ram, a very portly American Jew wearing an embroidered *kipah*—yarmulke to you, a couple of swarthy Sephardim and the Texan.

The reason Ron is surprised when he looks around in the sherut is that the passengers are exactly the same as that first time years ago. It's enough to make him suspicious.

But of what?

The big Mercedes, the kind with the three-passenger jump seat, just moving out of Ben Gurion Airport. Palm trees festooning soft brilliance of sunlit, slightly humid air.

"Your first time in Jerusalem?" The professor. "You'll see. The light in Jerusalem . . ." A loud BOOM.

"What?" Ron. "What is . . ."

"You'll see. Light equals time, of course. Time equals the

speed of light." The professor's cadenced voice. "That's why you might say Jerusalem is bathed in time . . ." A loud BOOM.

"What . . . ?"

"Don't worry." The swarthy Sephardi up front twists around. "It's not the [   ]s already. He thinks it's the [   ]s already." With a slight smirk.

"Don't worry, jet boom." The very portly American.

"Hot damn."

". . . bathed in time so once something happens it can't stop happening. It just drops into the pool and ripples forever. As it were."

The blond American woman with her frank good-faith face. "What do you mean by that?" Probably a Christian come to see where He walkethed, get baptized in the Jordan.

"What do I mean? Do I have to know what I mean?"

The sherut from the airport. Otherwise when Ron used to take the sherut, especially from the bus station in Tel Aviv, there were never any foreigners. Only Jews.

Get that? No foreigners, only Jews. The first time he catches himself thinking that, Ron is astonished.

Going up to Jerusalem this time he remembers the first time. And all the times. It's hard to remember which time is which. Israel, Jerusalem especially, is a place where everything seems to happen at once.

Ron sitting in back next to the window, only slightly crowded by the professor next to him. The big struggle always to get a comfortable seat, since they don't leave till they're jammed full. Including the jump seats and the seats next to the driver. This time the two swarthy Sephardim yelling and shouting about who sits in the middle jump seat. In Hebrew of course. "Ma-a-a-a-zeh? Ma-a-a-a-zeh?"

Ron thinks they're angry at one another till someone explains much later. "If someone who doesn't understand would listen to Hebrew, they'd think you were angry. It's an impolite language." Very abrupt, abridged. Almost a code.

The driver waits. Finally the Sephardim settle somehow and get in.

The big limo pulling out onto the highway, people start pulling out their shekels and passing them up to the driver. Someone asks him to turn on the news. He does. It sounds like praying.

On the shoulder of the throughway a green sign just like the States, but Hebrew letters looking like a quote from the Torah. The translation too: YERUSHALAYIM. The big car smooths out the highway spooled through deep greens of farm land.

Here and there on broad flat fields complicated irrigation sprinklers fountain and mist. Storks stalk the crops. Cranes glide and cluster tall amid the grain, a few white herons. Occasional orchards, orange groves, vegetable farming. Then lots of plots dense with citrus trees. Palms and pines oddly assorted in same landscape. Wildflowers at roadside.

Looking back, a hazy glimpse of grey-green sea.

"Where is the port?" Ron.

"Jaffa?" The professor. "The southern part of Tel Aviv."

"That's the old port?"

"That's the oldest port."

"In Israel?"

"In the world."

The road now a gentle upgrade, the landscape starts changing. The first hilltop village built of bone colored stone. From Tel Aviv to Jerusalem you go up several thousand feet, mostly in the last third of the trip.

"You're from?" The professor. Ron knows he's talking to the very portly American with the embroidered beanie because he's already asked Ron.

"Los Gatos."

"This is where?"

"Near San Jose."

"You mean the States?"

"I mean California."

"And your business?"

121

"Rabbi."

"You're a rabbi?"

"Reformed. Very reformed."

The rabbi looks more like a biker, pointy beard, Hawaiian shirt, gold Jewish star hanging from neck. A blue tattoo on his hammy forearm says, "Never again."

"Yeah, my congregation is strictly edge city. Silicon, genetic engineering, you know. Not exactly kosher types. *Glat* Yuppie. They're shooting for the big one now. The superchip, everything on one cookie. The big one is the little one."

"Communication instead of communion, huh?" Ron.

"Hey, you think it won't change religion? The micro wafer of macro communion. We're going to bring it all home. Here. We're working with fundamentals. I'm a fundamentalist. We work with fundamentalists in the States. Why not? We all want Eretz Israel. To hell with the [   ]s."

"The peaceniks here would disagree."

"They should be shot. But I'm not here for that. Just a little archaeology. Why did you come?"

"To find something.'

"What?"

"I don't know."

The road starts to climb. YERUSHALAYIM 40. No more palms. Bare green hills. More and more white stone scattered in fields like sheep.

"I was in New York six months just now." The professor. "I like New York. But to come back is not nothing. The State of Israel is a certain state of intensity. A farm here is not the same as a farm in the States where you throw a seed on the ground and it grows. New York is frivolous by comparison."

Barren hills, bone white stone. Off to the right perched on a high pillar an army tank.

"What's that on the pedestal? the tank?" The American woman.

The swarthy Sephardi next to her shrugs as if he doesn't

122

speak English. She repeats the question to the earlocked religious on the opposite end of the jump seat who speaks it fluently.

The earlocked religious turns toward the window, staring through it at nothing. Earlocked. When he turns his head back she repeats the question, he repeats the gesture.

"It's that he can't answer, Miss." The professor.

"Why not?"

"It's your first time here?"

"Yes."

"He doesn't speak to ladies."

One night Ron coming back from Tel Aviv with My Constant Companion. Completely dark. She's sitting on the jump seat next to another one of the earlocked Haradim. Suddenly from the back he sees her jump on the jump seat, break into laughter. Later she explains there was a hand coming from somewhere touching her breast. When she traced it back to the religious she couldn't believe it.

"Somehow this guy had gotten his hand back along the jump seat and up my other side. When I realized who it was I could only laugh. Then his hand disappeared fast. I couldn't believe it, he was feeling me up."

But he didn't talk to her.

A woman friend who lived in Mea Shearim, the Hasidic neighborhood, complained she had constant problems with what she called peeping Moishes.

Tales of the Hasidim.

Trees in the landscape again. Evergreens. And rocks. The banks of the road are steep cutting through the hills. Among pine trunks on slopes wrecked armored cars rusted red on right. YERUSHALYIM 20.

The driver shifts gears. Ear pop. Cypress trees prick up above road like needles. More abandoned armored cars on left. At a steep angle up to left a monument of metallic shafts, mammoth spears or rockets or bayonets. The walls of the pass heighten and close in. Evergreens. And rocks. A deep, deep stone terraced valley opens at right. YERUSHALAYIM 10.

Distant views of modern concrete housing projects high on hills to left. Swaying through a series of sharp curves. Immense building developments swing into view, white on distant heights, while down to left terraced along the side of a deep drop, low abandoned rectangles of a crumbling stone village.

Glimpse of urban mass white over stony hills, fortress like. Then a sharp curve, stone walls close on right, curve, trees, houses, Jerusalem.

The light is different. Maybe it's because the sherut has climbed a half mile up from sea level. Or because the air is desert dry. Or because everything is built of cream colored, sometimes rosy, stone. Light to be seen not merely through, or with, but in itself visible, the city smeared pale gold.

The sherut picks through auto traffic, buses, into an area of new apartment buildings between which flashes of wide canyon, distant hills. Then turns into an old neighborhood of poor three- and four-story attached houses.

Suddenly it's the Polish ghetto, narrow streets swarmed with bearded men in black overcoats and black felt or broad fur hats. Women in shapeless dresses with kerchiefs over hair. Paste-faced toddlers with ear locks, tiny adults.

The sherut lets the religious out at what appears to be a new community center. Ron notices a sign in the street that says:

PASSAGE PERMITTED
ONLY TO WOMEN
DRESSED MODESTLY
LONG DRESS Lower Than
Knee Length (No Slacks)
LONG SLEEVES
Beyond Elbow Length
CLOSED KNECKLINE

"They don't like to sit next to strange women either." The professor. "It's handy to know on buses."

She smiles. "I never thought of myself as strange." The blond American woman.

124

"You're not Jewish?"

"No."

"Here you're strange."

The sherut moving slowly along a shop-lined main street that could almost be any city. It stops at a tall modern building opposite a broad pedestrian mall.

"*Bevakasha.*" The driver.

"What does that mean?" The Texan.

"Out."

The swarthy men get out. The driver gets down their battered valises from the roof rack.

"Sephardim," says the professor.

"Schwarzes. As they're sometimes called." The hip rabbi.

"By you?"

"Only when I'm angry at their politics." Getting his bag to leave.

"How do I get to the Scottish Hospice?" The American woman.

The driver. "Find a taxi."

"Let's share one." The Texan. "I'm at the King David."

"Can you take me to Mount Scopus?" Ron. "The University?"

The driver. "Impossible." Impassive, dismissing the idea with a wave of his hand.

"*Beseder.*" The professor talks to him in Hebrew, the driver listens, nods. "*Ken,*" he nods.

"*Todah rabah.* Never mind, he'll take you. Here saying impossible is just a way of saying hello."

The sherut pulls out again. The professor still in it.

"You're going to the university too?" Ron.

"Why not, I'm at the university."

"At the other university I thought."

"So, I need the library. Research."

"What's your project?"

"A book."

"What about?"

125

"About the [   ]s."

"What about them?"

"Everything about them. Especially their religion. It's called *All About Allah*."

"My name is Sukenick. Ron Sukenick."

"You told me."

"What's yours?"

"I told you. Professor."

"Professor is your name?"

"My first name."

"What's your last name?"

"Hagamel."

"And you're at the university at Giv'at Ram?"

"I work there. I'm with the security staff."

"I see."

"You're related to the Sukeniks?"

"So far I haven't met a Sukenick I'm not related to."

"You should check it out, the Sukeniks here."

"I intend to."

Down a hill, up a hill, the [   ] section and the walls of the Old City, the sherut establishing that Jerusalem is a city as much of verticals as horizontals. The road winding up to Mount Scopus and the acropolis of Hebrew University.

"So you're going to be Writer-in-Residence at the university. You have fans here?"

"I'm not translated."

"You don't need to be translated to have fans. You should have a fan club."

"Nobody's read my books here."

"Why not? Everybody reads English. I've read them."

"Which ones?"

"All of them."

"What did you think?"

"I think they're written in secret code."

The sherut enters an underground drive and stops. The driver

126

unloads the bags and Ron pays the extra.

"Get a kabbalah." Hagamel.

"What do you mean?"

"A receipt."

Pass through a checkpoint for bag inspection, then swallowed up by the cavernous cement intestine of the modernist university complex. Emerging from an elevator near a terrace overlooking the city.

"This is the best view of the Old City." Hagamel.

With the walls it looks like a ship, the northeastern corner the prow, the Dome of the Rock the bridge. Jerusalem gleaming in the sunlight. Under a low blue sky that makes it clear it's closer to heaven than elsewhere.

Which immediately explains a lot.

There's a message at the desk of the university guest house. *Meet me at the windmill. Now. Keksana.*

"You know anybody named Keksana?"

"Sure. He's a character in that book by whatsis. Don something. How do you say it, Quickoats. The one with the Jewish mother." Hagamel.

"Cervantes had a Jewish mother?"

"You didn't know it?"

"You're a big reader. Where's the windmill?"

"All Jews are big readers. Anyone knows where's the windmill."

"Goodbye."

"You're going some place?"

"You are. And thanks for the help."

Ron leaves his bags in his room, catches a taxi down to the Montefiore Windmill.

It's a windmill. A big white one, in mint condition and obviously not used. Nobody much there, he walks to the edge of a parapet for the view. Down a steep valley and way out past whitish brown desert hills the mountains of Jordan at horizon gray through the haze of distance cup a piece of blue Dead Sea. Well below sea level. The low point of the world, Ron knows.

From around a corner of the stone terracing near the windmill a black hat emerges, long black caftan, earlocks. An ultra-Orthodox, but a young one, skinny, glasses, a yeshiva student maybe, green skin. You can see he's wearing a *kipah* under his brimmed hat. Ron wonders if this could be Keksana. He looks as out of contact with the world as Quixote himself. Ron observes him with undisguised skepticism.

He motions for Ron to follow him around the corner. He does. The kid turns, hitting him in the solar plexus with his elbow, hard, this really happened. Ron doubles over, is twisted off balance. Jew-jitsu. Gets a knee in his chest that knocks him backward at the same time he's somehow tripped, twists and falls at same time Hagamel appears running hard, the kid takes off Hagamel behind him.

Hagamel comes back, helps Ron up and gets him on his feet. But he can't stay there. Hagamel sits him on a step.

"That's Keksana?" Hagamel. "Try to walk."

"What was that about?"

"Mistaken identity. Your identity is a mistake. As far as he's concerned." He helps Ron up. Ron waves him off, starts wobbling toward the windmill.

"I'm all right."

"You're tilting."

"What impresses me about these ultra-Orthodox types is that they're so spiritual."

"They fight all the time." Hagamel. "Different groups. Believers. Because they think they're right. Never mind the [   ]s, they beat up one another's rabbis. I mean really beat up. Eighty year old patriarchs, kidnapped and beaten. Their beards cut off."

"Nice."

"Try to look at it this way. This is a patriarchy. One result of patriarchy is fratricide. Some of the Jews hate one another more than they hate the [   ]s. And the [   ]s hate one another more than some of them hate the Jews, the Sunnis and the Shi'ites just for one example. But I'm telling you one of the problems is it's simpler to hate the [   ]s. And for them to hate us. Otherwise it could get so complicated you could forget who you're supposed to be hating. My guess is he knew you were going to visit the refugee camp. The yeshivanik."

"How would he know that? And how do you know it?"

"As to how we know it, don't worry. We know. So why are you going?"

"Tourism."

"For tourism it's not on the map. It's not even on our mental maps. *Terra incognita.* But the Golden Calf we've heard about."

"What Golden Calf?"

"All right. I'll get you a taxi."

"No, no, I'll walk." Descending many steep stairs through the chic Yemin Moshe quarter goes down into the Valley of Hinnom, otherwise known as Gehenna, where children were once sacrificed to Moloch. Then up steep path under walls of Old City toward the Jaffa Gate. Where suddenly a mysterious sharp pain in his right foot and he almost falls.

Manages to limp up to Jaffa Gate. The wall there of various shades of large stone blocks in the pink to white range. Ashlars. Like many structures in the city, a subtle, rosy stone mosaic, gorgeous up close. Inside the Gate the serenity is palpable though he couldn't tell you why. He thinks it's maybe because however turbulent things get, the Old City is still contained, cut off from real time by its wall. Its circular flow outside and inside history at the same time.

Hobbles through the square along the moat and walls of the Citadel and turns into King David. The bazaar, the Suq. Sukenick tours Suq.

Stores he used to like sparsely stocked because of the Intifada. Merchants more sullen. [   ]s. As his friend Chaya Amir says, "It's been an average year. A little worse than last year, a little better than next year."

But that doesn't stop solicitations and sleeve pullings from merchants. Mostly though they're hanging around their store fronts talking to friends. Under the tin awnings protecting the narrow street from the weather.

Limping down the incline of the street. A basket of ornate canes catches his eye. Walks past regarding other merchandise in the stall with elaborate disinterest. Just enough to let the merchant know he's interested. Walks almost beyond, then as afterthought asks how much.

The [   ] merchant is not too interested in selling canes at the kind of unprofitable bargain prices that they're getting these days. It goes from there. He [   ]s me up I jew him down, Ron thinks. After a few minutes the price is about halved. Ron guesses he's still being taken, but not for much.

A nice light carved cane, elegant really. Quite pleased with it. Maneuvers down the steps in the sloped suq, through the crowd, among elbows and shoulders and the boys speeding down the street steering blue, green and red painted carts with no brakes, dragging tire on chain they step on now and then to slow. Better with cane. What walks on four legs in the morning, two at noon, three at night? Oedipus knew.

Makes his way down King David, between the Christian Quarter and the Armenian Quarter toward the Jewish Quarter and the [   ] Quarter. He's been advised not to go there in this atmosphere. Recalls the first time he was here with My Constant Companion, getting lost, the city getting dark, slightly terrified. Now he feels at ease, at home almost despite the atmosphere. No trouble finding his way through the labyrinth of the Old City.

He's come for something quite specific this time. Last time he didn't know what he was looking for. And he found it. His attachment to the place.

Turns right and quick left into the Street of the Chain and limps toward the Temple Mount. Past suspicious Israeli guards into a huge walled area open to the low blue sky and up the steps to the Mount. His foot hurts.

Glad to get his shoes off to go into the Dome of the Rock. A fairly recent antiquity, 691 A.D., its brilliant ceramic exterior reminds him of a giant gorgeous cookie jar. Inside the huge space it's a slow day. A worker is vacuuming the acres of Persian carpets covering the floor of the mosque.

Goes down the steps into a grotto under the rock. Just as he reaches the floor of the chamber a man interrupts his prayer, glances at him, abruptly walks up the steps. Passing Ron he slips something into Ron's breast pocket. Or does he imagine this?

Either way Ron wouldn't dare look at whatever it is till he's out of the mosque.

When he is, Ron fingering his breast pocket finds a clipping from the French newspaper *Le Monde*, a clipping which anyway Ron's already clipped.

> *UN "VEAU D'OR" TROUVE EN*
> *ISRAEL. A little idol representing a calf,*
> *made of bronze and perhaps also of*
> *silver and of lead, has been found*
> *recently in the ruins of a temple, prob-*
> *ably Canaanite, in the village of Ashkelon*
> *by archaeologists from Harvard, directed*
> *by Dr. Lawrence E. Stager. The statuette,*
> *in very good condition, appears to have*
> *been placed in a sort of "reliquary" of*
> *terra cotta of which the pieces were*
> *recovered. The ceramic accompanying*
> *the idol dates its fabrication at around*
> *1,550 B.C. It is probably the bull god*
> *(the "golden calf") of the cult against*
> *which the Bible fulminated many times.*
> *(UPI)*

Hobbles off the Temple Mount and down, past Uzi-toting guards at a narrow checkpoint. The Western Wall of Herod's Temple. High and massive, it's composed of giant, trimmed stone blocks dominating a large cleared plaza.

Coming down from the huge platform where the Temple had stood, sees the swarm of people thickening to a dense pack close to the Wall itself.

Picks up a paper *kipah* at the barrier to the main, of course, men's section. Now he plunges in. Everybody is doing their particular Jewish thing. Praying or dancing or crying or bobbing back and forth or singing or laughing or just strolling, alone and in groups, a bunch of Italians are conducting a bar mitzvah, the Haradim chanting and swinging.

At the Wall a group of men are shaking tambourines and dancing. Others are flat against the Wall itself, kissing it unabashedly, passionately or tearfully, others stick little wads of paper into its crevices. Messages to God.

The Jerusalem post office also gets letters addressed to God, according to the *Los Angeles Times*. They come from all over the world, often forwarded by local postal services. "Dear God, Shalom. I write this letter after deep thought. Please in your kindness and when you decide, give me the power to study the profession of chef." "Happy Father's Day. To the Angel of Death: pass over unless I say not to." "Please give money to the account of anyone who works for peace, freedom, good will." They go to the dead letter office, marked "insufficient address" or "addressee unknown."

Reaches out to touch the wall. "You promised," he says. Hot damn if he doesn't get some kind of current coming back though his hand, at least that's his impression. Cosmic energy? From a ruined wall that contains nothing? The empty box. The empty room, holy of holies, the lost ark. Probably some trick of psychology.

"You're screwing up," he says. Just for the hell of it. He wants to say "fucking up," but maybe that's going too far. "So what's the story?" he says, his palm still palpating the Wall.

As he's waiting for an answer he notices a fat man with a little beard and an embroidered *kipah* next to him sort of wallowing against the Wall, doing an obscene little belly dance with it, all the while staring sideways at Ron. When he catches Ron's attention, the fat man nods toward a crevice and sticks a folded slip of paper into it. As he disappears into the crowd Ron realizes it's the very portly rabbi from the sherut.

132

Takes the slip of paper from the crevice and unfolds it. It says, *Our Lady of the Spasm. Message 13 Arlozoroff. Get kabbalah.*

Tired now, foot hurts more and more. Pockets the note and walks up into the Jewish Quarter. Our Lady of the Spasm is a church associated with the Via Dolorosa. But 13 Arlozoroff is his own address, over in Rehavia. Ron's confused. Suddenly sees a herd of sheep galloping out of a narrow street, their noisy little hooves clattering on the paving stones across a square, disappearing down another street. Did this happen? He knows the effect on him of the Old City well enough to know that by this time he could be seeing things. Makes his way through the impressive and sterile-looking new Jewish Quarter to the Cardo, the excavation of a Byzantine era shopping mall turned into a modern shopping mall. Below ground level, stairs down. A very nifty looking Negroid young woman, judging from her costume a Felasha, a Black Jew from Ethiopia, gives him a thrilling look over her shoulder. Heads for her she saunters down Cardo, stopping at chic shop windows long enough to let him stay close as he hobbles behind her.

The Felasha woman goes straight up stairs out Cardo past Christian Quarter to the Via Dolorosa, disappears into an alley in the [   ] Quarter. Approaching favorite cafe El-Wad Road sees American woman from sherut at a table. Soon as she sees him she gets up, heads around corner for Our Lady of the Spasm, he follows. She goes to the door of the church, he follows. She goes inside he goes inside, she's not there. Who is there is the Texan from the plane.

"What are you doing here?" The Texan.

"I got the message."

"That was the wrong message."

"What's the right message?"

"The right message is the second coming is coming."

"Where's the blond woman?"

"She comes with the second coming. But when she starts coming you won't be here. Get going."

Ron goes. Limps back to El-Wad heads for Damascus Gate heart of [   ] Quarter. They told him not to do this he does it up steps finds a *kaik* vendor I beg your pardon no it's a roll not a role buys one. Eats it among money changers tables vending jewelery almost knocked over by swing of crate carried by donkey on way out Gate. Stops outside to admire its crenellated medievalness a beggar approaches checkered red Arafat handkerchief on head something warns Ron to be afraid an angry villainous face.

"You need a taxi?" Hagamel takes his arm helps him to black Mercedes, opens back door gets in driver's seat.

"What are you doing here?" Ron.

"Jerusalem is a small town. A small town with big ideas. It's no good to go to East Jerusalem now."

Tired, foot hurts, doesn't ask questions as Hagamel drops him at pedestrian mall central to West Jerusalem. Ben Yehuda.

Eats falafel in a hole in the wall, revives, buys *Jerusalem Post*, limps down shop lined pedestrian street to terrace of Cafe Rimon. In sun, terrace crowded, animated, orders coffee.

One In Seven Wives In Israel Is Beaten, it says in *Post*. And maybe as many as one in three. At least one hundred thousand battered wives in Israel, according to research funded by the Guggenheim Foundation, the actual number probably much higher.

> In Israel differences over raising chil-
> dren were a more common cause of
> conjugal violence than financial prob-
> lems, the most common causes of mari-
> tal violence in other countries. In the
> patriarchal structure that characterizes
> most Israeli families, women are ex-
> pected to be passive, family-oriented and
> responsible for the quality of life in the
> family. For the most part they are pre-
> pared to compromise, except on the
> issue of raising children—a subject on
> which they will not budge.

Suddenly Ron starts to wonder about his spontaneously crippled foot.

Sits there watching the variety of faces, afro dark and nordic fair, biblical and ghetto and cosmopolitan, mustached and bearded and clean-shaven, all Jews. Sips coffee and reads his paper in the sun as an energetic urban life seethes around him.

At some point looks up and there's an old Israeli friend from years back staring at him.

"Is that you?"

"Yeah, it's me." Ron. "You were expecting the Golem?"

Shmuel sits down. That's not his real name, I can't tell you his real name and besides he changed it when he made aliyah. His Israeli wife calls him Shmulie.

He looks weird though. Thinner, hollow eyed, nervous and hesitant, he used to be robust and outgoing.

"What are you doing here?" Shmuel.

"Looking for the golden calf."

"What golden calf?"

"The golden calf. Someone dug it up."

"What do you want with it?"

"I want to take it out of circulation."

"Why?"

"It promotes the golden rule."

"What's that?"

"Do unto others as you do to yourself. Fuck them up."

Shmulie is a moral philosopher. He understands. But he still looks nervous and hesitant. When he first came he looked robust and outgoing but that's what sometimes happens when you make aliyah. When you make aliyah you know all the answers about Israel then you become nervous and hesitant then you don't know any. It's a sign of intelligence.

Shmulie is strange, over-intense, haggard. He's working on a book. About the answers. He's finished working on the fall of man but he hasn't written the redemption part yet.

Maybe it's because he just got out of jail. For refusing to

serve in the army. Or maybe it's because he hasn't written the redemption part yet. He's bothered by the way prominent Israelis are beginning to talk about the [   ]. They talk about them as "two-legged animals," "grasshoppers," "drugged cockroaches in a bottle." He's interested in proving we're all still human beings. A hopeless task in Ron's opinion. If you have to prove it forget it.

He says anything having to do with the [   ]s is both happening and not happening at the same time. He keeps quoting one of Ron's books about things happening and not happening at the same time. He was in the States during Vietnam which was also something that was happening and not happening for a long time. Until it happened.

Actually in Israel everything is happening at the same time anyway because in Israel the past is the present. Recall is total, time is forgotten. That's why every new war is also an old war, every criminal act an act of revenge, every wacko cruelty a righteous vindication. Each day careens through a time machine where history is a geography of trauma.

Please give money to the account of anyone who works for peace, freedom, good will.

As Shmulie talks Ron is noticing a little scene evolving on Ben Yehuda. The scene is basically a group of very hip-looking Israeli girls. If Israel is a melting pot of the East and the West these girls are very West, like Greenwich Village already. They float from cafe to cafe that's why Ron notices their scene, because of their back and their forth.

Speaking of back notices especially one of them, blond and modelly, wearing jeans strategically torn just under a buttock exposing back and inside of creamy thigh. He has an urge to jump into her gene pool. This time she walks past somebody's arm around her shoulders the fat man. The hip rabbi embroidered beanie pointy beard Hawiian shirt and tattoo.

Leaves his shekels on the table hobbles after them. They disappear into a taxi at Kikar Zion. "Mahaneh Yehuda." The fat man pulling the door shut.

Waves to the next taxi gets in. "Mahaneh Yehuda." Mahaneh Yehuda he gets out just in time to see them disappearing into the crowded market streets. Guesses they're heading for the covered part of the market but he has a hard time getting through the shoving mass of shoppers anyway he doesn't find them there.

What he finds milling among market stalls is beards, moustaches, kaftans, military uniforms, black *kipahs*, embroidered *kipahs*, flat black hats, brimmed hats, Hasidic fur hats, stocking caps, rolled-up wool hats, yachting caps, kerchiefs, grey hoods, checked handkerchief hats, even red fezzes, tan fezzes with white cloth wrapped around, black burnooses, white handkerchief hats circled with plush brown cord. Every few minutes an announcement over loudspeakers warning about unattended packages that might explode.

Buys some fresh dates, persimmons, prickly pears, olives, goat cheese, pitot, fresh figs, blood oranges, eggplant, yoghurt, sesame cookies, tahine, grapes, Odem chicken broth, radishes, lettuce, strawberries, nut cake, poppy-seed cake, herring, tomatoes, fresh dill, St. Peter's fish, turkeyburger and decides to go home.

Catches the bus to Rehavia and walks to Arlozoroff. A settled old section of solid block-like houses. Palm, mimosa, evergreen, deciduous, birds singing in the yards.

My Constant Companion is there working and waiting for the three hours of heat and hot water to take a bath. She washes the fruit and vegetables in dish soap and feeds the stray cat that had kittens on the terrace.

He has a notice for a registered letter. Goes to the post office. The line is as long as usual he reads the paper while waiting. A squat hefty old lady bulls into line in front of him.

"You got in front of me." Ron.

"I didn't get in front of you. I got behind him."

She has the blue number on her forearm. He can see why she survived.

"You're ztill in line?" The man behind him. Short, rimless glasses, black hat, pointed little beard.

"How else would I get my mail?

The little man thrusts his hand out. "B. Frei."

Ron shakes it. "Do I know you?"

"Maybe. Fats fit your vood?"

"Nothing. It's hurt."

Ron is busy making the camp calculation. That's a calculation you make here with people of a certain age if they come from Europe. You make it automatically, subtracting backwards to figure whether someone was in the camps. If they were in the camps you know to expect anything. It's a survival mechanism in a country of survivors. A way of surviving the survivors.

"Tvistit?" Glittering lenses, laser eyes.

"I don't know whether I twisted it or what."

"Maybe you god a gompleggs."

"A what?"

"Fen you god a gompleggs, zum dimes id giffs you an eddypuss. You zpeak a bisl Yiddish?"

"No. I'm studying Hebrew."

"Hebrew okay. Bud vor a baragraph of Hebrew you need only a zentence of Yiddish. Vor a zentence of Hebrew a ford of Yiddish. Vinally fen you zpeak the drue mame loshn you don't need to zay anythink, the mother dong."

"If the tongue is the mother then who is the father?"

"The shlong. Abba Shlong. He's an Israeli."

By now he's next in line for the mail window. "Get a kabbalah." B. Frei behind him.

He picks up his letter signs a kabbalah. It's from B. Frei. He turns around. B. Frei is gone. Inside the envelope there's an envelope with a letter inside the letter says: "Dear Ronnie, I have a letter Uncle Ben wrote the last few days before he died. It would be for a best seller made into a book. Sincerely with love to the little boy (you) I bought a small typewriter it's so many years. Love, Aunt Bea Frey." There's also a poem, ending: "He saw the vision of death's shadow/ And immediately followed its trail." Ben Frey.

On the inner envelope there's a message scrawled: "Sukenick—Shep nakhes. Drey a kop. 'Get joy. Twist a head.'"

This means that he has to go down to the Dead Sea, Ron immediately realizes. "Death's shadow." What "twist a head" means he can't guess. He doesn't speak Yiddish.

He rents a car. Drives down to Derekh Yericho between the Old City and the Mount of Olives into the barren Judean Hills past the last [   ] village past the fortress-like Jewish settlement down into the Judean Desert occasional black tent of Bedouin camels staked nearby occasional clump of sheep down toward sign marking sea level heat increasing Dead Sea dead blue in brown baked hills ahead and south.

At the sign saying sea level a Black woman in veils and robes, ornate beads, the Felasha from the Cardo, waving. He stops she gets in fixes him with dark burning eyes directs him straight down to Dead Sea along shore under the caves where the Scrolls were found to a rocky beach tells him to disrobe. He takes his clothes off she leads him into the salt saturated shallows tells him to lie down scoops mud from the bottom cakes it over his body masks his face with it. The mud is simultaneously energizing and de-energizing it must have special chemicals. It saps the vigor of his genitals and as it dries he begins to lose consciousness. He feels her inscribing something on his forehead while intoning, "Now you are dark like me, the man of clay." Felasha means stranger.

Next thing he knows he's in a pool of clear fresh water among some rocks in from the shore, the clay washing off him and she's gone. He dries clean, gets his clothes on, drives north toward Jericho knowing without words he's made of clay he'll return to clay. The man of clay. He wonders if the Golem was considered Jewish. He knows it wasn't allowed to make a minyan. Because not a mensch. It couldn't answer for itself. More a wandering question than a stationary answer. Like Camus' Stranger.

Near Jericho past Israeli soldiers, tanks, the refugee camp over on the left. Remembering that an Israeli soldier was burned to death in a refugee camp in Gaza.

139

Picks up hitchhiking Israeli soldier asks him where's the entrance to the camp he gives elaborate directions gets off down the road Ron follows the directions finds himself not in the camp but in the middle of Jericho smell of citrus blossom date palms citrus groves intensely green in brown desert heading toward the Tel Jericho excavations. Wondering why can't Israelis give directions probably because they don't know which direction they're heading directionless trying to go every direction at once. But there are no directions. Not only is time in Israel such that everything happens at once but it also happens in the same place. Over and over.

Spots Hagamel stops walks over.

"Where is the entrance?" Ron.

"There is no entrance."

"To the camp."

"There is no camp."

"I just saw the camp."

"Well maybe there's a camp. I wouldn't know. But there's no entrance to it."

"There used to be an entrance."

"That's when there used to be a camp. Now that there's no camp there's no entrance. Or if there is an entrance there's no camp."

"How is that possible?"

"It's possible." He looks at his watch. "Excuse me I have an appointment." He leaves. Ron heads for the excavations.

Looking at the Eleventh Century B.C. tower part of the walls. Where is the entrance? Here the entrance was music. If you find the right music the walls crumble and let you in.

A voice over his shoulder. "We know where it is."

It's the fat man, the hip rabbi pointy beard Hawiian shirt gold star around neck. This time he's got his arm around the woman staying at the Scottish Hospice. What do they see in him? Probably they don't see anything in him that's probably what attracts them. A vacuum.

"The entrance?"

"The Calf."

"Where?" Ron.

"She'll show you."

"How did you find it?"

"The copper scroll, we have a photocopy. It gives directions."

Ron recalls a recent *New York Times* article:

> Dr. McCarter is quietly translating the
> Copper Scroll, one of the most intriguing
> of the finds. It is the only scroll made of
> metal rather than leather or papyrus, and
> it describes the locations of 61 caches of
> gold, silver and other treasures believed
> to have been hidden near Jerusalem and
> Jericho in the first century A.D.
>
> After examining photographs of the
> scroll taken under different lighting
> angles, Dr. McCarter said he has been
> able to correct earlier transcriptions and
> now has some definite ideas about where
> at least half of the treasure could be. He
> is not saying where that is, though, out of
> concern that it might encourage looting.

Ron is thinking, Israeli directions? Good luck. Out loud he says, "What are we waiting for?"

"She'll go with you." The fat man.

She tells him to head north, to Zefat. "Have you seen it?"

She nods. "It's three cubits high and solid gold."

"How high is a cubit?"

"Don't know."

"Where is it?"

"Under the Temple Mount. There's a tunnel. It branches off the Tunnel of Hezekiah."

"Is this true?"

"I don't know. They blindfolded me."

"How come?"

"They didn't want me to see the dynamite."

North along the green snaking Jordan up to Galilee. Brilliant blue of Lake Galilee-Tiberias-Kinneret rimmed with green. Through Tiberias, white cubes palm trees.

They take a lunch break in the nature preserve at Dan. An enclosed oasis of groves streams ferns glades reeds. According to legend the site of the Garden of Eden. Walk along idyllic paths to stretch, cool out, off, come back to parking lot the dude standing next to their car tall muscular blond crewcut scar on forehead devil-may-care grin big aviator style shades over his eyes but you know they're steel blue. Carries a very big revolver in a holster on his belt. She goes up to him flashes a Captain Midnight badge. He looks at his watch.

"Right on time," he says.

"Who's he?" Ron.

"This is a check point." She.

"Goylim," extending his shooting hand. "Captain Goylim. Why did you come? to Israel?"

"Business." Ron. "And pleasure. Besides, my father died. I thought it was the thing to do."

"Why?"

"I don't know. I couldn't tell you. This your job? Asking questions?"

"I'm the boss of asking questions, chief. I've done it all over."

"All over what?"

"All over the world."

"You're not Jewish?" Ron.

"I'm not Irish."

"That doesn't mean you're not Jewish. Why are you working here?"

"Where ever they need me, that's where I go. To do what I do."

"How do you do it?" Ron.

"I have something extra."

"How come you have something extra?"

142

"Because I have something missing." Captain Goylim. "When you have something missing you can do a lot of stuff you can't if you don't. Only I miss not having it. Sometimes."

"What is it?" Ron.

"If I knew I wouldn't be Captain Goylim. That's why I drink a lot." Looks at his watch. "Time to get on with it."

She. "What's the master code today?"

"The master code is three. You should be at Zefat at oh nine hundred. They'll give you the information you need. Get a kabbalah. Take off tonight."

> 'GOLEM' COMES TO LIFE. The
> Jewish Golem, the creature raised by the
> Rabbi of Prague to succor the Jews, is
> made of the common clay from which
> Adam was created. But the Golem,
> battered emotionally by impressions and
> feelings it cannot understand, uses
> violence and the threat of violence to
> gain its ends. Finally, it turns on the
> community it was created to protect, and
> the rabbi must destroy his creation to
> avert further tragedy. (*Jerusalem Post*)

They take off. Into the mountains of Upper Galilee to many levelled Zefat.

Oh nine hundred. Narrow walkways pedestrian stairs flowery courtyards stone walls mountain light. Mystic synagogues of Isaac Luria and the Kabbalists who gathered here.

"Why are we here?" Ron.

"Here comes Tex. He has the pictures."

"What pictures?"

"They took of the Calf."

The Texan from the plane. He's carrying a manilla envelope. "You want to see them?"

"No." Ron.

"Why not?" Tex.

"I have a theory about the Golden Calf. It demands sacrifice. It takes more than it gives. It leads to the golden rule."

"What's the golden rule?" Tex.

"The rule of gold."

"Just take a look at what's in this secret envelope." The Texan whips the photos out. "The famous Golden Calf of Aaron. We've won."

"It's beautiful." Ron. "Let me see those."

"Yee-hoo!"

"I want it." Ron.

"Of course you do"

"No, I mean I need it. I'm addicted. I need to have it."

"Sure you do. And you will. We're gonna give it to you."

"When?"

"Soon. Very soon. Let's drink to it." He holds up a thermos. "Martinis." He pours into plastic cups. "With or without an aleph," he winks.

They visit one of the Luria synagogues, the Ashkenazi one where in a corner the great rabbi once studied. Inside Ron buys a book about him, the attendant hands it to him with the receipt, "Here's your kabbalah." It marks a page with some lines checked: *The first step is withdrawal, Luria says. Interior exile. In the Book of Life you are then one with the Aleph. A nest of possibilities. Things don't have to be as they are. (On the Book, see Sukenik.)*

The best way to see Sukenik on the Book, Ron knows, is to go back to Jerusalem and visit the Shrine of the Book housing the Dead Sea Scrolls the archeologist Sukenik and his son Yadin recovered. Besides, he has an appointment to see the Tunnel of Hezekiah, his chance to take the treasure branch of the tunnel and beat everyone to the Golden Calf.

Goes back to Jerusalem gets a taxi to the Shrine of the Book. Shaped like a huge chocolate candy kiss, insofar as a candy kiss resembles a breast, except it's dazzling white. In the main chamber, round with a hole funnelling up through the ceiling, there's an item directly in the center on a pedestal, a stylized penis sticking up.

If you think about it you might get the idea that this is supposed to be one handle of a giant Torah. So you're in the Book of Life, living it not reading it. Knowing it in the biblical sense. Which is a good thing, because he realizes he forgot his glasses.

Ron is surprised, even embarrassed, by his erotic reading of the holy book in its conception here. But he feels he's being drawn into some holy intercourse.

The penis is sticking straight up toward the sensuously contoured hole. The Shrine is an Ark, it holds the Book, it couples the species. The Book is not about anything it engenders everything, joins everything with the Word.

Hobbles around with his cane, vexed because without his glasses he can't read in the Shrine of the Book, aware his painful foot is worse. Now he can barely walk five minutes without needing to sit. He withdraws from the pain in a kind of trance, when he comes to he doesn't know how much time's passed, wonders if he's been joined with the Word. Whatever that is.

Finally walks out in a pain daze sits down on stone bench. When he gets up to start walking again, his foot is much better. His gait gets better and better as he walks. Soon he doesn't need his cane any more. He has no explanation. Another holyland miracle?

Only later does Ron learn of the kabbalistic interpretation of the Aleph as illegible but as the mother of all intellegibility. Meaningless but pregnant with meaning. Interpretations. Translations. Possibilities. Things don't have to be as they are. The master code is Aleph.

He thinks of an Israeli play he saw in Tel Aviv called *Frodo*, the dialogue done completely in an incomprehensible tongue composed of many languages that you could comprehend anyway through your linguistic sixth sense, if you have one. He thinks of a news flash he just heard on the radio that the first world wide computer plague is possible from a virus discovered in Australia, originating in Israel, called Frodo. It renders all programs illegible.

* * *

In 701 B.C. the Assyrians came down like a wolf on the fold to besiege the city of Jerusalem. Sennacherib had already taken all the other Jewish cities, but on the advice of the prophet Isaiah Jerusalem resisted.

Before the arrival of the Assyrians, King Hezekiah had a tunnel hacked through solid rock to channel water from the Spring of Gihon to a pool that would be accessible to the Jews during the siege. Because Jerusalem had water it was able to hold out, the Assyrians eventually withdrew, and so it was the Tunnel of Hezekiah that literally saved the practice of monotheism for subsequent history.

The tunnel is about 585 yards long, shoulder width at its straitest and less than three and a half feet high in places where the water runs up to your knees and you have to double over like a foetus to squeeze through. It empties into the Pool of Shiloah, where the opening in the rock from which the clear water still flows is extremely vaginal, as even postcards of the site plainly show.

Looking from Mount Scopus across to Jerusalem with its dry, visual clarity, its hard definition, redefinition, over-definition of the holy turf, gems heaped on a pale table refracting sharply but differently from different perspectives, the Dome of the Rock, the Western Wall, the Holy Sepulchre, the aggregate repetitively disintegrating into a jumble of pure competing details numinous and hypnotic, resembling the jewel-like birds that inhabit its parks—bulbul, hoopoe, sunbird—each monopolizing the attention in turn with its dazzling, singular and dominating brilliance, the contrast with Tel Aviv, hazy, amorphous, voluptuous and Mediterranean, could not be more striking.

A one-god town with too many gods, too many tribes, each obsessively drilling its own tunnel to the light, tunnel vision obscuring insight that light is indivisible. This is why it's the Holy Land. It's full of holes tunneling toward our missing whole.

Ron is on the terrace cafe of the University at Mount Scopus. He's with a young American widow recovering from a case of

146

mono, a survoluptuous lady of a certain age who babbles like sea surf lapping the sand, incessantly, and an Israeli writer admired abroad as much for his sabra dash as his talent, but known in local polyglot intellectual circles as Jerusalem's most illegible bachelor.

Their guide has just arrived, a *Yekke* archaeology professor with whom they are to penetrate the Tunnel of Hezekiah. *Yekke* is Hebrew slang for German Jew and is an acronym, some say, for the phrase "Jew hard of understanding."

The survoluptuous lady, who had the sense to come here as a small child from Rumania before being wiped out by the Holocaust, has enormous breasts. Ron keeps identifying her with Jerusalem itself which is an architecture of breasts, the pervasive domes vying with the male thrust of spire and minaret, the mammoth cock and balls erected to house the YMCA. In sheer volume she is an overwhelming mother, and like Jerusalem, relentless in her demands.

If you live in Jerusalem you don't live in a mere city, you live in an inexorable situation. Jerusalem is a problem without a solution. Like life.

Much to the shock of his Israeli friends, Ron had once gone to a [   ] refugee camp near Jericho for tea. It seems that his friends are not so much afraid of the [   ]s as that they just don't see them. They seemed to be shocked mostly at his having seen them.

He'd had a long, pleasant talk with his host and his host's family. How did he like Palestine? Was he Jewish? The partition of the country was unfortunate but it was to be hoped that Arab and Jew could live in peace. Could he help his host emigrate to the United States? His mother couldn't shake hands with him because she had already prepared herself for evening prayers. It had been an extremely civilized occasion.

He left and got into his car parked among the alleys, low houses and packed earth. In the dust of his windshield a finger had written: "Jews into the sea."

"Get me another coffee, please dear." The survoluptuous lady. "And a glass of water."

"We have to leave." The *Yekke*. "I can't take all day."

"I can't last all day." The widow recovering from mono. "My energy is limited." She seems a bit maniacal about her mono, to the point where Ron suspects it's psychogenic.

"Enjoy the view," says the dashing, if illegible, bachelor. "This is the best view of the city." I wonder why he's coming along with us. The monomaniacal widow is quite sexy.

Among the five of them assembled for the penetration of the Tunnel of Hezekiah, the lingua franca is English. But in the group there are native speakers not only of English but also of German, Rumanian and even Hebrew. As in Israel whose native speakers represent languages from all over Europe, North Africa and the Middle East, the lingua franca is Hebrew. As in Spain it was Ladino. As in the Diaspora from Russia to the Americas, the lingua franca was Yiddish, the *mame loshn*, the mother tongue.

Language is an ocean, a womb of the possible. Not any particular language just the fact of it. Though it needs to be written. Otherwise you're left with babble. But how do you get from babble to bible?

To go down from the ivory tower of Hebrew University on Mount Scopus to the multilingual fratricidal Babel of Jerusalem is like plunging into a sea of babble. Today they'll stop short of the usual penetration of its walls to park outside them at the Spring of Gihon.

As they ride down the Mount of Olives in the car to Gihon, which is on the edge of Kidron Valley just outside the limit of King David's Jerusalem, the illegible bachelor sits with his arm grazing the shoulders of the monomaniacal widow in the crowded back seat.

It's obvious that she is attracted by his blond, blue-eyed sabra dash, the very image of the native Israeli that official Israeli tourism promotes, with its ironic note of anti-semitism, since few Jews, including Israelis, actually look "aryan." Not to say that Israel dislikes Jews, that would be going too far. Though its attitude toward the Diaspora is another matter.

Every now and then Ron goes to visit the [   ] novelist Anton Shammas, an [   ] Israeli whose intricate soft irony Ron finds so much more Jewish than the aggressive assertiveness of the Israelis. Shammas no doubt finds it so much more [   ]. Though he writes in Hebrew. A Jewish Israeli acquaintance in Shammas' autobiographical novel calls him "my Jew."

In contrast with the illegible bachelor, the monomaniac widow looks exaggeratedly *yiddishe meydl*, black hair, whitebread skin, big brown eyes, high nose—a look Ron associates with victimization. There's a sexy vulnerability to her body, emphasized by her insistent claims of weakness due to convalescence, that Ron, with his writer's x-ray vision, sees as an instinctive way of hiding her strength.

Maybe it's her strength, not her evident weakness, that the illegible bachelor with his own x-ray vision sees and that attracts him?

But Ron, his x-ray vision rivalling the illegible bachelor's, picks up in him—despite his attractive image, his obvious intelligence, his demonstrated talent, his status as accomplished artist and even cultural spokesman—a self-defeating passivity that courts contradiction, submission, even failure, which Ron finds odd, and oddly familiar.

It's a quality reflected in his writing, the illegible bachelor's, what little of it is translated, by a style that tends to cancel itself out, that intimates a story then denies it, that formulates an idea and simultaneously dissolves it and that, above all, creates a kind of poetic language tending to lapse into apparent incomprehensibility, if not downright meaninglessness.

They say that not only is his style less lapidary than the older generation of Hebrew writers, something they say is common among younger authors. They say that in the original Hebrew, his style atomizes the typically concrete imagery of that language into drifting vagueness. One of his Hebrew critics told Ron that he subverts the virile thrust of his native tongue with a kind of semiotic hysteria. Whatever that means.

And yet it is his virility for which he is known. The constant scandal is that he has a long-time, generally well-liked mistress whom he refuses to marry, and an incessant string of incidental conquests. This is a syndrome common to quite a few writers and which Ron has never completely understood, even in himself.

The survoluptuous lady has a voice best described as booming that fills the car when she talks, and she doesn't stop talking as she drives them down from Mount Scopus. She looks at her watch and turns on the news, an Israeli reflex. Her driving makes Ron a little nervous because she looks everywhere but at the road as she talks, and the road is in places winding and precipitous, impeded by pedestrians, goats and even an occasional camel, not to mention auto traffic.

She seems to be driving at the edge of disaster, but Ron's x-ray vision tells him that she's completely in control, that the way she's driving is a way of unnerving them, a way of imposing control on them, done not intentionally but by the compulsion of her nature.

"Israel!" she scoffs at the radio. "The Sephardim look at Menachim Begin and see, my god, King Solomon. And the American Jews who come here with all sorts of ideas in their heads. They don't see that this is a poor country living beyond its means, broken into endless factions, quibbling over stupid superstitions to the point of death, with an impossible political situation in a completely hostile region. No! They see the land of milk and honey. Right. Goats and bees. They see Eretz Israel, they see the fatherland—the fatherland! father of which land? of Latvia and Yemen? of Kracow and Morroco? of Algiers and Auschwitz?"

"Please, watch the road," says the *Yekke*.

She grabs the wheel as the car veers. "Jews are not supposed to be stupid, but here Jews are becoming stupider every day. And do you know why? American money. Every stupid mistake here is underwritten by American money. American money makes us look smart but it's buying a dream world based on stupidity.

With every dollar America gives Israel, Israel grows a dollar more stupid. We don't even have to think any more, all we have to do is buy. The American disease . . ."

The brakes scream as the car skids to a jolting stop on the shoulder, cut off by a Mercedes that stops just ahead. A dark young man gets out each front door and runs back to their car. Ron sees one of them is holding a short club. They start banging on the windshield and the driver's window, the hood, shouting in gutturals, enraged. The writer, the *Yekke* and Ron, all sitting next to doors, open them almost simultaneously and simultaneously, as if in a dance, the men retreat, walking backwards, snarling menacing gutturals all the way to their car.

"Who are they, [   ]s?" Ron asks. "What do they want?"

"[   ]s? These are Jews!" exclaims their buxom driver scornfully. "These are North African Jews. They don't like women. They don't like women driving."

"They don't like women driving badly," says the Illegible.

"Badly or well, they don't like women. Not outside the home. If you were driving they would never stop. You know it! They beat only women, with men it's just ritual, like snarling between stray dogs."

"*Schwarzes*," sneers the *Yekke*.

"You Ashkenazi are just as bad," she bellows. "Men I don't need in this country. For men I go to Italy. Israelis are almost as bad as [   ]s when it comes to women. Moronic. Sometimes here I have to look at a man's foreskin to convince myself he's a Jew."

"[   ]s aren't circumcised?" says the Illegible.

"[   ]s she wouldn't look," says the *Yekke*.

She starts the car and pulls onto the road. Buli is such a nice guy, Ron is thinking, thinking about the novelist A. B. Yehoshua. Yehoshua, whose family has been in Israel for generations, once let Ron know in the nicest possible way that Ron is not really Jewish because the only real Jews are the Israelis.

The Israelis are now in the business of telling others they aren't really Jewish, the Orthodox tell it to the Reformed, the

Hasidim tell it to the Orthodox, the white Jews tell it to the black Jews. When did it get so popular all of a sudden, being Jewish? Ron, who grew up fearing the question "Are you a Jew?" now has to contend with the answer that he's not.

The question to this answer occurs to Ron, as it might, sometimes, in despair occur to you, Buli: Are Israelis really Jewish? And whether or not, do they herald some unforeseeable transformation?

Meanwhile, the Monomaniac sinks back against the arm of the Illegible, staring with big eyes out the windows at the walls of the Old City, above them now. "It's so beautiful," she sighs.

"Beautiful, yes," says the *Yekke*. "But there was a time here when life was not so beautiful. When it was not possible to go into the Old City. When you had to dodge machine gun bullets just to go into the street."

"Jerusalem is a dangerous place in many ways," says the Illegible. "It has always been a dangerous place. That's its main function, to be a dangerous place, a place of destruction, and still more dangerous, a place of reconstruction."

"Listen to the prophet!" says the Survoluptuous. "It's the most peaceful place in the world, it's a place where your soul can be at peace. You know this if you have travelled. Everybody recognizes it. I don't know why it is, but it is."

"It's both," says the Illegible. "Peaceful and dangerous."

"My god," says the *Yekke*, "listen to these philosophers. Even if the [   ]s wanted peace, which they never will no matter what they say, and they don't even say it, it would still be war here. We would fight just as bitterly among ourselves. As they would. This country is so complicated that anything you can say about it is true. Except what outsiders say about it, which is always too simple. If there is one thing we cannot afford here it is simplicity. Simplicity, you Americans will kill us with your stupid simplicity."

"Unless we die of complications first," says the Illegible.

"I like being simple," says the Monomaniac. "I thought I came here to be simple. To start over and be simple and live on a kibbutz. To be one with a people and a land and a country. Isn't that simple?"

"Yes," says the Survoluptuous with the maximum possible sarcasm.

"You might not like being simple, even if you were," says the Illegible. "Simplicity is a complicated business here. One god is a great simplification, a big improvement over the old, bickering pantheon. But what happens when everybody has a different one god?"

"We're here," says the *Yekke* as the car slows to a stop. "You are about to enter the realm of silence. And darkness. Everybody gets one candle."

He hands out thick candles as they get out of the car. He's a man past middle age but in evident health, with a supercilious air and a rigid military carriage. A survivor so he's probably a little crazy, his childhood blighted in the camps. It's probably hard for him to understand why he likes to take people through the Tunnel of Hezekiah, which he's done many times, but that's why he's a *Yekke*, to be hard of understanding.

Though Ron will have a good intuition about why after the fact. As a writer you develop a sixth sense which others call imagination, though imagination, as far as Ron is concerned, is the shtick of fashion designers and advertising types. Writers deal with language. Screw imagination.

They go up to the Spring of Gihon and those not wearing shorts roll up their pants. The Monomaniac strips off her skirt under which she wears the bottom of a bikini. They're all wearing expendable sneakers. They step into the cool stream running from the pool and the *Yekke* lights their candles.

The cool water makes Ron think of the warm, peaceful Mediterranean, and he suddenly wishes he were on the beach in Tel Aviv, swimming in the carefree ocean, cradled on its solvent swell, rather than sloshing through the steady, determined current of this stream. The ocean is a solution without a problem.

As they approach the dark opening Ron perceives a tightening in his stomach and inconveniently recalls that he's sometimes prone to attacks of claustrophobia. He's distracted from panic, however, by vexation. How could he be so stupid as to forget this weakness when he agreed to the expedition? And yet he did want to come and, he knows, wouldn't have had he dwelled on his fears.

The Survoluptuous plunges ahead like a hippo, her hippo hips churning ahead of Ron as she pushes in behind their *yekke* guide, while the Monomaniac falls in behind him, and the Illegible follows her rear.

"Mah-yeem! De l'eau! Wasser!" exclaims the Survoluptuous as they enter the tunnel. "I love water. I love anything wet, even moist. Water is life, when you live in a desert country you understand that."

"You've never been to the Dead Sea?" The *Yekke* over his shoulder.

"The Dead Sea is different. The Dead Sea is a cloaca, the asshole of the Holy Land. Don't talk to me about the Dead Sea."

"I like the Dead Sea also." Ron. "It buoys you up, it's supportive, maternal, you can float on its bosom and go to sleep without sinking."

"The Dead Sea is disgusting," she insists. "It's unclean. It's sticky. If you stay in that water too long you simply dissolve in its chemicals. The living sea is sexy, it soothes, the dead one is stagnant and poisonous."

"The difference between a lotion and a potion." The Illegible. "One mothers one smothers."

"The ocean, the ocean, the mama lotion." Ron. "Let's face it, it does both."

"Dark in here." The Survoluptuous. Ignoring him. "It's restful, no? We should go back to living in caves, we'd be happier. Look, already the entrance is gone." Sloshing around a curve darkness closes in. They move ahead with their candles like a line of supplicants.

Ron considers making some excuse and going back but, stupidly, he doesn't. Moreover, he can tell from the way she talks that the Survoluptuous is feeling the same way he is, even more so, her babble factor is increasing as the silence imposes itself, the silence frightens her. Maybe she suffers from semiotic hysteria.

"On one occasion," the *Yekke* over his shoulder, "the water in the tunnel rose unexpectedly while a troop of boy scouts was going through. It got higher and higher. It was almost up to the top by the time they got out. Can you imagine it? They had water up to their noses at one point."

"How often does this happen?" The Survoluptuous.

"Not often." The *Yekke*. "It's unpredictable."

Ron feels a current of panic. He thinks about the ocean, the expanse and aimlessness of the ocean. He looks behind him. Things have been rather quiet at the rear. He thinks he sees why. By the light of the candles it seems to him as if the Illegible is walking with his hand in the Monomaniac's bikini bottom. She has a kind of abstracted look on her face. Innocent. Ron thinks about the ocean and its rocking motion.

"The waters of Gihon are supposedly where the Virgin Mary washed her infant's clothes." The *Yekke*. "And where Jesus made a blind man see. Stupid."

Though Ron persists in seeing a bright side to stupidity, especially since there always seems to be an inexhaustible supply. He knows that's probably stupid of him.

The rough walls of the tunnel, moist and glistening in the candle flicker, close in as the passage narrows and lowers. The Survoluptuous ahead of Ron, churning through the water now risen from ankle level and moving up their shins, seems to be in the grip of some sort of low key logorrhea, going on about all kinds of irrelevances, sometimes in more than one language, and occasionally humming snippets of song.

Everyone else is quiet. The tunnel winds through the rock mass. Deep in the womb of Gaia, spawn of Chaos. The walls seem menacing with brutal chthonic powers, the tunnel dead-ended, labyrinthine, the Minotaur, Zeus as bull, the Golden Calf, gods of the underworld demanding blood sacrifice, holiness broken down into component parts.

Suddenly the Survoluptuous stops talking. The silence puts the fear in Ron. Claustrophobia closes in and a feeling that he can't breathe. He has the sense that divinity, whatever that is, is coming close, and he doesn't want it to.

Then he remembers from drug experiences how the best way to handle breakdown is go with it, it's worked before. He takes a deep breath and goes. The claustrophobia recedes. He breathes again, again. Whatever happens happens. He thinks about the ocean and its rocking motion.

The water is now up to the middle of their calves, he doesn't know whether the tunnel floor is dropping or the water is rising. It's impossible to tell how long they've been walking. He wishes the Survoluptuous would start talking. She's having some trouble pushing her bulk through the ever-narrowing passage, sidling sideways, swivelling her heavy hips. Ahead, the *Yekke* stops.

"Now. I want you to experience the darkness here. Absolute darkness. The darkness of death. Just for a moment I want you to extinguish your candles. When I give the command."

The two behind Ron don't wait for the command. They blow their candles out right away. A sigh sounds above the rushing of water.

"I don't want to." The Survoluptuous.

"Just for a minute." The *Yekke*. "You'll ruin it for the rest of us."

"No. Please."

"You will do it. When I tell you. Now!"

His candle goes out, Ron blows out his own. Hers remains lit, illuminating her heavy face, in the flicker a mask of fear.

"Ach-tung! Now! Schnell! Schnell!" The *Yekke* bends and blows out her candle.

Total nothingness. A long, absolute silence, impossible to tell how long.

The voice of the *Yekke*. "You see. There is nothing to fear. There was never anything to fear."

A wild scream rings through the tunnel.

"Light the candles." Ron. "Light them."

The *Yekke* ignites his with a lighter. "Let me light yours," he says to the Survoluptuous. But she just stands there with her mouth open, as if still screaming, which startles Ron with the impression that they are all screaming.

The *Yekke* passes the lighter to Ron who lights hers and his own and passes it back. Nothing further is said. They move on through the rising water, now up to their knees. The Survoluptuous whimpers occasionally.

Gradually, as the water deepens, the roof of the tunnel gets lower, so that now it grazes their heads. Again the *Yekke* stops and holds his candle up. They see a passage off the main tunnel.

"They started digging from both sides. They didn't quite meet so that, as you see, those digging from the city hit the side of the tunnel coming from the spring, leaving a blind passage, a dead end."

The route to the graven image, Ron remembers, the polymorphic bull god, the calf, the golden idol. But he's too spooked to dwell on it, much less penetrate it. He thinks of the ocean, the mama lotion.

They move on. The tunnel narrows and gets so low they have to stoop to get through. Ron thinks about the ocean and its rocking motion.

"The next section is very low. But don't worry. Just bend over and you'll get through."

Ron notices that the candles behind him have disappeared, did they take the dead end? Are they clued into the treasure, the Golden Calf? But he doesn't have a chance to say anything because just about then he finds he has to double over to get through, so that the water, which is now above his knees, is just below his nose. Almost simultaneously, there's a cry from the lady in front of him.

"Oh my god! Oh my god!"

"What is it?" Ron. But he sees what it is. She's stuck.

"Oh my god! Oh my god! I can't get out! Oh my god, oh my god. Do something!'

She's doubled over in front of him, her body curled over the water. Her candle drops from her hand and is snuffed in the stream.

157

"Don't panic." The *Yekke*. "Don't worry. We'll get you out. Try to squeeze your shoulders together. Breathe out, breathe out. Push her," he yells to Ron. "I'll pull."

To have two hands to do this, they have to blow out their candles. Ron puts his in his pocket and in utter darkness gropes her survoluptuous body till he finds a firm handhold, he thinks it's her ass. Her voice subsides to a low, repeated moan. He plants his hands solidly on her buttocks and pushes. It's like pushing jello.

"Are you pulling?" Ron.

"I'm pulling. Push harder." Her moans get louder. Oddly, they seem to have developed an echo in the tunnel.

"It's not working." Ron. "You push, I'll pull."

Ron gropes her blubbery flesh for handholds, loses his grip on what feel like breasts and belly, finally grabs what must be thighs and pulls backward. The moans increase in volume as the echo amplifies.

"Are you pulling?"

"I'm pulling. Push harder."

"It's not working. You push again."

Ron puts his hands on her buttocks and pushes.

"Push harder. Push. Push."

She moans.

Suddenly there's a release, Ron falls forward into nothingness, into water, she screams, and he hears a male grunt and a female cry from somewhere behind him that is definitely not an echo.

When he gets up out of the water the candles are lit again both behind him and in front of him, the Survoluptuous is free, and they quickly move past the narrowest and lowest part of the tunnel.

Nobody speaks except the Survoluptuous, and she isn't really speaking, she's doing something you might call uttering but not speech, her babble now broken down into baby talk, soft vocables that make no sense at all and that sound something like, "Vasht niet vilsta, ach zuup schmach gehonicht shlups, where ist, ma-a-a-z, oola basta in la neige mit hagamelbruder, dodo ma dovay ich . . ." Frightening and soothing at the same time.

It seems like a long time, there's no telling how long, the lady still babbling, before they begin to see light and finally come to the place at the tunnel mouth where the ancient plaque commemorating its completion was discovered.

Walking through the shallows of the pool of Shiloah the sunlight is dazzling. As soon as they hit the light the Survoluptuous stops babbling. She stands in the middle of the pool looking around her, dazed.

The *Yekke* looks at them, flicks a wan smile all around. "You see?" he says. But he looks somehow defeated.

Though the rest of them have the look of people who have accomplished something, it would be hard to say exactly what. A sense of renewal, maybe? Or is it just relief? The Illegible and the Monomaniac have their arms around one another shyly in the light, complicitous, she blinking fixedly up at him as if she's found her only one, her messiah, her idol.

And suddenly murmuring liquid nothings the survoluptuous one opens her moist arms to Ron with an all-inclusive embrace in which he stupidly allows himself to be swamped. As she rocks him in her blubbery arms he smells the saltiness of her sweat and within her billowy, asphyxiating bosom for a moment feels the stubborn difficulties of life drown in humid exhalations and wave on wave of undulating flesh.

Ghost Ghetto

Many years later he returns to Venice, a changed person, a mere ghost of his former self. In the interim he's been invisibled, not only by a luckless profanity of events, but also by his own prejudice against projection of image, of any counterfeit, including imagination's slight-of-mind. But by now the scarlet of his invisibility, I mean the small scar, not the color, has become an emblem of holdout against an idolatrous, icon conned, oscar crazed hollywooden world. As the rabbi said after the briss, can it be long now? His scarlet letter, his Aleph, marking him an E.T., an alien. In case he were thinking of idolizing himself.

So that in answer to Kafka's question, What have I in common with the Jews when I have nothing even in common with myself? he might reply, What self?

The more so, then, that on vacation, sitting in his apartment in a poorer quarter of Venice, overlooking the canal, the quai-like fondamenta, the bridges, the Venetians, the tourists following their various tour generals holding aloft banners of scarf, ribbon, chapeaux on umbrella or cane, or rapt in the gleaming gondolas, black as death, his life is an absence from his life.

Invisible, a nobody afloat like the gondolas drifting by with no idea of what will happen next, his invisibility, in fact, is simply an extension of his normal situation—the consequence of obscure critical esteem for his literary work, buried by myopic media hype for his more journalistic, if ostensibly profitable, output as a writer—an invisibility recently more painful as a result of deaths, divorce and geographical circumstance, by the removal, in short, of all those who had been closest.

It is a condition to which Venice, however mistakenly, is meant to help him reconcile or, at least, to ballast the kind of rapidly progressive instability that isolation can breed, since in a city so full of thereness his presence isn't necessary, allowing him to vacate, hopefully reach for a tonic vacancy as the vegetable boat scuds the corner full speed, the man on the high bow doing some drastic ducking so his head doesn't get knocked off by the bridge, the grocery boat pulls up to the store downstairs, its pilot has a long discussion with the storekeeper about accounts, pulls out, a garbage boat goes by, loaded high with trash.

A cat licks itself in the sun across the canal, beyond the blue, the red, the teak boats tied up to plain wooden poles at the fondamenta beneath the tall windows with the geraniums on the balconies on the walls faded maroon, green, ochre, plaster scaling off to exposed salmon hued brick that he looks at over his own geraniums in his own tall windows.

Somebody's houseful of furniture floats by on a moving van boat.

A teak water taxi churns through, cabin lined with white sofas.

He goes down to pick up his shoes from the blind shoemaker, around the corner down the fondamenta across the wooden bridge to the right, where they were supposed to be ready yesterday and weren't.

Today the little man in the store looks alarmed.

"After lunch," he says.

"No, I need them now," Ron says, "I'll come back in fifteen minutes."

"No, a half an hour."

"Okay, a half an hour."

A sweet little old man, yesterday he gave Ron a shine, refused money.

Ron comes back in half an hour, he's working away at them. Okay, Ron will go get a haircut he's been meaning to.

Ron comes back after haircut, he's just starting second shoe.

Ron goes to get bread, comes back, he's got the heel on and fixing sole. Ron stands in doorway watching people come down the narrow street. A tourist asks for directions in broken Italian, Ron gives them in broken Italian.

Now he's back on first shoe perfecting his work. His meticulousness is becoming fascinating. Ron's impatience gives way

161

to absorption in his unbelieveable perfectionism with awl, glue and nail.

As he works he talks.

He grew up in Toronto, taken there by his anti-fascist father. "Mussolini niente!"

Still working away from within a different sense of time, out of another world. When he's finally done he gives a big smile. He's very pleased with himself, showing Ron the shoes.

There seems to be an otherworldly concern here for the soul as well as the sole, the way you feel, your state of being.

Venice is a practical town, but the unworldly, not the pragmatic seems fundamental, and the pragmatic in any case is founded on the visible ongoing decay of this world, the mouldering fondamenta, the rotting timbers, the crumbling masonry.

If you feel bad, stop for *gelatti*.

Or, more to the point, Ron sees a man run into a hotel and yell to the desk clerk, "Where's the nearest church?"

The Pope was just here with much hullaballoo, and among other things visited a woman's prison on Giudecca across the Lagoon.

"Don't get demoralized," he told the inmates.

Don't underestimate this advice.

One day Ron wanders into the Hotel Falier around the corner and down the fondamenta, he doesn't exactly know why, a sudden impulse of curiosity about that class of hotel—third, probably—in this kind of slightly decaying lower middle class neighborhood, or maybe the vaguest mental tide, like the tidal current that seems to run through the canals slowly flushing out all the trash tossed into them.

This is the floating world, not in the Japanese sense of a world of pleasure though that too in a more subtle way, but as a world adrift from the mainstream, eddying, insular, isolate, labyrinthine, intestinal, encoiled, amnesiac, amniotic, curled into itself like a foetus or a brain.

(Why else would Ron's friend, John Tytell, who did his doctoral thesis on Henry James, end up by coincidence in James' old hotel room when he comes to the city, a city that generates resonances like an echo chamber?)

In the Hotel Falier a young man is talking to the desk clerk in pidgin Italian, a very thin young man with very black hair and water green eyes reminiscent of a certain Titian, an anonymous portrait of a young man called simply "The Man With the Green Eyes."

The young man is having an altercation with the clerk about giving up his room in the Hotel Falier because there's now a place for him in the youth hostel on Giudecca.

There's a very nice youth hostel on Giudecca with a great view of the Lagoon, very cheap but always full.

Ron recognizes the altercation instantly and finding the situation oddly painful immediately walks back out to the fondamenta, remembering suddenly his own first visit to Venice almost thirty years ago, arriving as a kid in a vaporetto at the same hostel on Giudecca with a painful injured eye and no money to have it cared for but so superexcited that he wasn't worried about it, sensing with a certain amount of accuracy the invulnerability of youth, when without preamble a large, muscular, golden haired, handsome young man, somewhat older than himself, with a strange accent, on his way to the same hostel, began to inquire about his plight and on hearing it, made him the loan of a, for Ron, large sum of money so he could go to the clinic.

And then curiously Ron never saw him again, not on the boat, not even at the hostel, as if he'd evaporated into the mist-bright air as abruptly as he'd appeared.

Ron went to the clinic and the doctor probed his eye, finally removing an embedded cinder.

Ecco! said the doctor, and Ron experienced an immediate sensation of relief.

That's how Ron learned the meaning of the word *ecco*.

Ron considers the amusing possibility that the opportune

appearance of the golden and muscular young man represented an intervention by the gods, the kind of gods we don't have anymore, especially not in the secular States, who used to go among men, and women too, and talk with them, and help them out or punish them, and love them. This used to be their territory. *Ecco*!

The next day Ron goes to the ancient Jewish Ghetto, speaking of old gods, the Venetian Ghetto having the distinction of being the first in the world, established in the sixteenth century, giving its name—from the word for the foundries that were originally there—giving its name to all subsequent versions.

The Ghetto is way over to one side of the railroad station where off a lesser canal an alley-like viale begins.

Ron turns to the right into the viale and notices on the left-hand wall a marble plaque above the doorway of number 48, not as he first thinks an apologetic memorial to the miseries of the Ghetto, but the actual edict establishing the Ghetto, as it were still edicting, fierce with warnings about Jews being prohibited from leaving, threats of prosecution and provision for informers contacting the authorities about violations.

Then he penetrates the Old Ghetto square, surrounded by shabby buildings very tall in terms of Venetian architecture, very plain, with none of the lacy decoration of the Venetian style, the Ghetto still another world, and not in good repair, a picture so oppressive that Ron can't get himself to take a picture as planned.

The Old Ghetto's tall buildings, no doubt to increase population capacity of compressed space, look like the predecessor of Ron's long-time neighborhood in New York's old Lower East Side at its worst.

He meanders past a bakery featuring matzos Italian style— "our bread contains only flour, water and olive oil"—baked in a beautiful latticed, lacy open-work shape, into the New Ghetto, more spacious, houses in better condition, a series of monumental plaques to the Holocaust, and still oppressive, claustrophobic.

He goes into the little synagogue-museum in the Ghetto Nuovo, against his better judgment because now all he wants to do is get out, and discovers that while the museum isn't much, the interior of the actual synagogue is an architectural gem, a baroque oval surrounded by a railed balcony no doubt for women worshippers.

And there he discovers, engaged in conversation, the dark, green-eyed boy from the Hotel Falier, and seeing him, feels a sudden tug of attraction, an inexplicable, spontaneous, almost embarrassing pang of feeling, like an evocative but isolated musical chord implying a phrase, a composition whose sense hangs in the air.

The boy is listening to a middle aged man telling him, in broken phrase and bad grammar, with an Ancient Mariner urgency, how he came to be here, in this synagogue, through a twist of absurdity, an absurdity emphasized, Ron notes, by what looks like a folded dish towel or large handkerchief perched on the man's head as an improvised yarmulke.

He had been brought up completely secular in South Africa, the older man is saying, gone there as an infant with his mother, an old atheistic Italian Socialist, when she had remarried.

One day, after he had grown up and his mother long since died, he received notice from Italy that the cemetery in which his family was buried had been hit by an earthquake and the graves had to be moved.

On coming to Italy to see about the situation, he was told by the authorities that the graves had to be moved to the Jewish cemetery.

"The Jewish cemetery! Why?"

"Why! Because they're Jewish, of course!"

He was astonished, but on reflection realized he had always suspected something.

The man pauses.

"And you?" he asks the boy.

"Yes," he answers. "But not a believer."

Nor is Ron—short of an earthquake.

He again feels an urgent desire to get out, get out of the

165

synagogue, get out of the Ghetto itself.

He leaves the synagogue, takes one of the bridges out of the isolation of the Campo da Ghetto Nuovo and heads for the vivacity and color of the Rialto and the world as quickly as possible.

He walks for about five minutes, he turns a corner and with a shock realizes that he is once again in the Campo da Ghetto Nuovo.

Dumbfounded!

He has no memory of heading back here, he would have had to return on some of the same streets, the same bridges by which he came.

He had been walking directly out of the Ghetto and then suddenly, as if his trajectory had been that of a ghost, he is back in it, how was it possible?

It's as if a certain period of duration has disappeared, unaccounted for, during which he was transported back here in a wink of time, and he is not so much back where he started as back when he started and it occurs to him that the real meaning of labyrinth is time warp.

Conversely, ghosts are not creatures that have returned after their time, but those who have lost their way.

So this mystery is his little, ambiguous miracle of the day, as if some magic rabbi had waved his hand and conjured an angel to fly him back, its wing veiling his consciousness to make him aware of something that consciousness itself renders invisible.

What?

The next day it's raining, the drops pocking the canals, Venetians go about their business in bright over-all slickers and high rubber boots, boatmen bail rain water from boat bottoms, so he goes to the Scuola San Rocco, which is near where he lives.

The Scuola San Rocco is where you go if you want to see Tintorettos, they're on the walls and on the ceilings, especially one immense crucifixion covering a whole wall to the ceiling.

Crucifixions give Ron the creeps, barbarous and sadomaso, spiritually tacky, and yet an effective way to evoke empathy for suffering, the Holocaust for example, too big, it cannot be imagined, the crucifix provides a human focus.

As he approaches the huge painting he notices a slim silhouette of a male figure, almost swallowed by the vast canvas, shoulders up, head and neck thrust forward, mouth sagging open, eyes slightly popped and staring intensely at the painting in total empathy as if he sought to absorb it completely, an impression so striking Ron actually checks back to the painting to make sure it's still on the canvas.

By this time Ron is not surprised to encounter him, he's begun to accept these intersections, it's as though they've been programmed for the same itinerary, it's not that unusual when you're touring, there are just so many sights to see, so many tour books.

But he's become intensely curious about the slim boy and, he has to admit, more than curious, definitely attracted, and he would like to strike up a conversation, find out what he's about, except that the strength of the boy's scrutiny, his attention to the painting in front of him, definitely forbids it.

For Ron, on the other hand, once so avid an explorer of the European cultural heritage, coming back here yet again is more like an exploration of his own past, what he had originally sought in the classics evidently already found or, perhaps, not there, not ever there.

Now, as he turns at a right angle to gaze, a little absently, at the beautiful, small "Christ Carrying the Cross" kept behind glass on an easel, the one attributed indecisively to Titian or Giorgione, Ron's always thought Titian, he senses to his right the boy turning also to look at the same painting, turning quite simultaneously along with him, and Ron decides this time, after a minute's hesitation, to breach his privacy.

"You know," he says, "in the sixteenth century it was thought to have miraculous powers."

The boy, the young man, his age is actually not clear to Ron, or rather he seems to look different ages at different times as if he's not quite in focus, turns his head toward him with a slight, ambiguous smile, not totally unlike a sacred subject by the great Venetian, Giovanni Bellini, gazing into another spiritual dimension, and seems to stare past him actually, without the slightest acknowledgement of his remark.

And then Ron realizes, and it's a little scary, that he's looking through not past him, that he literally doesn't take in that he's there, and this with such an absolute quality, that for a second Ron has to wonder himself.

Ron looks back to the Titian/Giorgione, the shrewd, secular face of the older man focusing on the young god whose gaze scans eternity.

Is the young man, by force of youth and innocence, staring into another spiritual dimension, one in which Ron no longer exists, lacking the purity and disinterestedness of the blind shoemaker unconcerned with production obsessed with essentials like good work, like truth?

Essentials are of the other world, maybe a better one, but you can't walk around without shoes these days on the fondamenta.

There's much to be said for the crumbling perfection of Venice but it now requires high tech methods of preservation and, while it's true the ghetto blasters are beginning to move in with them, who needs the ghetto?

Ron moves down to the first floor of the Scuola, leaving the young man at peace in dream time, and goes to take a look at the various religious articles exhibited, among them a reliquary from within which a dead saint's shrivelled finger beckons.

But when he leaves the Scuola the rain's stopped and the sun breaks loose, causing all the birds threading the air to join with the city's innumerable caged canaries which, like the gondoliers, are always singing.

It's almost like being back in the stream of history again except, at the same time, he's still eddying in a lagoon of internal exile, apart from all that, in an old world he'd thought he'd left

168

behind, as if his people had never passed through Ellis Island into modern time.

In the Piazza San Rocco, across from the Scuola, six or ten cats lounge near the fence, one of the packs of street cats fed here and there through the city, outside restaurants, churches, sometimes even by citizens lowering food in baskets from upper-story windows, to keep the rats at bay, he supposes.

The cats look at him out of their timeless world, reminding him that Venice is a city of a thousand years that has, like an eddy in a river, evolved its own rhythm of time, in-turned, reflexive, self-referential, a reflecting pool in which a traveller may reflect.

It isn't for some days that Ron catches his next image of the boy, though he had expected it sooner than the evening when from some unexpected back-street pool of silence where he had stopped to reflect on the chat of aqua with fondamenta, a twist in the viale brings him suddenly into the uproar of Piazza San Marco, harmonized by the whining violins and old tangos of the small orchestras playing on the terrazzi of the cafes.

There, in one of the cafes, Florian, the most famous one, he spots the object of what he by now jokingly thinks of as his fascination, at a table eating *gelatti* with a wide-eyed brunette young woman whose half smile and constant glancing about the Piazza imply a frank reach of wonder.

She's arrived in Venice only recently for the first time, Ron guesses, still overwhelmed by the initial impact of the city, and on Giudecca was swept away both by Venice and his young man at once.

Her long, full, brown hair, thigh-length skirt according to a once again new style for kids, and a generally unbound look under loose cloth, that, or maybe some openness to experience that she projects like an invitation, creates for the observer an immediate aura around her.

This is just the right place for her, Ron speculates, just the right moment at just the right age for a flowering presumably offered to her companion that gives him a shot of envy, even jealousy,

169

though for exactly what it's hard to say, since though Ron might want to be in his shoes, then again, he doesn't want her, however attractive, between the boy and his growing, maybe even unhealthy he has to admit, obsession with him.

But her refreshing presence, like the breeze now blowing off the Lagoon, it being unusually cool here for the start of tourist season, serves to distract him from the somewhat fevered solipsism of his concern for an unknown boy who is really little more than an artifact of his imagination.

Her quivering sensuousness even as she moves in her seat, inspires Ron to take a table in good view of her, and tantalizingly close to hearing distance of their probably amazed conversation about the scene around them, from which several things become likely.

First, that they seem to be lovers, or about to be lovers or, most likely have just become lovers, almost purring at one another, even on a honeymoon perhaps, and that part of their wonder, and especially hers, over the city is an extension of their own sensuality which Venice, certainly, helps to arouse.

"This is the sexiest place I've ever been," he overhears her voice. "All the buildings are wearing lace nightgowns."

The metaphor suddenly sets him off on a revery in which she is his poetic travelling companion on a shoestring tour of Europe which she is seeing for the first time so that for her, and for him because of her, the Old World is an endless succession of opening doors again instead of a dead end whose main interest lies in investigating the series of mistaken turns that led into it.

Here in the midst of the detritus of a tradition, her enthusiasm would help him collage together all sorts of hopeful possibilities, following the example of the great generation of permanent tourists, those modern Americans from between Wars I and II.

He imagines an itinerary through the museum of Europe in which a process of continuous edification is relieved only, if very frequently, by sex, which is in fact the way he travelled once, and having once done so wonders if he could do it twice.

What she would have thought of him then, or now in those circumstances, might resemble the prestige of a soldier heroic on both fronts, with consequences sometimes known as love, a word that might have been used to describe the relation between himself and, at the time, his wife.

His imagination has already embarked on a journey echoing the original, together again for the first time, when the couple in question give signs of disembarking, and he has the almost panicky idea of offering them a room in his apartment, there's plenty of space.

But just then, their lire already on the table, they get up and slip into the stream of pedestrians in the crowded Piazza, and are quickly lost to his view.

This loss of an elusive nostalgia, however, gains his attention to his current actual situation, which is that he's lonely and horny, since all issues resolve in the here and now, do they not, because what is not cannot be clearly understood, even if how much there is to gain from what is understood is itself quite relative, though relative to what is also a question.

In the here and now, the next day, his fluid itinerary brings him once again to the splendid equestrian statue of the warrior Colleoni, brutal image of self assertion so unchangingly there that its magnificence seems quixotic on the blackboard of history.

Then in the flux of the morning he threads his way through the narrow alleys leading to the Rialto, and as he stops to look into a shop window showing an impressive array of thick, soft badger shaving brushes, the unmistakable accents, female, of an American trying to speak Italian, strike from close range over his shoulder, and it's almost certainly the young woman from Florian's last night.

"Scusi, signor. Dov'e Ca D'oro?"

"Do you speak English?"

"Yes."

"American?"

"Yes."

"I happen to be heading in that direction. Why don't you come with me?"

Certainly it's the same young woman, though it's true that people under a certain age are starting to look the same to him, young people in general starting to resolve into types rather than individuals, a situation that has resulted in more than one embarrassment.

As he heads off with her at his side toward the Grand Canal, he can't help thinking that it's a perfect pick-up situation although he knows, of course, that she's not in the market for being picked up in that sense.

She's just as appealing at close range as she was at the table last night and yet different, because chatting with her a bit, it seems she's no gaping tourist, the same gawking quality he noticed last night deriving rather, it soon becomes evident, from a fine sensibility and a quick sense of wonder.

"Are you staying, then, at the Hotel Falier?" he asks her.

"You mean as opposed to the Hotel Success? Is there such a place?"

"I thought I saw you there. With a young man?"

"Oh, is that how you say it? I guess I started there. The young man is a writer. I suppose that was an inauspicious place to start."

"I don't know. The United Nations was started at a place called Lake Success. And is this the first time in Venice for both of you?"

"For me yes. For him no. But the first time he was here he was having some sort of eye trouble and couldn't see as much as he wanted."

"Isn't that always the case?"

"Maybe. But that's not because of eye trouble."

"True. They say that people believe what they see. But in fact most people see only what they believe. The second time I came here was with my then wife, but though I could see, I really couldn't see. Much less believe."

She doesn't respond to this, probably losing interest in view

172

of the flood of new and beautiful things to see, while he, barely pondering the news that the young man is a writer, starts to feel the pull of a magnetism as powerful as it is apparently baseless, since its source is a girl about whom he knows nothing and yet with whom he feels an immediate coincidence of rhythm, an empathy, an intimacy almost, so that it would seem the most natural thing in the world to ask her up to his apartment, to sit with her on the chaise, to put his arm around her as they talk together effortlessly and luminously.

And he, he flatters himself to believe, intuits, though surely she has no thought of acting on it, that she is feeling the same thing.

So that by the time they climb the steps up to the summit of the Rialto bridge, the various vaporetti and motor barges and long-oared vessels weaving wakes below on the Grand Canal, and he stops to point out the Ca D'oro to her, he hasn't the slightest idea of what he might say, and she, with a look in her soft brown eyes of both expectancy and prohibition, no idea, certainly, of what she might hear.

He turns to point up the Canal to her goal, explaining the route which he has no intention of letting her pursue alone, and when he turns again to her the space she occupied just a few seconds ago is vacant, and in fact she's nowhere in view.

He quickly looks around the other side of the line of shops, glances down both sides of the bridge, behind the shops on the other side of the bridge and she is nowhere.

Disappeared in a wink of time.

He doesn't quite believe it, and more mystified than insulted, he wanders down the other side of the bridge, invaded by a wholly disproportionate sense of loss, of roads not taken, and of roads taken that wind back on themselves, leading nowhere, or that lead through marvelous landscapes that themselves are lost.

Stumbling among the shoppers and vendors on the other side of the bridge, he wonders exactly what it is of which he feels the loss, and he thinks it's that, from her wonder over the spectacle of the city, she is as he once was, a believer, not a believer in anything particular but one credulous about belief itself, a faculty hard to come by, but without which, as now, there's little but empty air inhabiting your dreams.

But having come to Venice for vacation, for the pleasure of vacancy, and not for work or thought, he's content to let the whole episode drift by without further analysis. Besides, he has the intimation that though there's something doing here, for him, other than the pleasure of mere doing, it will emerge only if he lets his normal analytic habits of mind become undone, giving himself up to the apparently aimless drift and eddy of incident, the profane course of event which, faithful to nothing, comprises nonetheless a kind of fateful language if you know how to read it.

What follows then is unpredictable, once he decides to give in to the natural flow of things.

Whether the consequence of one of those waves of fatigue that suddenly looms in the course of the touristwork, or a riptide of spiritual origin, an overwhelming current of hopelessness catches him and sweeps him along, pulling him helplessly like drifting garbage in the canals without destination, a surge of despair denoting the final uselessness of all effort—why keep going, why not die?

Staggered by a vacuum emptied of hope that leaves him breathless, he reels to a table in a café and sits down abruptly.

The waiter comes, he orders a café *macchiato* and, looking around, sees that the café is quite singular in that it's populated largely by old people. Old, but animated, vivacious, talking and gesturing and calling from one table to another and bantering with the waiter.

The vigor, the good humor of the old people some of them obviously quite handicapped, illumines his melancholy, relativizes his dark humor. One ancient gent in particular sporting a beret and cane, lively but with a thoughtful eye, he sees wishfully as himself in the labyrinth of time.

Whether it's the tonic effect of the jocular septuagenarians or simply the rhythm of his own psyche, he recalls himself at a happier time in this city, sitting at a café table with his young wife.

In particular he remembers sitting at a table bordering the Lagoon, at night, having a private celebration of sorts because he had just sold his first story.

He felt rather smart and success, whatever that meant to him, was almost palpable, in view of which he seemed to himself quite worldly-wise.

At a certain point in the evening he even literally saw himself as a successful author twenty years in the future. Whether he projected this apparition onto another client sitting in a dark corner of the café or whether it was a materialization of alcoholic intuition hardly mattered.

Whatever the case, in his innocence this vision of himself gave him a shock, to the point that he dropped his glass on the floor of the café, because it wasn't what he thought it would be, success, it looked more like obscurity, like failure, something he was willing to accept but reluctant to understand.

Now, remembering that apparition, he recognizes himself.

In remembering who he was going to be, he begins to remember who he is.

Energized by the recollection that once upon a time he had a vision of himself, and that, however ambiguous, it still is him, he decides that a little sun and exercise will do wonders, and when he leaves the café he's already plotted an afternoon on the beach of the Lido.

That afternoon, having taken a beach cabana at the Hotel Excelsior, he's walking down the strand past the domes and minarets of that pseudo-Arabian monument, along the endless line of cabanas with their colorful striped poles, when he spots the young man who has become the subject of his Venetian meander, in a swimsuit walking toward him down the beach.

This time he resolves instantly to engage him, hoping to illuminate, through conversation, the source and reason for his fascination.

As the boy approaches Ron notes his dreaming gaze out to sea, thinking if he is a young writer it is indeed the look of one better able to deal with a landscape of imagination than of reality.

Before the boy reaches him he stops on the beach, looks back and down, smiles and speaks, presumably to his young wife or girlfriend, his body turned in profile.

Thin, thin as a stick, it's hard to believe he's so thin.

It's a leanness Ron immediately associates with spiritual purity which, if anything, increases his desire to interrogate him.

But as Ron approaches his now stationary figure, the boy looks up at the sky and, since in following his gaze Ron spots nothing, he looks down and realizes the boy's suddenly grown taller and then looking down at his feet he sees that's not it at all, it's that there is an undeniable and growing space under the soles of his feet relative to the sand.

Stunned, Ron continues toward him, knowing this couldn't be happening but too dazed to pause and take stock, and the closer he comes to him the higher he rises, like a kite or a balloon, already his knees are at the level of Ron's head, and as he ascends his arms stretch out to the sides, his ankles cross, his head rolls against his shoulder, his eyes look up from under his lids, levitating more quickly, soaring, then evaporates against the blue-white sky, gone.

For some reason equally confused and embarrassed, Ron looks around to see if anyone else has witnessed this prodigy, and seeing nothing but cabana life as usual, looks down to seek the girl on the beach, and discovers that, yes, she is there, but only in effigy, her seeming likeness spread comfortably on the beach, but sculpted from, or turned to, sand.

Ron hardly knows what to think of this episode if, in fact, stunned as he is, he's capable of thinking anything at all, but the first thing that occurs to him, however absurdly, is that, since such a singularity could only be a caprice of visual imagination, the young man has been looking at too many Tintorettos.

Then, of course, it occurs to him that maybe he himself has been looking at too many assumptions, resurrections, ascensions, annunciations, apotheoses, transfigurations, epiphanies and other magical subjects.

And then the true reading of these events comes to him, which is that whatever their presumable source they signify expanding contact with the other world so aptly signified by Venice, and that this rapidly growing contact might be as much cause for alarm as for—how would you put it?—anticipation.

And that conversely, if he is, as he is beginning to suspect, on the brink of insight, it is one that brings him also, perhaps, to the brink of sanity.

Next day, hoping to understand the effect on him of the city and its culture, and so get his feet back on the ground, he goes once more to the Accademia, which contains the essence of Venetian painting, if any single place can be said to do so.

There, in a room dominated by Giovanni Bellini, standing in front of "The Tempest," one of the few certain works by Giorgione, his contemplation is invaded by a tour group whose guide, lecturing in poor English, is giving a florid and undoubtedly cribbed interpretation of the achievement of the Venetian School.

"The Venetian of early Cinquecento founded harmony between the form and the color, and so in various vibration of light the fervid intensity of life, reasons, and principle which is why her painting was flourished amidst our lagoons will shine eternal. The one whose intimate contemplative desire founded the inspiration of every living thing in color, in man and her plants as if the other world is all we have and it is this one. The first to see. This the first essentially modern painter rose to being universal art. *Ecco*, Giorgione!"

The tour moves on, leaving him with this new information to contemplate by way of getting his feet on the ground.

The other world is all we have and it is this one.

Maybe he was talking about Venice itself, which exists largely in the other world, apart from the eroding undertow of history.

History defeats itself.

He looks back at the Giorgione canvas, beautiful but cryptic in its imagery, which his guide book refers to as a "fine nude woman" and "a young man calm and serene" against crumbling towers and stormy sky, all of which conveys "a lofty expression of universal beauty." *Ecco*, Giorgione!

Ron rather thinks of the imponderable black cloud in the painting with its improbable bolt of lightning as a miracle that intensifies the landscape, a phenomenon not unknown, if unpredictable, in his own mental landscape. Annunciations, they come lightly, and if he's not attentive the carrier pigeon is gone before he knows it's there. The message is adrift in the bottle—where are you in the riptide of history?

The next encounter, and by now Ron's Venetian odyssey has clearly taken its measure from these encounters, is at night in a spectacular canal-side café extending out from one of the luxe hotels, with the shiny, black, coffin-like gondolas sliding by on the glinting wavelets reflecting artificial light beyond the flowered border of the balustrade edging the terrazzo.

Way off to the left on the Lagoon an illuminated cruise ship at its mooring, lights strung along its masts and cordage, marks the perpetual holiday in which the city lives, set apart from the normalcy of the quotidian, and across the mouth of the Grand Canal, the ornate, improbable, floodlit mass of the Church of the Salute marks the occasion of yet another miracle.

Here as he huddles in a corner of the nearly empty terrazzo, the two of them come in together with a conspiratorial air of taking a "big splurge," as the student guide books categorize visits to more expensive establishments.

"A step up from the Hotel Falier," she remarks, as they take a table beside the water, close to his but less in the shadows.

"Yes," he answers. "But if preferable in the long run is another question."

"Maybe not. But good for a celebration."

"I suppose it can't hurt," he says. "For an evening. Visiting the fauna of this kind of world is like going to the zoo."

"I like the zoo."

"The animals can't hurt. In the real world they do."

"Then I appreciate your preference for the other world," she says.

"The one you can't see?"

"Can't see? Can't see what?"

"That's the question," he answers.

"Anyway," she says—their drinks had come—"here's to the sale of your first story. Your first move into the real world."

"I'm not sure that's reason for congratulation."

"As long as you don't forget that, it's okay."

Ron would be charmed by their innocence if he were not anxious for their fate, and finds himself musing over speculations as to why that, in fact, should be the case, when he's shocked to attention by the sound of one of his own titles, an early piece written long ago on the subject of the visionary.

And then, as if continuing from previous discussion: "So that was why you didn't see much the first time you were here?"

"Right," he affirms.

"And what did you do?"

"I went to the emergency room of the clinic. Some young doctor simply put anesthetic in, probed around, and pulled out this large cinder. '*Ecco!*' he said as it came out, and I felt an immediate relief. I'll never forget it because the eye had been very painful for days. I'd almost gotten used to it, in fact. And then of course there'd been another kind of pain, the pain of being in a wonderfully visual place and not being able to see it properly. I was lucky."

"You're always lucky."

"Practical. Everything depends on that. You have to be shrewd. You can't live entirely in another world. If you want to survive in this one."

By this time Ron is almost standing in his dark corner, trembling in a half comprehending panic, impelled to say something

179

though he can't imagine what, while they, totally unaware, gaze across the Lagoon.

Finally, almost choking, he manages to articulate a strangled warning: "The other world is all you have!"

But there's no reaction, he imagines they haven't heard, or that he hasn't articulated after all, or that they're aware of nothing more than someone coughing in the corner.

Besides, he knows perfectly well the boy won't see through the false sophistication of his innocence—the worldly-wise pose of one gifted with an opening to the unworldly in a world that can't honor it, can see it only as failure.

Nevertheless, as if in a dream he approaches their table, trying to speak but incapable, gesticulating, yet they see nothing, the girl looking out across the water, the boy staring right through him.

Suddenly the boy focuses, pales as if he sees an apparition and, looking into its eyes, green as his own, goes rigid, his glass shattering on the terrazzo.

"What?" cries the girl.

"I just dreamed I saw myself twenty years from now."

"But you weren't asleep."

"Right."

But having looked at my reflection in his eyes for that instant, I at last understand without innocence.

That I myself am it, for him, at this moment as twenty years before, that ghost and warning of another world I once merely intuited.

Ecco!

Blinded by this vision, I finally see my own invisibility, as he, miraculously, fades and disappears into passing time.

After the Fact

The trip begins in the Olympic Stadium in Berlin. Even empty, its vastness, like the footprint of a giant concrete boot, crushes the spirit beneath its monumental cement.

I'm standing there within the walls of the Olympic Stadium with Federman while he describes to me, in his dense French accent, with a kind of perverse admiration how the Nazis used its huge scale to crush the individual ego. My silent reaction is, we have met the enemy and he is us.

Because like the fascists we all understand this now, we've all been through the ongoing ego smasher of the history the fascists helped to unleash. Besides, how could one assume the arrogance of individual identity after all those identities exxed off the surface of the planet since the year of my birth, 1932, the year Hitler assumed power? How could one even presume to be a person after all that, or even a human?

And how much less so Federman, whose family were among those abruptly exxed? In fact I'm not an individual, I assert it now, I'm just as much Federman as Federman is, and I'm others too and they are me, whether they want to understand it or not.

That's up to them, it's none of my business and I really couldn't care less, it's simply a question of being passive enough, that is, receptive enough. Invisible enough, invisible as my shadow. The shadow knows.

You read all this with skepticism, he's dealing in metaphor, you think, okay it's metaphor, this isn't science fiction. But it's not merely metaphor. The only thing totally individual about me will be my death, but on the other hand the one good thing I can say about my death is that I won't be there.

I know very well that Federman will be annoyed by this because he resents the way we're always twinned, by the literary critics that is.

[REAL TIME WINDOW: Contrary to
what I say here about his being annoyed,

181

in response to a draft of this manuscript,
Federman writes, "I am of course honored to appear in person (with my real
name) in Ron's new novel. It's really a
great honor to be a character in a novel,
it's like acquiring a kind of immortality.
And just think, suppose the book becomes a best seller, I'll be famous."]

This is just like Federman, to use my novel for his pursuit of
fame. Just like Federman, but is it Federman? Or is it just his way
of being annoyed?

And in fact aside from fiction we're very little alike, we're
more like opposites, Federman's ebullience nothing like my slow,
sullen pace, and even in fiction there's little resemblance,
Federman's fascination with absence, the absence of the exxed,
having nothing to do with my indifference toward the progressive
ebbing of my self and the aggressive presence of everything else.

The real problem is not merely whether I'm Federman, by
virtue of my progressive invisibility I'm pretty much anybody,
anybody who gets close enough to allow my antennae to receive
their ectoplasmic transmissions, man, woman or child.

Or animal. And when I say ectoplasmic I'm just kidding, I
don't know what the hell it is or why it kicks in, probably cyber-
netic would be more accurate. I don't want to give the impression I do this for fun, either, often it's not fun, quite the reverse,
sometimes it's unpleasant, or worse.

I'd avoid the whole business if I could. Or if I could I'd
figure out how it works and take out a patent.

Anyway, obviously, I always know what Federman is thinking, and what he's thinking as he gives me his impressions of the
Olympic Stadium is that if he arranges the day's schedule right
he might be able to get me to come with him to the gambling
casino in the evening.

Because one of Federman's ambitions in life is finding the
Golden Calf. Finding it and at the same time losing it. That's
why he likes to gamble.

And that's what he's doing here in Germany. Pursuing the Golden Calf. Which he doesn't really want. That's not it, that's not what he's after.

What, then, is he after? Maybe this is my chance to find out.

And so standing there now with him in the wall of the Olympic Stadium, one of the few remaining monuments of Nazism left by the war, where Hitler held his giant rallies designed to ensure that we don't exist as individual egos or, in our case, at all, Federman snapping my photo to show that after all we do, I'm already aware of what's going to happen during my brief visit to Berlin.

> [REAL TIME WINDOW: Just this
> minute, as I revise this to send to him,
> Federman calls to ask me among other
> things when I'm going to send it to him,
> the revised version, and I'm revising it in
> fact, as fast as I can, because I want to
> get it to him within the next two weeks,
> before he has to go into the hospital for a
> potentially serious operation.]

I'm already aware of what's going to happen during my brief visit to Berlin because this has already happened, though it hasn't happened for you until I tell you it's happened.

And even then it will only happen for you in Virtual Time. The rest of this trip is in Virtual Time. Virtual Time is a hologrammatic projection of the times we live in. It looks real, it feels real, it smells real. And it is real. It's a real projection.

What will happen next is we'll get into the car and drive toward the Brandenburg Gate, parking some distance away because of the general congestion, since the fall of the Wall will have been only two or three weeks past during the time period we'll be moving through. As we walk toward the Gate, we'll start hearing a certain sound, a clinking, chinking, chipping sound, clink, clink, chip, chink.

"What's that?" I'll ask Federman.

"You'll see," he'll say.

And when we reach the Wall I'll see a grafitti-swashed page of cement, an endless concrete page unscrolled as far as eye can see crammed with multicolored multilingual writing, the writing on the wall an incomprehensible babel of symbols, slogans, signs, messages, epigraphs, pictograms, hieroglyphs, riddles, runes, alphabetic jocularities, plays on words and words playing on themselves, what you might call concrete poetry, all hacked and pocked and pitted and peeled through layers of painted and petrified palimpsest with hammer and chisel and crow bar and drill and pick by memento seekers and souvenir merchants to the skeleton of reenforcement rods and through to air on the other side, click, clink, chip, chink, chunkachunk chunk. Be frei.

These chippers are called Wallpeckers, a coinage. I pick a piece of Wall from one. One mark. For Julia, My Constant Companion. Back in the States. Julia B. Frey.

From the Wall we'll go back to Federman's apartment where the formidable—in the French sense—Erica waits, and where we'll chat and nosh, me, Federman and his wife, she too among the fortunate fugitive few of the European fascist years, whom I sometimes think of as Eroica, or even as Europa, gathering our forces for the next lap in our Berlin adventure.

It's during this conversation, according to my notes, that Erica will describe a scene that strikes me as the vivid emblem of the fate the human ego endured during the duration of cataclysms of the last half century.

Her five year old eyes record, as a torpedoed ship filled with refugees is sinking, the water filled with struggling bodies, the image of men, women and children trying to save themselves from drowning, caught up in the stern wheel of the very ship trying to rescue them.

We no longer talk so much about the end of the world because at heart we realize the world as it used to be has already ended. And this is it, caught as if on film. Even efforts to save it help to destroy it.

184

When we strike out into the city again, our goal will be the Gestapo Museum.

All the while Federman will be telling me how he's closing in on the Golden Calf, meaning in this case his literary successes in Germany, his German translations, his prizes, his best sellers, his radio plays, his films, his fellowships, his photos, his translations, his portraits, his admirers, his Italian translations, his Spanish translations, his Polish translations, his pesetas, his lire, his zlowty, his deutschmarks, till I have the feeling that basically he's in the running for an eventual Academy Award.

I know, by contrast, what Federman thinks about me, and I'm sure he's correct, that I don't promote myself, that I don't know how to sell myself, that I'm commercially backward, that I'll never get anywhere the way I proceed, and consequently he's always trying to help me in my own pursuit of the Golden Calf with this publisher, that translator, this fellowship, that magazine, and it never does any good of course, or rarely, and especially not when it has to do with getting anywhere.

Because where is there to get?

Which Federman well knows and is what makes him the manic gambler that he is, because a real gambler is in it not to win money but to play with it, to turn it into something other than an instrument to further ends, to transcend it exactly, or no, to transmute it into something infinitely more valuable than the original material, because a gambler is a kind of artist is what a gambler is, who knows how to win and lose at the same time, who knows that the opposite of losing is not winning but finding.

Which is why when you go to a casino with Federman you can never leave because either he's winning and he can't leave or he's losing and he can't leave, maybe you can only leave when you're breaking even, but then why go at all?

What we'll find at the Gestapo Museum is the shell of the former headquarters of the Gestapo, its bare walls exhibiting a selection of photos showing what the Nazis did to the Jews, some of the very best photos no doubt, some are even familiar, they must be prize specimens, one more heartbreaking than the next, but I don't know, I'm sort of tired of all that, why do I have to look at it, imagine it all, yet again?

But Federman will point out to me that it's not tourists that one normally sees here but the Germans. He'll point out one young woman, very pretty in the best German style, slim, buxom, sensitive, *soignée*, looking at the photos with tears streaming down her face.

And I'll realize, not just then but at some time in the still unspecified future, remembering this, that it's a reaction it never occured to me to have, tears, that it always seemed to me a response too superficial, too simple, for that enormity, almost a diminishment or even an insult simply to cry, while remembering at some subsequent time that young woman for that moment reduced to her tears it will come to me it's probably the only reaction simple enough to be adequate. Even though it's not adequate.

Federman will point out to me, besides, that there are Germans and Germans, there's Bavaria with its neo-fascist political party led by a former SS officer, and Austria, where an old woman on a train told him and Erica, "If you Jews don't like it here you can go back where you came from," and there are others, especially younger ones, like us trying to take in what happened in those days, trying to account for it.

And then Federman will tell me a story, not just then but at some other time in the future, a story about his father long ago before he and the rest of the family were exxed in the camps.

This is during the Occupation, when they were hiding out in the countryside somewhere in the west, in Normandy or maybe Brittany, and they were very poor and hardly had enough to eat and his father could barely make a living and I think was sick on top of that.

When suddenly, some of the German soldiers stationed in that part of the country, three or four, black marketeers maybe, started coming to the house with a truck loaded with coal and provisions every so often, to the point where the neighbors thought that rather than a family of hiding Jews, these must be secret collaborators, since nobody could understand why the Germans came with all this stuff.

And Federman as a child remembers how the German soldiers would talk and talk all night with his father, and each time, just before they left, they would all get up, raise their arms in a clenched fist salute and softly, in very low voices, together, sing the Internationale.

So the Germans are not unsympathetic, depending on the Germans. How could they be, given their enthusiastic response to Federman's innovative and not always easy-reading books?

But what they're trying to do through his books, Federman explains to me, is to conduct a sort of autopsy. Now that they've killed off the Jews, they're interested in finding out what Jews were, what it is that they're now missing.

What it is that they're missing, Federman thinks, is humor.

Just what was this supersexed seducer of their women, this economic infiltrator, this clever entrepreneur, this subtle, subversive intellect, this bignosed alien from another cosmos, this self-conscious, ironic, in-turned, unhealthly mentality, this dirty Jew?

Did you take a bath this morning?

Why, is one missing?

Next we'll head for a café, or maybe a sports club, or possibly an excellent restaurant in Federman's Mercedes, or BMW, or possibly a Porsche this time. There in the cafe we're sure to meet one of his female admirers, one who is interviewing him for a newspaper, or another who wants to make a film of his life, or one of his students working on a study of Federman.

She'll be young, no more than thirty and maybe less than twenty, and she'll be part of his exuberant pursuit of the Golden Calf—give me money, or if not money fame, or if not fame sex, or if not sex my exxed family and lost childhood, or if not that something else from your horns of plenty.

He's not very French, finally. He's more like a French translation of a Russian novel.

It will be that second night in Berlin the bad dreams will begin. That night it will be the wan young girl, blond, prepubescent, thin, something fine in her eyes, caught with me in an air crash. I struggle to rescue her from the flames which are engulfing her, I know I can't though I try. But she doesn't die, she evaporates as I reach out for her. Then the plane crashes again, she's caught in the flames again as I try to reach her and she evaporates again. The plane crashes still again, she's burning, I try to save her and she evaporates. She's caught in the flames again, I try again, she evaporates again.

I have the impression her name is something like Birken, Birchermuesli. Birkenau?

The next morning we'll go to the suburb of Wannsee, passing through one of the few sections of Berlin not destroyed during the war.

This is and was a wealthy section of the city, many Jews lived here, and it will be interesting to me for more than its handsome, various and individualized architecture.

You sense here the presence of an idea.

It is a neighborhood that must have implied an idea of a life, comfortable, secure, private, an idea of stability and continuity. What could possibly happen to people living in such a neighborhood, beyond preoccupation with their bank accounts and the well-made plot of family life with its inevitable melodramas and tragedies?

The presence of an idea and an absence of thought.

There are still places in Berlin that remain unreconstructed rubble, and there's nothing like the rubble of a city to get you thinking. To get you thinking that ideas are frozen thought and cities concrete expressions of it.

The neon jumble of rebuilt Berlin, with its tacky glass office buildings, will strike me as the revenge of the Bauhaus, a good idea at the wrong time, bankrupt modern skipping sixty years, confirming that what happened here couldn't have happened, even though it did.

All ideas are wrong. Especially the right ones.

That afternoon we'll go to East Berlin.

We'll be astonished that we no longer have to buy a certain amount of East German marks, apparently it's the first day or two of new currency regulations. That, and that the border guards won't be sullen, they'll be almost friendly. These are things that won't be believable till they happen, and even then they'll be hard to believe.

We'll head for the Jewish cemetery, which is on that side of the wall. Don't forget that before the war, eighty-eight percent of the Jews in the world lived in Europe, and among them Berlin was the most important and successful community of all, Berlin and Vienna. So I'll expect the cemetery to be august, even flashy. Or alternately, devastated, desecrated.

But it's neither. It will turn out it's subdued, not poverty-stricken for sure, but almost modest, with a share of somewhat magnificent monuments, and the rest discreet, correct. There are a lot of trees and greenery, slightly overgrown.

People stroll through its paths with a meditative look. Here and there a row of small headstones covering a whole family, two and three generations, with inscriptions all reading, "Died at Auschwitz, 1944."

It will come to me, as we stroll through, that the cemetery is devoted to two kinds of death, that of individuals, and that of a long history dead-ended, a community, a whole culture disappeared into a black hole.

But unlike Auschwitz there's something peaceful here, oddly benign, something laid to rest, as they say.

It will be the first time I've been in a cemetery since they buried my father. They uncovered the coffin there so we could get a last look. His face looked greyish, it had a distinctly frosted look, he must have been in cold storage. My mother kissed him and broke down, then they nailed the lid shut.

I say nailed but really I have no idea, my own brain was in a sort of cold storage too. Here in the Jewish cemetery of Berlin it will defrost a bit, and one of the things that will come to mind will be the difference between dying and being exxed. My father died. Federman's father evaporated without a word, without a trace.

Not only that, but my father was able to choose his death. Pills. And given the state of his health I couldn't have argued with him. "Goodbye Cile, I love you."

Somehow, he spelled my mother's name wrong after fifty-eight years.

And he was even able to speak a few last words, by way of final advice: "Go home and go to bed."

It rained, it rained hard. I remember that much of the funeral. I remember I'd been away, because the doctor said there was no predicting how long he'd last, weeks, days, hours.

It turned out to be hours. I still feel guilty about that. But I remember it. What does Federman remember? Being pushed into a closet when the Nazis came. Then, many years later, going to Auschwitz to search the records, only it was Sunday and the records were closed.

There's a frontier style restaurant where I live in Colorado where if you wear a tie they cut it off. This is meant to be profound Americana, and it is. The basic American experience of immigration is one of cutting ties.

And it illustrates why Jews have gotten along so well in the United States. We're used to having our ties cut. But the moment we have our ties cut we start extending ourselves to re-establish connections as soon as possible. We know that's our only salvation. It won't be long now.

No one's ties have been cut as abruptly as Federman's. It will occur to me that Federman has been kicked out of the ghetto by history and in the most brutal way possible, as have for example most Israelis. For them the ghetto is dead and gone.

I know other Jews will assure you that they have eliminated the ghetto in themselves, especially the Israelis. It reminds me of a story the Uncles used to tell about a man who went to a doctor to complain he could hardly get it up any more. So the doctor tells him, "What do you want, you're eighty years old."

"But Cohen is eighty-five," says the man, "and he *shtups* his wife seven days a week, sometimes twice."

"How do you know?"

"He tells me."

"He tells you, so you tell him."

I've always lived in our world. I have no allegiance to the ghetto. So I'm surprised whenever I feel the undertow of its invisible existence. But what you don't see is what you always get.

That's why I've at times been fascinated with writing and rewriting my autobiography, there's so much of it I don't know anything about.

As a result of these autobiographical investigations, which are something like Federman's work, the next time I'll see him it's again in Germany at a conference on autobiographical fiction. In Mainz. This will be an intensive four days with so many things happening that I'll barely remember any of them.

Luckily, I'll take notes. The only problem is they seem to be written in secret code. Tough notes to crack. And then piece together.

Making plans to go to Mainz. I'll start trying to coordinate arrangements with another invitee, Serge Doubrovsky, French autobiographical writer of what he calls "*auto-fiction*," since both of us will be going via Paris.

Doubrovsky, to begin with, having been invited to Mainz thanks partly to my efforts, won't be able make up his mind whether to go. This, if you know him as I do, you will recognize as typical Doubrovsky behavior. Just arranging with Doubrovsky to go eat in a restaurant can be such a production, with his precise requirements for cuisine, diet, quality, price, time and location on a particular night, that negotiations can go on for a week and even then are liable to complete change at the last instant, if not cancellation.

Finally the only way to do it is to do it his way.

[REAL TIME WINDOW: After reading
this, Doubrovsky responds in a letter by
calling my practice of putting other
writers into my writing "cross-fiction."
And it does make him cross. Among
other things, he writes about the above
that it applies "literally and equally to
you! In Lacanian analysis it's called the
'blind spot.' Not seeing that what you
blame others for doing is exactly what
you do." Further: "I found parts of your
text concerning me kind of abrasive and
offensive and in return I penned a somehow bristling epistle to couch my own
reactions. Today, I sat down and perused
the same chapter again without experi-
encing the same sort of mixed feeling.
Very weird. It's as if, at first, I could
hardly tolerate to see my self transported
or deported from auto to heterofiction!"]

Transported or deported indeed. But weren't the camps literally a deportation from one's own ego?

On the other hand, going to Germany will be horribly complicated for him both because of his experiences as a Jew during
the war, and because of his Austrian wife, recently dead. Ilse. A
friend of mine too, and more so of My Constant Companion,
with whom I'm travelling, their marriage and her sudden, ambiguous death in her mid-thirties the subject of his noted autobiographical novel. The guilt-ridden, heart-broken *Le Livre Brisé*.

A prize winner. And a best seller.

Ambiguous death because it wasn't clear whether it was
caused by pills, alcohol, pills and alcohol, accident, suicide, or
whether Serge had a part in killing her himself.

Bernard Pivot, on his famous French interview show "Apos-
trophe," more or less accused Serge of killing her.

192

Sometimes Serge seems to agree.

But the matter is not simple. And here comes one of the problems of autobiography. Since Serge's novels are meticulously factual, and the premise of the novel in question is, at Ilse's request, that it be about their life together, his and Ilse's, including, foreseeably, her alcoholism, it's hard to know how much of a role he and the novel itself played in her death.

The novel which when finished would end with an account of that death.

Because though he showed her the part of the manuscript dealing with her alcoholism just before her death, and she was upset by it, who can say objectively, least of all Doubrovsky, how much that had to do with a death that is to begin with only ambiguously a suicide?

But it's just such heartbreaking ambiguities as this, included of course in the book, that make it interesting as literature. And as an exemplary autobiographical novel. Because what person knows the whole story, even of his own life? Especially of his own life.

One might have known something was wrong. Even beyond the drinking. But who could have predicted that, that suddenly one day I would get a card that looked like an invitation, or an announcement of a birth, the birth of the child she so much wanted to have, and looking at it not being able to comprehend that in fact it was an announcement of her death?

Serge not only is Jewish, he looks Jewish, as he was made so well aware by Nazi propaganda during the Occupation. And he's alive, like a number of French Jews who survived, thanks only to a gendarme's discreet visit letting his family know he'd soon be back to arrest them.

And Ilse was Austrian, from a family with Nazi connections.

A bright, pretty young woman, for Serge a late happiness after a long, disastrous relation with another woman. Which was the subject of his preceding novel.

So you see, things are not so simple. Not simple for him to

come to Germany, to hear her language, literally a language of love and of hate, pathos and fear. To read to the Germans, of all people, for the first time out loud about his life and her death.

For years I've been wanting to get Doubrovsky and Federman together, I've known each of them forever but, surprisingly, they hardly know one another at all, maybe they've shaken hands once or twice in all these years, and never with me around. Surprisingly, because they have so much in common.

On the other hand, they're total opposites. Doubrovsky, his family having survived, if just, graduating from the elite school for French intellectuals and shuttling back and forth from his job in the States to France, writing in French, Federman, whose whole family was exxed, growing up in the Black section of Detroit, writing in English. Then why is it Federman who has the atrocity of a French accent still? Federman the jock, who looks like he just got out of the Foreign Legion, Doubrovsky, who looks like the complete European Jewish intello. Federman, the writer obsessed with innovation, Doubrovsky, the conventional writer whose obsessions force him to innovate. Doubrovsky who, in his writing, is compelled to tell you everything, Federman who is obsessed with telling you nothing. Doubrovsky the loner, Federman the convivial, Federman the hip, Doubrovsky the bourgeois, Doubrovsky who likes to make money, Federman who loves making it and even better, throwing it away.

> [REAL TIME WINDOW: Doubrovsky
> objects, quite justly, that "to be anti-
> bourgeois has become a bourgeois
> cliche. So I am, indeed, bourgeois,
> because I have a steady profession and
> income. So do you and so does Federman.
> And insofar as 'bourgeois,' historically,
> has always been connected with acquisi-
> tion and ownership, since I don't own a
> thing in the world, except for a car and a
> few pieces of furniture in Paris and have
> no landed interests, I possess no house or

apartments, I am in a deeper sense far
less bourgeois than you or Federman."
As if the three of us, despite complete
assimilation, are in competition for
status as outsiders.]

These two old friends of mine, so similar and so different
I'm often surprised I can be friendly with both. And my relations
with them ambiguous to begin with since, wanting to be more
like Raymond, I'm probably more like Serge. Serge is right, after
all, this is my "blind spot"—not seeing myself in him.

Serge and Raymond will seem to get along fine, from what
I can see. I'll hear Serge promising to send Raymond a copy of
his novel. I wonder if he has?

[REAL TIME WINDOW: He hasn't. He
promises to have a copy delivered to me
to send on to Federman. He doesn't.]

The next day one of the hazards of such conferences will
threaten to get out of hand. Girl (or boy, choose one—or both)
chasing. That is, them chasing us. Luckily I will have My Constant Companion along to ward off evil, I can't speak for the others. All men and women of the pen, no matter how unattractive,
and literary types are notoriously unattractive, become cocks and
hens of the walk in these backyards through the law of eminence
in our domain.

So though I'll see Doubrovsky coming back from a trip to
the Lorelei with an elegant admirer late one night, looking a lot
happier than when I'd seen him the evening before, this will not
alter my sense that he's still grieving deeply over Ilse's death.

This day's performances will confirm several of my mounting convictions, namely that we're all more alike than the creed
of individualism permits us to admit, that I'm growing increasingly invisible and that I'm becoming everybody else.

One illustration is that host Professor Hornung will give me
a long, wonderful introduction but in which he calls me Federman.
Another is that me, Federman and Doubrovsky, it will turn out,

choose to give readings heavily freighted with the Germans' role in World War II regarding the Jews. Still another is that I'll find that Maxine Hong Kingston, with whom I'll expect to have very little in common, has stylistic ambitions in fiction remarkably like my own rejection of the merely imagined in favor of fact.

Finally, when I find that I've accidentally walked off with Hornung's notebook and look to see what's in it, I'll discover copious notes on everyone else, and my name followed by a completely blank page.

But Federman, every time he burps now, somebody here publishes it. He gives a few lectures, he writes them down, Suhrkampf turns them into a book. And I, of course, am writing down his private interchanges with me to publish in my book. In fact the Germans are going to write down and publish this entire conference.

So what is there left that isn't written down and published? All that remains is the book of life, and I try to get that into print as quickly as possible. So that nothing remains hidden. So I can tell you the true story. Like Doubrovsky does. So that the published book reflects the book of life. Well, reflects on, maybe.

But to get back to the true story, I will introduce Federman's reading that day, beginning with our visit to Wannsee.

"It was only later, much later and back in the States, that we remembered that Wannsee was where it all began: the Wannsee conference where the idea of the final solution was endorsed as the right one for their Jewish problem and set in motion by the Nazi elite.

"Reflecting on this now it becomes impossible to maintain that Jews are European, even European Jews like Federman. Yes, many Jews have European reflexes, those Jews with long histories of European evolution. But then Europeans by now have profoundly Jewish reflexes: relativity, consciousness of self, collective social responsibility, via Reb Karl, Reb Albert, Reb Sigmund, to name just a few from the merely recent past.

"But Europe is just one part of a long story. And the story

Federman tells is the end of the chapter or rather, what happens after the chapter has ended. The characters have disappeared, the tragedy is over, the stage is bare. Even Samuel Beckett, Federman's friend and great model, has finally effaced himself for the last time. Fifty million people have been slaughtered within six years. The great tradition of Humanism wasn't worth shit in a chateau, a fox hole, a death camp, a stately state palace. Never mind post modern, we're all post humous as Europeans, including the Europeans themselves. Post human.

"One day, Federman, who must be twelve or thirteen at the time, is in the apartment with his family, poor, relatively recent immigrants to France, when the Germans come, he's pushed into a closet by his mother, and suddenly he's an orphan, a fugitive jumping from freight train to freight train, a farm laborer in the south of France, a factory worker in Detroit, a white named Frenchy in a black ghetto, a jazz musician, a paratrooper in Korea, a student in New York, a poet, a jock, a professor in California, a novelist in Buffalo, an honored literary guest in Germany. A great story but what's the plot? and which one of the above is the hero? and where's the verisimilitude? and when is the beginning, the middle, the end? and why should this irrational discontinuity be related in sequential sentences from left to right, left to right to the bottom of the printed page? and how in the name of probability can it be called real?

"No, the book of life cannot be paraphrased, it cannot be prescribed, it cannot be predicted, it cannot be dictated, it cannot be imitated, it cannot resemble some other book, it cannot begin, it cannot end, it cannot be made up, it cannot be about major characters or minor characters or any characters other than those of the alphabet, it cannot be about the right ideas, it cannot be controlled, it cannot be about reality, because life is not about reality. It is it. If it weren't, what would be? There is only one thing you can do with the book of life: add to it. Federman writes books that add to it, that's why they don't seem to be like other books, why they're sometimes strange, because life is sometimes strange. Stranger than fiction, as they say.

"And now, stranger than fiction, Raymond Federman!"

It will be obvious from the response to Federman's reading that he's by far the great favorite here. But I've heard him reading many times and never Doubrovsky, who though far better known than either of us in France, is little known in Germany. So I'll be eager to hear him read, and especially eager to get Federman's reaction to his performance.

But it will be Maxine Hong Kingston who will read first this night, and her reading will make me think how un-European we all are. Even Doubrovsky, who spends half his time in the States, has moved so far to the edge of French literary decorum that the French are scandalized.

But the French like to be scandalized.

It will come to me that in comparison with the Europeans, none of us Statespersons are miming real life. Why try to imitate the inimitable? We're all engaged, like Dr. Frankenstein or the Rabbi of Prague and his Golem, in creating life.

In making things happen. Things not necessarily in our control, and it can be dangerous. As it's proved to be for Doubrovsky.

It occurs to me that that maybe Jews were never really Europeans. Certainly not in the ghetto. Certainly not any more. No more than Maxine Kingston.

Doubrovsky's reading will turn out to be an eruption, an explosion of emotional and stylistic violence, a confrontation with his guilt over Ilse's death and his hatred for the Germanic society that created her. He'll tell them that though today they celebrate him, yesterday they were trying to reduce him to ashes. He'll say he's not a Jew but a Kike. Later he'll tell me how he really gave it to them, even called them Boches, which he says they hate.

By the end of the performance he'll be exhausted. During it he'll break out in tears reading the story of his wife's death. The impact on the audience will be such that they can't applaud at the end, it would be like applauding at a funeral. Doubrovsky will appear to be in such a state that we fear for his mental, even his physical health.

Shortly after in the men's room of the restaurant we go to, he's asking me about the publication possibilities of the book in the States, and whether it wouldn't be feasible for my press to translate it. This will be Doubrovsky the literary figure talking, not Serge the grieving husband, the one who refuses permission for a German translation for the sake of Ilse's mother, or who refuses to use the profits from his book about Ilse, putting them instead into a trust fund for his daughters. These two Doubrovskies don't have much to do with one another, and even less with Serge the writer, not to mention Doubrovsky of the Lorelei.

Meanwhile, I'll have been wondering about the reaction of Federman to the reading. But it will turn out that Federman didn't attend. He had something else to do. Federman's expansiveness is his way of avoiding things Raymond the dreamer prefers not to confront.

Raymond is a seeing eye man. In order to see some things others don't you have to be blind to some things others aren't. While I, with my fetish of transparence, refuse to see I, forcing others to see through me. A mere scribe ascribed to be the medium for the tribe.

Serge himself will be wondering what the effect of his reading was, especially on the Germans. At a certain point he'll call me up.

"I don't suppose you were able to find out how the Germans liked it?" he'll ask.

"Well as a matter of fact, I did get some reactions."

"Because I was really hard on them, you know. They might not have liked that."

"Well I did ask some of them about it."

"Although I used the German word for peace at the end. That was intentional."

"I did ask them," I'll shout into the phone. Serge is a little hard of hearing.

"Hornung and some of those people."

"I believe I asked him . . ."

"Well I guess I'll never know."

Serge is a hearing ear man.

Before he leaves Serge will advise me that life is not all work and no play and that I should profit from the trip and not miss going up the Rhine to visit the Lorelei. Raymond will give me the name of an editor in Paris who he assures me wants to publish a translation of one of my books. It moves me to see how my two friends try to take care of me.

Even though they can't.

    [REAL TIME WINDOW: The next chance I get to see Federman it's at another conference a few months later. He tells me he's waiting to hear about the need for some potentially serious surgery. Then he tells me a story about meeting someone he knew as a kid in France and hadn't seen since, now both of them grey. The first thing the guy said to him was, "Ça va vite, la vie, hein?" It goes fast, one's life, eh?

    Then Raymond added, "And I suddenly got so scared . . .

II. WRITING

PROFITS

One of our personalities is a *tummler*. A comic, a crazy. At a precocious age he wanted to be a wild-tongued word twister like Danny Kaye who was from his Brooklyn neighborhood. Or a suave ventriloquist like Edgar Bergen. Or even a dummy like Charlie McCarthy. But a star. Some kind of star. To loudmouth his way out of Brooklyn. Or talk softly maybe but with a big shtick. Marathon mouth. Now that he's escaped we're not sure what he gets out of it. Maybe it's just his bent. If not his warp. Or his kink.

Because comics are kinky. You need to be the tattler of dirty secrets, the more so the *tummler*, the killer kike. To joke about the shit, you have to get into the shit. And that's no joke, that's sad. If not sadistic. Fear, hell and death is the scummy underside of all those laughs, a side that comics and hellfire preachers best portray. Which is why they often stray. Godliness is the cover, as is funniness. You have to kill off authoritarian cops and pops to get on stage and grab the mike, and the king is first on the hit list.

"Once I find myself on a boat from Morocco to Spain. A group of refugees clustered on deck with their belongings attracts my attention, because though dressed much like rural Berbers and obviously lacking means, they exhibit a certain ancestral elegance.

"Me. 'What's their story?' In Spanish.

"'*Ellos mataron al Re*,' answers a sailor, crossing himself.

'They killed the King.'

"We're not talking Elvis."

He waits for laughs. Doesn't get any. "Elvis was called the King," he says. "Get it? Elvis Presley, p, r, e . . . Oh, you know? You don't care about him? Right, all he had was money and fame, who cares about that?

"Do I hear a snicker?"

To a certain extent we all have the same story so that his story is the story of the refugees on the boat. But his story is that he wasn't there. It's an alibi. He didn't do it, it wasn't his fault. One of the things they always tell you is that you did it. But he didn't. "Screw that. I wasn't there. It wasn't me." That's his usual story.

Though maybe it's time to change his tune, what the hell. "Sure I killed him. I'd do it again. Because I'm pissed—he has it coming after twenty centuries of grief. Let him show his face. Christ the Butcher."

His bit is to retell the old stories.

"Who was this messiah anyway? He had twelve followers and one was unreliable. The rest was marketing."

"Yeah."

"I bet you didn't know Elvis was Jewish. On his mother's side, that's what counts. It's a proven fact, look it up. You thought it was a religion? What makes you think it's a religion? Being Jewish is an art," he says. "You got to have talent."

"What if you don't have talent? Hire a boy. What, I'm the boy?" he asks, pleading innocent.

He who? What's the difference? He gets on stage, he tells his joke, he takes his bow. He favors gags because he's chronically disgusted and when he gags at least he doesn't puke. There's not much difference between laughing and puking, laughing and puking and crying, they all come from the gut. Besides, gags stop you from saying what you really feel, and saying what you really feel is not advisable. Blind rage gets you nowhere, look where it got Samson. Freud didn't invent the Id, he just dropped the Y.

He can't say what he really feels because he's not a real person. He doesn't really feel anything. He's a dummy. A manikin. An android. An alien cyberpod. Slapped together. Mosaic man, the man of parts. Ceramic. Or silicon. Prick him he doesn't bleed. He who? The Jew. Of thee I sing.

Sometimes he's invisible. Now you see him, now you don't. He's got a disappearing act. He may be a dummy, but he's not stupid.

You say he's hiding. What else? Dr. Joker and Mr. Hide. It's the old story. Part of the mosaic. Preprogrammed. He has a factory installed Read Only Memory and he only knows what he reads. They say he was hiding in the reeds. He had to be invisible. Because he knew they would have killed him. They were after our boys.

But our boy was after an oscar. Despite the language capability built into his operating system what he read was mostly comic books and funny papers, later on *Rolling Stone*. The golden image was graved on every page, cast on every screen. He dreamed of being a star. Elvis. Isn't that what he was supposed to dream? But that wasn't in the script. The only star for him would have been the yellow one. He didn't understand. He knew he had a problem but it wouldn't compute. His bar code wouldn't scan. "I must be from a different part of the pluriverse," he tells people.

"Stop bitching," you may want to tell him, "Jews have more fun."

"Jews have more fun, yeah," he would probably say. "But do I have a choice?"

No choice. You're it.

He knows. He likes to tell a story about two Jewish bees flying through the air when one rummages around, pulls out a yarmulke and puts it on his head. The other bee asks, "How come all of a sudden you're putting on a yarmulke?"

The first bee says, "Because I wouldn't want to be taken for a wasp."

"I thought we're supposed to be humble," says the other bee.

"Not humble, you turkey. Bumble."

Stories, stories. He doesn't think, he relates.

Like the one he tells about the Golden Calf. This is a history rap, an example of what mavens of his style call speculative jocularities, while more learned exegetes talk about stochastic extrapolations. A form of archaeology. It expands the screen, adds definition, more pixels to the inch. Some people even call these riffs prophetic. Wrong. The famous surgeon, Dr. Goneff, coming out of the operating room, was asked what he had operated for. "Money," the doctor replied. He tells stories for money. He hopes to get a screen play out of them he can vend to Hollywood. It's the profit motive. Pure exploitation. He exploits himself. The plot he stumbles on in his wonderings could be called *The Raiders of the Lost Calf.*

The scenario opens in Granada.

"Granada was once known as the city of the Jews. At one point it had a Jewish Archbishop. Under the Arabs the Jewish community had grown rich and sophisticated. It was a center of learning. There, certain fathers of the community revived the biblical worship of the Golden Calf in an anti-Mosaic form of Judaism, calling themselves Aronians, after Moses' brother Aaron. The fathers were on the gold standard because, shit, that's reality. But Moses didn't have a father. It was said they actually were in possession of an ancient calf icon discovered in an archeological excavation near Caesarea in the Holy Land. It was said that many of these Aronians became Marranos, Christian converts, at the time of the Expulsion in 1492, and prospered as crypto-Jews from 1492 to 1942. It was said that Francisco Franco was one of these crypto-Jews. *Marrano*, literally, means swine. Then, in 1942, the Golden Calf was stolen by a Nazi sect believing that we live in a hollow universe in which cosmic rays emit gnostic wisdom crystallized by certain visible icons like the Golden Calf. Right. But in the chaos of the final days of the war, they too lost it, the Calf. It is said that the trail leads to Malta, that's all we know.

"Except," he says, "a mysterious international neo-Christian group called the Bond appears to be on the trail of the Lost Calf. The secrecy of the Bond was broken when an executive in a communications company called ComPost®, named Strop Banally, was stopped at customs in Kennedy Airport trying to smuggle fragments of unpublished Dead Sea Scrolls in the heels of his cowboy boots. Banally claimed the boots were nothing but a sort of cowboy mezzuzah but then they discovered he wasn't Jewish. And wasn't a cowboy. He resembled an astronaut, that sort of overbuilt, robotic look.

"The Mossad stepped in and claimed that Banally was the kind of agent known in the trade as a golem. They said a golem is professional jargon for the kind of psychopath adept in worldly affairs willing to do what you can't or won't do. Sort of like a shabbas goy. Uncircumcized. They said a golem will work for anyone who knows his bar code. They said Banally's bar code was three martinis, but this is thought to be a wisecrack. They said Banally's handler was an ambiguous genius named Dr. Frank Stein, a rogue microbiologist known as a brilliant but maverick gene splicer. But Banally had a reputation for getting out of control. A golem out of control wanders around like a dog without a nose. I once had a dog without a nose. How did it smell? Awful.

"The Mossad was involved because the Bond was reported to have formed a coalition with fundamentalist Evangelicals and ultra-nationalist Israelis working with a Jewish terrorist organization known as the Bang Gang to dynamite the Temple Mount in Jerusalem where they think the Golden Calf is buried. Right.

"But the Golden Calf locks into the Dead Sea Scrolls. Why do you think they didn't want to release the text of the unedited Scrolls? What do you think they really say? Why do you suppose the leader of the team of scholars editing them was making antisemitic remarks? Why was he was fired? Who do you think is behind all this? Why do you suppose the Scrolls were housed in the Rockefeller Museum in Jerusalem? What does this have to do with the Tri-Lateral Commission? What was the reason for turning over interpretation of the Scrolls to Harvard Divinity

School? Why were no Jewish scholars among the original group? Who tried to claim that the skeletons found at Masada were Byzantine monks? Why do they insist that the scroll site was a monastery? How do we know we're getting the complete texts? Why are the Scrolls being treated as if they were themselves divine, as if they were icons, occult, not simply a code to be broken? Is it because they include directions to ancient Jewish treasures that must be veiled in complex mystifications?

"The truth is that the Scroll photos at Claremont College, one of three sets then in existence, were secretly copied and bootlegged years ago by a fanatic hit squad of crazed Lubavitchers trained in the martial arts. They found that the Scrolls give directions to the original Golden Calf of Aaron. They found that the Scrolls prove God is an E.T. and religion should really be a branch of astronomy. According to the *London Sun* they found that Elvis is mentioned prominently, but this is clearly tabloid hysteria. They also learned that what we call people are interchangable genetic accidents and that they can move from one identity to another, including sexual identity. They can even become animals, but this we knew. Though most people forget their other identities when they feel committed to a particular role, we all have the potential for multiple personalities. It all depends on how well you know your alter egos.

"But the real secret of the Dead Sea Scrolls is they're written in genetic code," he says. "This was discovered in collaboration with scientists through computer studies at the Weizmann Institute in Israel. Did you know that there's already a dictionary of the genetic language? The language is called Gnomic. The name was chosen at the Weizmann Institute. If you don't believe me look it up. It's called Gnomic because it's the language of the genome, the aggregate genetic matter in cellular nucleii. And because the Greek root means to know. And because the gnomes write secret scripts with silver pens at midnight. Sound crazy? Check out the *New York Times*, July 9, 1991, page C1. The scientists say it's a way of distinguishing the genetic language from the Babel of background DNA. They say it's a language that far outstrips the subtleties and complexities of any human language, proceeding by puns and triple or quadruple entendre. Something like *Finnegans Wake*. They tell us that the discovery of Gnomic as the underlying language of the Scrolls uncorks a bottle of knowledge that can never be closed. Because Gnomic is the secret language that establishes the missing link between mind and body. They claim that Gnomic is the true sacred language. They say it's a language beyond the comprehension of conventional intellect. Or even supercomputer. Too eccentric. Too spontaneous. The genius of the genus is finally out and it turns out the genetic genie is quirky but ingenious. Even though real people aren't ever that smart."

Though remember, he's not a real person, he's a dummy. Like Bergen and McCarthy.

But maybe the ventriloquist is also a dummy. A puppet. The problem is, who's pulling the strings? He may be paranoid but that doesn't mean there isn't a plot. Do you think coincidence is purely coincidental? Intelligence is interested in the Golden Calf. It wants to destroy the Lost Calf because it's an icon. Because intelligence is iconoclastic. Because it doesn't matter what icon I con you with there are always strings attached. That's why Moses was an iconoclast. That's why he destroyed the Calf. Because if there are strings attached you're still a dummy. Easy to control. Born to lose.

Maybe that's why he's so zany, trying to break loose. He's the type of comic they call a crazy. They call him "the typing tummler" because after wandering from place to place for years with his song and dance, telling his stories, he's decided to put them on paper. The rumor is he's working on a novel called *Great Expectorations*. Mavens say the stories always have an argumentative bent, even though nobody's arguing. He says his stories don't have a bent, they just seem twisted because folk wit always seems crazy and even dangerous to sophisticates. He says the comic's job is to de-escalate the language of the elite. In fact he denies he's a comic he says he's a cosmic, just a cosmic peasant from the interstellar boondocks of the galaxy. On occasion he's referred to himself as a "hermonaut." His shtick is how to be Jewish.

This can be a question of life and death. So let's get the story straight. Where did he come from? Where is he going?

"Jews come from another planet," he says. "Not in this galaxy. That's the short answer. As aliens we try to adapt to this world, with more or less success in different countries and different epochs. You think this is a joke? Hey, where do you think Yahweh comes from—heaven? And the moon maybe is made of green cheese?

"Where we went wrong in paradise was when Eve and Adam thought they could ditch their preprogrammed factory-installed Read Only Memories and simply see right and wrong for themselves, as they could in the old galaxy where everyone had x-ray vision like Superman.

"'You want to be androids forever?' asked the snake. They were sitting under the apple tree.

"'Have a bite,' said Eve.

"'Why?' asked Adam.

"'Information is power.'

"'I don't see it,' said Adam.

"'You don't want to see it,' said Eve. 'Seeing is believing. And remember, what you see is what you get.'

"'And what do I get?' asked Adam.

"'You get me, babe. Random access. In virtual reality and hologrammatic I-max 3-D. Colorized. With quadraphonic superwoofing sound.'

"'Will you keep your eyes open?' he asked.

"'Yes.'

"'Will you look right at me when I do it?'

"'Yes.'

"'Sexy. But Mr. Big says it's a no-no,' said Adam.

"'Mr. Big? You mean Mr. Huge.'

"'He says we'll be outlaws,' said Adam. 'That would be a shame.'

"'Mr. Huge is only my inlaw. Outlaws have perspective because they're outside. We'll be able to see what's right and what's wrong. And then who needs inlaws?'

"'You can't get outside,' said Adam. 'Or if you could you wouldn't want to.'

"'Afraid to know the awful truth?'

"'I'm not afraid of anything,' said Adam. 'Go for it.'

"So Eve took the big billion K bite from the apple. And that's why Jews are outsiders. We know the awful truth. What happened was they were trying to see what can't be seen. The apple was good for eating and a delight to the eyes, as it says in the book. But what they were trying to see is inside, not outside. Invisible.

"Said Mr. Huge: 'ROM you had, RAM you get.'

"From Eve and Adam Jews know that there is another world that they can think about, and talk about, and write about, and hope for but that they will never see. Not here and not in Jerusalem. Not even in Eretz Israel. Like Moses, you will die before getting there. Clay to clay. That's the awful truth. That's the secret of being Jewish. So that even as we chase after the Golden Calf, we know that's not the oscar we really want to win.

"That's the short answer. Short but grave. As in cemetery."

Which explains how we got into this, but not how we get out. How do we get out?

"They say," he says, "that long before the Rabbi of Prague made a Golem, the Rabbi of Chelm made one too. It was a work of genius. Like the Rabbi of Prague, the Rabbi of Chelm took some clay, modeled an android bound together with iron, recited the kabbalistic formula and placed the secret word on its forehead. The secret word is AMETH. Truth. The Man of Clay arose, invincible and just, saviour of the Jews, a sort of Frankenchrist. The brain child of the rabbi, you might say he was a creature from another world, a walking idea realized sensationally.

The Rabbi of Chelm considered himself in the running if not for an oscar then for some other graven image of celebrity. The distance from a man of clay to a calf of gold is not really all that great.

"The problem was, the Rabbi of Chelm had a Golem Complex, a bad case of Golem envy. The rabbi himself wanted to be a Golem. In creating the Golem he was creating himself. As Dr. Frankenstein was really his monster, or wanted to be. Because the monster was dumb and didn't think before it did. Because he envied its strength, its invulnerability, its emptiness, even its innocence. And he was terribly jealous of its essential banality. There was an oedipal situation there. They were competing for Mary Shelley, the monster's mom. The monster wanted to sue its mother. For alienation of affection. That's what was monstrous about the monster. That, and that it wanted to dust the doc. Regarding this the doctor was afreud. If not a Faust. After all, he wasn't blind. But he persisted, despite everything. More body parts, Igor.

"True, the Golem couldn't speak. But it could write. And it could sing, though not in words, it sang in a variety of percussive grunts and hums like a synthesizer, gyrating on its ball joints as it strummed, sometimes sitting in with local klezmer bands. So while the rabbi could speak for it, it could also communicate the rabbi's thoughts and feelings at the level of public expression, even though it hadn't the slightest idea of what it was expressing. And there were a few other things. Our superhero was sometimes invisible, so only the rabbi could tell where it was. It couldn't make love, though this wasn't a disadvantage, at least for the rabbi, and was probably even preferable from the rabbi's point of view, resulting in a creature something like a very large prepubescent teenager.

"But there were some other little problems which raise the suspicion that maybe the Rabbi of Chelm didn't get the formula quite right. After all, the residents of Chelm were widely known for getting everything wrong. Even so, how could the rabbi have predicted his idea would backfire? The Golem didn't know how to deal with human emotion, that was much too complex for it, and this led to all sorts of blunders. So our clay-footed superhero turned out to be something of a klutz. Its klutziness was literally magnified by the fact that it was so big, a huge fellow. There was something pathetic about this prodigy, for all its talents.

"But the Golem was a necessary monster and its klutziness wouldn't have been so bad but for the fact that it was growing. What's worse, though it grew slowly at first, the bigger it got the faster it grew. That in itself would not have been a disaster except for the circumstance that the Man of Clay was, as mentioned, occasionally invisible, so that nobody could tell where the monster was at any given time and the townsfolk couldn't stay out of its way. As a result whenever someone bumped into something, had an accident or even tripped over his own feet he would say, 'It's him.' Sometimes it was. Things quickly got out of control, the creature ran amok, and the rabbi soon realized that the only remedy was to put an end to the android's life. But to do this he had to alter the secret word on its forehead, which he could no longer reach.

"So the rabbi had to find a very high ladder, and when he found it he rested it against the monster's chest and plucked the aleph from the secret word on its brow, which then became METH. Death. The Golem immediately became mere inanimate clay, but because the rabbi was balanced precariously on his ladder there was no way he could protect himself when the monster collapsed and buried him under its huge mass, ending the rabbi's life along with its own.

"Luckily, the Golem of the Rabbi of Prague, which was very like that of Chelm, was much more successful as his agent in the world, though the rabbi had the good sense to decommission his boy when it got too big for its britches. Unlike the Rabbi of Chelm, however, the Rabbi of Prague took the precaution of affixing his Golem to a wooden cross by its feet and outstretched hands so that it wouldn't fall on him when it gave up the ghost. This event used to be known among local Jews as the affixion, or affiction or, possibly, affliction. However, they say that the Golem lies in the attic of the Prague Synagogue ready to be summoned again to become the saviour of the Jews once and for all, an advent known locally as the second becoming. They say that the rabbi explained all this to the Golem before decommissioning it, but that the Golem didn't like being decommissioned any better for understanding, and that it gave up the ghost with a combination of defiance, pain and forgiveness that was almost human.

"And they also say that the Golem of Prague, though sterile, was not impotent, far from it, and in fact was quite sexy a la Arnold Schwarzenegger. Only as an android, unfortunately, it was not programmed to enjoy it. And they say that, though it was sterile, it also had cloning capabilities by which it created other men of steel and clay whose offspring roam the earth today."

Elvis was seen late last night in a small bar in Rohnert Park, California, singing to the gentiles. The singer stroked his golden instrument, flitting around the room on glittering sequined wings attached to his shoulder blades. "But I noticed that his boots were smeared with clay," said the bartender.

Elvis' manager, the Colonel, an alien from another land, though this isn't generally known, couldn't do it himself so he invented Elvis. Elvis saved his ass. Or did he save Elvis' ass? Either way, they say he destroyed Elvis in the end. Or did Elvis destroy himself in the end? Get too big, or at least too fat, for his britches? In the end. Whatever, he got out of hand. Elvis dies. Elvis lives. It's all standard operating procedure. Part of the program.

A teen age girl in Lubbock, Texas found Elvis climbing down her chimney on Christmas Eve, dressed as Santa Claus with a halo over his Santa hat. He was doing "Love Me Tender." As she was phoning her girlfriend to tell her he levitated and disappeared, his chin immortally defiant, his lips curled like a cherub's, agony rippling his sullen cheeks, his eyes filled with pity and fire.

"What's your story?" you may ask. "You, the ventriloquist. With whom do we have the pleasure of interfacing, masked man?"

Maybe I'm it. It's him, he's our boy, the invisible nomad, the dummy. But he's also me.

Though his story is misleading anyway. Because it's not his.

214

He's not his own master, masturbator of his fate. His destiny is not his own. He's not himself today, nor any day. Why? Because he's a Jew, in a word. And a word can change everything, whether you want it to or not. Not up to you. Or me. I'm not in control. No. I am who I am. Like Pop Eye the Sailorman.

When do I finally get back to the real me behind this mask in the mirror?

Not today, not tomorrow. No. Where ego I go.

But every Jew has a secret scriptural name, like Maimonides is RaMBaN. This secret name is a jack into the invisible. The secret name ascribed to him is RaMSCaN, an acrostic of his given names, Ronald Martin, and his family name. Some would say it's RaMSCaM. Thank you ma'am. RaMSCaN's function is to scan his memory, decipher the Gnomic. Till he finds what's hidden there. Because he's it.

Because he's it, his profits don't count. No oscar could make a difference. And besides, he doesn't make a dime. He's never propheted. So what does he get out of this?

He is basically a Jew de mot, an author though he declines authority. There are too many things he doesn't know. He's a medium for events he can't comprehend. He's known as a writer but thinks of himself as a teller. Like a bank teller he gives you an account of certain exchanges. He tells your fortune. He keeps the books. He's a scribe prodding the tribe to remember itself against the progressive alzheimer's of history, recording what he hears and sees and the voices in his head. We have met the writer and he is us.

It's not his business to make things up. The best stories are old and often told. He takes tales wholesale and tells them retail. Paper, xerox, FAX, computer disk, audio tape are his crystal ball, his handwriting on the wall. If they're not adequate for him as a medium, he might just call you up. If you're in the book. Of life, that is. You, the reader. He can feel your breath on the page, your eyes on the print. Your ectoplasmic vibrations.

Your invisible self.

HAND WRITING ON WALL

Dawn over money. The sun is coming up over Wall Street. It comes up over time and over space, it comes up over history. The Egyptian pyramids, the Greek acropoli, the gothic spires, the Roman portals, the Rosicrucian temples, the Florentine stonework, the scalloped towers, the immense mirrors glass and silver, the somber metal boxes, the Mayan pent houses, the deco decorations, the bauhaus grids, the moderne geometries, the pomo parodies, the corbusier concretions, the copper green Napoleonic roof palaces, the crenellated sky castles, the streamlined futurescape facades, the Babylonian terracing, the Ionic columns, the Corinthian cornices, the Colonial cupolas, the Victorian fretwork, the heavy arches, the brutal brick shafts, the water towers, cooling units, skylights, ventilators, the block and girder of new construction go livid at the edges, casting pale shades and ghostly shadows, steeping the narrow streets below in permanent gloom. The graph-like walls of the World Financial Center buildings multiply one another with reflections of wealth and power, Luxor on the Hudson. And looming over all, the two silver louvred vertical grids of the World Trade Center thrusting up off the chart.

What we have here is the ongoing urban mosaic. Of histories and geographies. That we call real time.

In our thirty-sixth floor apartment in Battery Park City, a.k.a. the Space Bubble, one curved wall all windows, even this pallid morning is a luminous eye opener.

Sliding our thick royal cherry terrycloth robe on, we peer out the window at the eastern sky as the curtained sun seeps through the towering cityscape to the glassy Hudson. The light in our room is amplified by the mirrors, it's a small apartment so there are lots of mirrors, floor to ceiling.

We activate Mr. Coffee and shave our face, micronuke a frozen bagel and throw it in the toaster oven, break out the cream cheese and run an orange through the electric squeezer. As you read this you too might want to whip out a little snack to keep by your side, some low cholesterol dry roasted peanuts, why not nuke some popcorn?

We turn to the work-in-progress on our desk. *Great Expectorations*, a mythological detective story. Simultaneously a segment for a TV serial. Though the tube is a problem for us because we're allergic to mimetic images. We begin to sweat and our forehead breaks out in rashes, often alphabetical in configuration. But the written word is a mental antihistamine, and with it you can reconnect the visible with the invisible and reclaim the superficial. All wrapped up in one neat package. Though as with all serials *Great Expectorations* is ongoing, no beginning, no end, just an endless middle of shticks, bits, gags and routines. Like the media environment. Just tune in where ever, tune out whenever. In medias res.

+

The package, neatly wrapped, arrived yesterday from Istanbul. It was left with the doorman, addressed in crude handwriting to "Ram Shade, Dick." A red, official-looking stamp said, "Don't Open Till Xxxmass." Today was Christmas. I didn't know about Xxxmass, but I knew enough to be paranoid about mysterious packages from Istanbul. Istanbul was the source of most of the illegally traded antiquities on the market. Read smuggling. If I opened it I could be in trouble.

There was a label on the wrapping that said, "Genuine Calfskin." It was a rectangular package wrapped in heavy brown paper through which you could feel a cardboard box of the distinct

218

size of a pair of cowboy boots. That was my best guess. Very heavy cowboy boots. But cowboy boots from Istanbul? I couldn't get a fix on it by hefting it or shaking it. A boom box, maybe. When you opened it it went boom.

I knew I had a tendency to jump to contusions. It was the paranoid in me. But in the shamus trade paranoia was a sign of intelligence. Okay, maybe it wasn't a boom box. But if it wasn't cowboy boots what was it? I had a problem on my hands.

Just then the doorman called and said there was a fat man downstairs, a Mr. Malte. I said send him up, straightened my tie, shoved the glass of booze behind the TV, stowed the package where no one would find it and nuked a cup of left-over coffee in the microwave.

The first thing Malte said when he came in the door was, You have something that belongs to me.

You don't say.

Oh, but I do say, dear boy. And I'd like it back if you don't mind.

I didn't reply. Malte's cheeks quivered when he talked. He looked like a fat Sidney Greenstreet. After a silence, he said, All right, how much do you want for it?

Since I had no idea what it was I made a stab in the dark. Five, I said.

Five thousand? He brightened. I was actually thinking five hundred but this gave me a clue.

Hundred thousand, I added.

Malte didn't flinch. Have you ever been to Turkey? he asked.

No. But I'm thinking of going this fall. I've always wanted to spend Thanksgiving in Turkey.

He didn't crack a smile. I could see my wit was lost on him.

In Turkey when merchants bargain in the bazaar they always begin with an absurd price, Mr. Shade. You are Ramsey Shade? We are in a certain way merchants, Mr. Shade, are we not?

Supposing we are. So what? I'm getting tired of beating around the bush.

So am I, dear boy, he said, producing an automatic from inside his ample jacket, So am I.

+

We see in the mirror this morning as we shave that the mark on our forehead is getting bigger. And reddish, "angry" as the dermatologists say. Angry at what?

We wonder if our acquaintances have noticed our increasingly hyper-rational behavior, as if we're turning into a robot, all brain no beast. They call us Shylocks but it should be Sherlocks. That's our generic vice. It's the kind of behavior that solves problems by creating bigger problems. The head getting out of hand. The intelligence rationed by the rational. But it improves focus, zeroing in.

We're here on top-secret research into the Third Temple Conspiracy. For *Great Expectorations*. Several of our personalities are involved, at least one of which is female. The Space Bubble is plugged into the electrosphere via the giant antenna on top of World Trade One across West Street. The FAX is connected to the modem, the modem is connected to the PC, the PC is connected to the telephone, the telephone is connected to the E-mail, the E-mail is connected to the internet and god knows where it all ends anymore. In the information network we use our secret name. Just compose RaMSCaN on your touch-tone and hit the pound sign.

We note as we eat the coffee and bagel that we have the headache and it feels as if we're going to have a case of the dreaded lockjaw. TMJ. Thermonuclear jaw. The Golem couldn't speak, Frankenstein, barely. They both lived in a stupor. Like Gary Cooper. In Tombstone or Prague there's always reason to grit our teeth, to keep our upper lip stiff, to grimace and bear it.

Glancing up through the curved glass wall we see that the tops of the twin Trade Center towers are invisibled by greyness. Then we notice something's come out of the FAX while we were dreaming. We go over and blink at it. Looks like bits from the book. This book. Jewish rules. Chips off the old block mosaicked together. Laws of mosaic.

Rx: Two Tablets
you Are, therefore i Am, therefore i Am you
make no image of the empty box
kill a Being kill a world
things don't have to Be as they Are
obey the letter, break the law
memory Is after the fact, but history defeats itself
the other world Is all we have, and it Is this one
twist your head or someone will twist it for you
value the golden calf but cleave onto it not, lest it
    cleave onto you
the mean justify the end, the generous don't need to
+

On to the day's work. I have an appointment with Dr. Frank Stein, Strop Banally's handler. I put on a black Joyce Leslie polka dot number, business-like, but subtly sexy, and hop a Five to Doc Stein's office in the East Seventies.

On the subway I review the secret intelligence dossier, prepared by a private dick named Ram Shade. It's a little fanciful, Shade went off the deep end in my opinion. But I suppose he had to justify his fee.

Doc Stein is a genetic engineer, according to the dossier. But unlike most genetic engineers, he received his doctorate in engineering rather than biology. His microtechnical skills are nevertheless so superior that he quickly came to dominate the field of designer genes. He was the geneticist who spliced a fly gene with a cock gene to produce the first really zipless fuck.

The plan to penetrate the Third Temple Conspiracy was Frank Stein's baby. The Third Temple Conspiracy refers to the complex of plots to destroy the Dome of the Rock and replace it with the Third Temple, using fundamentalist Christian and Jewish groups, each of which participates for its own competing reasons. Stein's reason derives from his endorsement of the Vampiricist Thesis which holds that the so-called blood libel accusation, i.e., Jews needing Christian baby blood for their rituals, is basically a cover-up for a highly influential vampire sub-culture spread by the Knights of Malta during the Crusades, drawing on barbarian traditions of magic specifying human blood as part of the alchemical recipe for turning lead to gold, through an intermediate substance not yet known as uranium. This tradition is not unrelated to the foundation of Christianity itself on a blood sacrifice. According to the vampiricists, Rabbi Loew in response to a dream question received a kabbalistic directive to create a robotic homunculus or Golem to fight the vampires on the grounds that it took a fabricated clay, read silicon, Frankenstein creature immune to vampiric blood sucking Christian Draculas to save the Jews. The directive to create the Golem was said to come from Elijah and was one of the many bulletins concerning the Messiah released by that optimistic angel.

Elijah was in the picture because in this tradition Aaron was said to be Moses' creation, a sorcerer's apprentice or robotic big brother who kept running amok and going over to the goyim, compulsively producing golden calves every time Moses turned his back in a rebellious attempt to assert its own human identity, an identity which however hard it might try to assert, alas, was one it didn't have. One of Aaron's calves remains and was supposedly presented to Rabbi Loew by the feckless Prophet Elijah for safekeeping on the occasion of his marriage. The rather dubious idea seemed to be that if the vampires could be kept away from the Golden Calf they wouldn't become infected with gold fever leading to bloodlust. In any case, according to the vampiricists, Rabbi Loew used Moses' Aaron technology as preserved by the Kabbala to fabricate his Golem.

As a result of his theories Stein was a natural recruit for the Raiders. Of the Lost Calf, that is. Funded by mysterious private foundations promoting a doctrine they called Democratic Fascism, this was Guy Lobe's cell representing the Bond within the loosely organized Third Temple Conspiracy. Though Stein considered Guy Lobe a pig spawned by the Inquisition, the new demofascist inquisition, that is, he knew the advantages of mutual exploitation. He'd looked into it. Columbus sailed the ocean blue for gold. Five hundred years ago. That was the first step. Trying to make up for loss of Jews in the Expulsion. Four percent of the population, they had paid twenty percent of Spain's taxes. The Cathay shot was the first multinational corporate venture. In the name of the cross.

God is one. But one what? Multinational interplanetary conglomerate?

Now, though, the Third Temple Conspiracy has gotten out of hand, the Lost Calf is being pilfered by one player from the next like a loose hockey puck and kindly Doc Stein probably works for the Mossad.

I wonder what Doc Stein would do if he knew I, Rona Fray, am really a fighting reporter doing an investigative story posing as part of the Third Temple Conspiracy? Even though Doc Stein and I are ostensibly on the same team, I suspect I can't trust him. I know for sure he can't trust me.

Why does Strop Banally always turn on us, Dr. Stein?

It's our fault, Rona. Some authorities say that all golems are ingrates. But that's not it. It's that he senses an ambivalence in the relationship between us that makes him very uneasy. It presents him with emotional demands he doesn't know how to handle and our only resort is enemas and mustard plaster.

Enemies and violence, it doesn't help.

It doesn't help unless you want to control everything no matter what. I want to control everything no matter what and the devil take the hindquarters.

What he tells me next, though, is surprising. The Lost Calf has been seen in a shopping mall in Secaucus, New Jersey, at an Elvis look-alike contest. What would Elvis look-alikes have to do with the Golden Calf? Despite their glittering gilt and sequins these grunt and grind look-alikes are little more than lamé ducks.

While talking, Doc Stein has come around his desk and slipped behind my chair. He puts his hands around my waist and slides them up. I don't move. I know he's metempsychotic.

223

He's transmigrating. As a conglomerate personality he's going through one of his normal series of leveraged identity raids, borrowing one image after another from junk media sources with little credit and less credibility. I stay still. I know that he's testing my identity for possible metamorphosis.

+

She's always said she wished she'd been born old and then grown backward, younger, until she disappeared into the womb. She looks like a foetus in the hospital bed, sleeping curled up on her side. Like our father in his death coma. But she's due to get out this time, she's still strong at ninety, and she looks well, aside from the missing teeth and the extensive bruises covering her arms, they say from the IV she tore out and her successive successful struggles to escape the restraints that keep her in bed and the injections and the blood samples they took and god knows what else.

Strange. Even to recognize her as our mother we have to twist our heads a little bit.

It's so good to see you, Ronnie. I feel so forsaken.

+

We look up Kleist's essay on puppets, and there we find the reason for our attraction to androids. The Noble Robot. Their deadhead gestures demonstrate a banal innocence, a crude grace otherwise found in animals and idiots. Charming and thoughtless, invokers of cliché. But they deal in dead letters, parroting folkwit, outwitting wit, engendering nitwits. Oilem goylem. All the dummies. Hoi polloi. Endangering our species. Pleasant crazies.

Peasant Crazies, in contrast, are annoying and unpleasant. They prophesy in conundrums, riddles, nonsense, stupidity, slapstick, wordplay, clowning and quips, sometimes in rhymed or alliterative verse. The Peasant Crazies are urban peasants often squatting in subway stations vacant warehoused apartments cardboard boxes over steam grates or even university campuses, or where ever possible in the interstices of the network. The Peasant

224

Crazy today, ostensibly backward, defective, or even weird or crippled in some way, psychotic or moribund, childish and hyperactive, is an entertainer in the court jester mode. Jerry Lewis, for example. Jerry's Kids. Their only reward disabled parking permits, but it's a biggie.

You ask, Who are some famous Peasant Crazies of yore? The peasant crazy answer is Yorick, Sterne, Schweik, Charlie, Groucho, Harpo, Costello, Abbott, Cantor, Benny, Bergen, Brice, The Three Stooges, Rumpelstiltskin, Rumpelthrillskin and Rumpledforeskin. All slapstuck and chapfallen.

+

Another message on the FAX, this time in handwriting:
> columbus sailed the ocean blue for gold
> a dime, a dime, a dollar, two cents

What in hell is that supposed to mean? And whose handwriting is this? Do the Peasant Crazies now have a FAX? Improbable. Of course as Doctors of Philosophy we recognize the second line as a modernized translation of the biblical handwriting on the wall. It reminds us that on Black Monday, when it is recorded that people were careening around the floor of the Exchange like a swarm of ants trying to evade extermination, a graffiti appeared on Wall Street walls that said *Mene, mene, tekel, upharsin.*

+

IMPORTANT NOTICE: Today we have to interrupt the book to bring the Mother to the Feast of Thanks for the Giving.

We go to fetch her from her Home in Rockaway. Her conversation is, Did you get permission for me to leave?

Yes mother.

Did you tell them where we're going?

Yes mother.

I'm so frightened, Ronnie.

Yes mother.

Will we go back soon?

Yes mother.

Will you take me home later?
Yes mother.
Do they know where we're going?
Yes mother.
Where are we going?
Yes mother.
Is this the right road?
Yes mother.
Did you get permission?
Yes mother.
You look so handsome.
Yes mother.
I'm so sorry for spoiling everything.
Yes mother.

Or as our sister says to her as we enter the Brooklyn-Battery Tunnel, Relax and enjoy the view.

+

We sometimes come across Peasant Crazies at literary gatherings and the other day we run into one of our acquaintance, a poet, who fixes us with eye glit and beard scrag. There is an old woman who lives in her shoes, he says.

It reminds us that My Constant Companion has discovered an Unseeable living in his shoes thirty-six floors beneath our luxury condominium apartment on an abandoned highway ramp. Well, not only in his shoes actually, but in his copious bundles and plastic bags. Day and night. It's dropped below freezing at night lately. This morning we go to the window to peer down at him, but all we can see is the bags and bundles and maybe a figure under some green blankets on or in an orange sleeping bag. Unseeable.

We're going to have to buy a telescope. That's when we understand the situation of the do-good intellectual.

The next morning his space seems to be neater than usual, the bags and bundles organized in some cryptic way, the sleeping bag made, as it were, with a rectangular area of green at the top and an orange area ranged at the bottom, very esthetic, and in the middle a square of black on white. A newspaper? My Constant Companion brings up the possibility of giving him some money, then wonders whether we could give him enough to make any difference.

Next day we buy a telescope. It brings his nest into close-up, thirty-six floors below. It's a mess, his nest. An amazing collection of sacking and plastics and miscellaneous junk. He's not there. Unless he's somewhere under the junk, which is so copious it's entirely possible.

Later in the day it's raining, he's nowhere in sight.

Does the Unseeable live in the same world as us?

Why is there a helicopter circling low over the building?

Finally through the scope we see the Unseeable reaching for something to drink, picks a container out of somewhere, shakes it up. The hand is black.

Fact: The death rate in East Harlem approaches twice that of wealthy areas of New York, infant death rate is more than three times as high. A black man in Harlem is less likely to reach sixty-five than a man in Bangladesh. Sixty-eight percent of very poor urban black children have lead levels in their blood beyond the danger point. Four times as many newborns in Harlem have very low birth weight compared to wealthier neighborhoods, a condition leading to serious disease, mental retardation and learning disabilities. Blacks in our nation's capital are four times more likely to die prematurely of heart disease, cancer, etc. Boring? It's getting more boring every year.

We have to face the possibility that the species is destroying itself in some century long Malthusian spasm. In Sao Paolo they're shooting homeless children in the streets like rats.

+

All right, I told him. It's in my car. Now, you can bump me off and try to trace my car, or you can make a deal with me. And if I'm lying at least I'm still alive. If I'm dead you got a problem.

You are an astute man, Mr. Shade. He put his gun away.

227

Where is your car?

I don't know.

He pulled his gun back out. Would you care to explain why you don't know where your car is?

Certainly. Last night I was stuck real bad for a parking place and I parked it in a Tow Away Zone. So either it's there where I parked it or it's over at the police garage on Twelfth Avenue and Thirty-eighth Street. If it's over on Twelfth Avenue then you need my driver's license and registration to get to it. The registration is in the car and the driver's license is in my wallet.

Hand it over.

Sure. But it has my picture on it.

You're always a step ahead, aren't you Mr. Shade? He put his cannon away again.

I try to be.

Where did you park the car, dear boy?

It's at the corner of Walk and Don't Walk.

Meaning?

Meaning you'll just have to follow me down to it.

What Malte didn't know was that I didn't own a car. When he found out he was going to be upset. So was I. But the package in question was burning a hole in the freezer where I always cooled hot goods, and I wanted to get him out of the house. Just then the door latch clicked and in walked a guy who looked like the world's nerdiest nerd, grey suit with narrow lapels, striped tie topping red sweater, short colorless hair, big glasses and white Reeboks, except there was another guy behind him who looked exactly the same and they were both toting uzis, barrels up.

Undeterred, I didn't hesitate to make unfriendly inquiries about how they got in there. It was my apartment, after all.

We have our ways, said nerd one.

I'm Rom, said nerd two. The only difference between them was that nerd two wore a black beanie held on by a bobby pin.

They are calling me Ram, said nerd one.

They call me Ram too, I said. Ram Shade. Are we related?

Are you Jewish?

I'm circumcised.

They looked at one another. If he would be a golem a minyan he couldn't make, said Ram.

If he would be Jewish we would know about it, said Rom.

Maybe we could give him a bar mitzvah? said Ram.

The kind of bar mitzvah we could be giving him, believe me, he shouldn't want, said Rom.

See here, what's this all about? demanded Malte.

Mossad. Israeli secret service, said Rom. You have something that belongs to us.

Just then the buzzer buzzed. So answer it, said Ram.

I pressed the button. There's a Miss Shane down here, said the doorman. There's a Miss Shane down there, I said. The nerds nodded. Send her up, I said.

I didn't know you and Miss Shane were acquainted, said Malte.

Neither did I, I said.

Just then the intercom buzzed again. I pressed the button. There's a Mr. Banally down here, said the doorman. I looked at the nerd twins, they nodded.

Send him up, I said. I'll break out the potato chips. It buzzed again. There's a Mr. Drackenstein down here. Yo, I said. Maybe we better send out for Chinese.

Just then the doorbell chimed, I opened it, there was this classy blond babe in a navy-blue business suit, a genteel white blouse and a string of pearls. Mature, but zaftig. It was the first time I ever saw a business suit and pearls look like a sex number.

And how can I help you? I asked.

I received an invitation, she said.

Well then, by all means, come in.

Just then this tall blond guy showed up at the door, good-looking, but with a funny Gorbachev mark on his forehead, much smaller, but a lot redder. Gorby has a red A on his forehead, take another look at his photo.

Strop Banally, he said. I got an invitation.

Well join the party.

He walked in behind the woman but as soon as she turned around he said, Hey, I know you.

Really, she said. How well?

From Paris. Remember Art, the poetry readings at Shakespeare and Company?

Yes, I still harbor a certain attraction for the Bohemian life. I invest in paintings.

There were some painters on the scene too. But it was mostly young writers, as I remember.

Ah, yes. My springtime in Paris.

Right. Remember that wild *Paris Review* party when you went off with those creepy preppies?

Creepy? she said. What was creepy about them?

Well I mean, I don't know, they . . .

Some of them are still close friends. Or at least business associates, she added, as if not wanting to be misunderstood.

No, I mean the guys who, uh, I heard . . .

I know, I know. They really laid me down and straightened me out. Besides, I'm not really sure exactly what happened that night. Are you?

No, ah . . .

I had so much to drink, all I know is I woke up next morning with a hangover and all these damp dollars strewn about, she said with a little smile. But they made me realize what's important to me, those fellows. I dropped Bohemia pretty fast and came back to the States. That was my ticket home.

I see.

Yes. No, they were really very nice young men, and they all made it big, that bunch. Very successful men. One of them was in the Reagan administration, and one of them was indicted in a big S and L scandal involving millions. Maybe even billions. A very charming fellow. A real gentleman. So cordial.

+

We hear the the distinctive ring of the FAX phone and watch as it prints out. There's only one line, in handwriting again:

number way divide. Huge.

As Doctors of Philosophy we recognize this as yet another rendition of the handwriting on the wall, but to what point? We call a Peasant Crazy of our acquaintance who says it's a message from Mr. Huge. It means count your blessings and give some to me, he says.

Why you? we ask.

It doesn't give reasons and I don't ask.

Well how do you know it says that?

Number is meant as a verb, like count. You're supposed to count your blessings and weigh their importance.

Where do you get weigh?

It says.

It says way.

It's misspelled. Once you count and weigh your blessings you give some to me.

How do you get that?

Divide.

But why with you?

Who else is here?

But why should I give them away?

Maybe you have too many blessings for your own good, how should I know?

I know I may be too happy, but life will soon fix that.

No pain, don't complain. Give to your local Peasant Crazy.

You know, you Peasant Crazies aren't so crazy.

We aren't peasants either.

He hangs up. Divide, we reflect. We can't help thinking of our local Unseeable. Why should we not just go down and write him out a large check? or simply hand him a substantial sum of cash? And then the practical difficulties begin to intervene.

"At times the truth shines so brilliantly that we perceive it clear as day," wrote Maimonides. "Our nature and habit then draw

231

a veil over our perception, and we return to a darkness almost as dense as before."

How to proceed? Obey the letter and break the law. So the Peasant Crazies say. This is the only way to jack into the outlaw frequencies that circulate fragments of the dark matter, the ninety to ninety-nine percent of matter that has been erased from the universe. What comes in when you do is small pieces of a huge mosaic, part of the master code that is a key to the whole. The mosaic code is very Peasant Crazy. Cryptographers say that the mosaic code is written in Gnomic, like the genome. Cryptographers know that deciphering the genetic code reveals the crypt. The Peasant Crazies say, Decode life you get death. That's their theory. But the Peasant Crazies also contend that a given theory is always wrong, or if it's right one minute it's wrong the next no matter what you may have thought. Thought is for the student, thinking for the teacher, or so the Peasant Crazies say. They also say, When the law kills the letter gives life. And make no mistake, the law can kill as soon as it's written. They have another saying that goes, Lasting truths are writ in invisible ink.

+

The next person through the door was this doll-like creature in a Brooks Brothers suit for ladies, complete with a tie, all of which made her look like Marilyn Monroe in drag. The first thing she said to me was, I've finally figured it out. We're all in a movie. That's why nothing seems real.

I assumed she was disturbed so I ignored the comment and asked if she had a name.

Yes, I have a name.

Would you mind telling me what it is?

Not at all.

Okay, I'll bite. What is it?

It's Ronda Fry. I got an invitation.

Just then this tall, husky, well-dressed gent appeared behind her and put his arm around her waist, guiding her into the room. As in small fry. Right, Ronda? He was wearing an English suit

232

and a gold watch fob, but with pocket handkerchief, tie, shoes and accessories very gucci-pucci. Hair, what was left of it, grey on grey. Furrows flicked across his highdomed brow like figures flashing on a cathode ray tube. His accent was more or less British, with an admixture of something vaguely Transylvanian. Boris Karloff lightly seasoned with Bela Lugosi. He wasn't exactly your man in the street but I knew I'd seen him before.

Hello, Rod, she said. Rod's my current mister.

Rod Drackenstein, he said. Initials R & D. Research and Development. That's what we stand for. We've all had a lot of fun with Ronda. We've researched her thoroughly. But she can't be developed. She's a doll. Do your trick, Ronda.

Among the most active issues, Ronda recited, Exxon was at thirty-three and one half, down ten and a quarter. IBM was at one hundred and three and a quarter, down thirty-one and three quarters. American Express twenty-two and a half, down eight. Ford sixty-nine, down fifteen and a quarter. USX twenty-one and a half, down twelve and a half. Volume was six hundred and four point three million. The day's losses came to more than five hundred billion, and since last summer losses amount to more than one trillion. The Dow Jones average of thirty industrials closed at one thousand seven hundred and thirty-eight point four, down five hundred and eight points.

She's just kidding, said Drackenstein. She says those figures unaccountably flashed through her terminal one day and she never forgot them. If I thought they were real I'd be the first rat off the ship. Ramsey Shade, I presume?

That's right. I assume you got an invitation.

No, I sent the invitations.

Oh. Well in that case maybe you can tell us why we're all here.

Of course. In due time. First you should notice that I have no shadow. That's because I'm not real. I'm realer than real. Bigger than life. I'm CEO of XXX, Ltd.

Which is?

Triplex, as it's called. A benevolent multinational interplanetary conglomerate dealing in space exploration, newspapers, biochemicals, computers, armaments, aircraft, breweries, publishing, transportation, food products, cigarettes, banking, gambling casinos, real estate, pet food, petrochemicals, pharmaceuticals, construction, bakery goods, shipping, sports, oil, farm machinery, containers, sex, soft drinks, entertainment and communications. We're a wholly owned subsidiary of a division of Huge Industries. Which possesses, I might add, a substantial interest in Mr. Banally's ComPost®.

As he talked Drackenstein somehow gave the illusion that he was growing in stature.

Why benevolent? I asked.

By benevolent we mean malevolent, said Drackenstein.

You know Guy Lobe? asked Strop Banally.

I think he works for us, I'll have to look it up, said Drackenstein. So does Romulus Malte here. Since we've all arrived I think I'll let him explain.

As you wish, said Malte. He pulled out a very large handkerchief, wiped his brow, cleared his throat. Hem. Once upon a time, while Yahweh was busy writing on Moses' tablets on top of Mt. Sinai, Aaron was down below conniving with the Israelites to make a Golden Calf. Hem. This you know. But what you don't know is that after Moses destroyed the calf and had the Levites put three thousand Israelites to death, Exodus thirty-two twenty-eight, he went back up the mountain to get the word again, and in the meantime Aaron, with a certain amount of R & D, managed to manufacture a new and better, or at least more durable, Golden Calf. The proof is that Yahweh erased two of Aarons's sons for absolutely no reason, or rather there was a reason, but it doesn't make sense, Leviticus ten three, unless you assume that the so-called alien fire was a new experimental process they discovered through R & D and used in helping their father mold another calf. Hem. But that wasn't in the book, it was erased, it was erased along with Aaron's two sons. It was erased because while Moses was on the mountain Yahweh told him he was going to erase those who had sinned from the book he was writing, and he erased the sin along with the sinners. And Aaron was silent, it says in the book. No doubt a guilty silence. Which is further proof. Hem. Malte popped a cough drop. But just because the calf was erased from the Book of Life doesn't mean it doesn't exist. It exists as part of the dark matter. But this is merely theoretical proof.

Malte was getting agitated as he spoke. He kept his handkerchief in his hand and mopped his brow every thirty seconds or so. Regardless of how pretty all this is as literary theory, and allow me to say that I was a young poet once, when I was young, as sure as my name is Romulus M. Malte, I assure you that the thing exists as a verifiable historical entity. The key is the copper scroll. Despite efforts to retard dissemination of that and other parts of the Dead Sea Scroll materials, after consulting them the Lost Calf came to light again in a dig some say under the Temple Mount others say at Caesarea. This is a well-known fact, it was in the newspapers. Hem. Then, just as mysteriously as it appeared, it disappeared, only to surface again in Istanbul in the possession of a Palestinian antiquities dealer who said he bought it from a Bedouin. He said the Bedouin claimed he found it when his camel stepped through a hole in the ground while grazing near the nature preserve of Ein Geddi above the Dead Sea, a dubious story. I actually had the thing in my hands one evening in his shabby hotel room. It wasn't large, but it was incredibly heavy for its size, even assuming it was made of solid gold. Furthermore it vibrated and buzzed, I felt as if I were holding a nuclear bomb or something that was alive in some bizarre inanimate way that I couldn't comprehend. It was like a magnet, a gorgeous magnet. Hem. An unforgettable experience, I should say. It must have been the product of a very sophisticated technology.

Malte paused, mopped, popped another drop. I had delivered a certain substantial sum to the dealer, on account as it were, and was to return the next morning with the rest, in exchange for the goods. I knew there was a certain Lobe who had gotten wind of the transaction, but I was confident I had beaten him to the punch. Hem. When I arrived at the hotel the next morning I found our dear Miss Shane here in the room with a note from the dealer that I was to give the rest of the money to her, and that she would lead me to the prize. To make a long story short, I did and she didn't. Instead it was put aboard a seagoing yacht that weighed anchor immediately, even though legend had it that the Calf brought fatally bad luck to the officers of any vessel who had the temerity to take it aboard. Legend notwithstanding, it arrived in New York. Then disappeared. So here we are.

If it's not found we're sunk, said Drackenstein. We might as well head for the Azores. He seemed to be growing again. Ballooning would have been the word for it. In fact he was starting to look like something in the Macy's parade. Frankly, it gave me the chills. It was unnatural. But the other people in the room didn't seem to be fazed at all. Well, they knew him better than I did.

+

Today it's raining. Down in the streets, we pass the Unseeable who camps below in his sleeping bag which he has moved today to the shelter of the underpass out of the Brooklyn-Battery Tunnel nearby. The words of Maimonides come back to us like a streak of light illuminating the dark matter and we change course to approach him and establish contact. As soon as the Unseeable sees us he gets a jumpy hostile look in his eye that clearly says, If you get much closer I'm going to kill you. We've seen that look in the eyes of street cats that are not going to live much longer because they've already been damaged too much.

The United States has more people in jail than any other country, more than in Russia, more per capita by far than South Africa during apartheid, the number of prisoners has doubled in the last decade, forty-three percent of prisoners are Black. And the murder rate is seven times that in Europe.

+

Mr. Huge lives in a hotel room way out in the network of interstates. No concessions in the furnishings are made to his tastes. He has no tastes. Except for speed and economy, because

236

that's what it's all about. Meals are no problem. He eats little and always the same thing. He sees no one, not even his wife. He communicates with the world by means of his Mormons. His image in the world is one of pure dash, a tall, good-looking man standing next to an airplane wing with his arm around a beautiful movie star, a golf club in his other hand. But he no longer touches anyone. Maybe he finds his Mormons to be sanitized in some obscure way, but he doesn't touch his Mormons either. He doesn't touch anything unless insulated by Kleenex. He doesn't wash or brush his teeth. He saves his urine in mason jars and suffers from monumental drug addict constipation. Gaunt, wasted, filthy, unshaven, with rotting teeth, bird-claw fingernails, his hair halfway down his back, his body covered with sores, he looks like a victim of Auschwitz. He no longer wears clothes. He works naked, and he works incessantly. No detail is too trivial, no sparrow's fall escapes his meticulous attention, as he sends and receives data through his inconceivably complex but beautifully simple network. He maintains total isolation because he is intensely careful about germs. He's phobic about infection, about catching what someone else has. Or is it about others getting what he has? Only the innocent expose themselves to germs, because they don't know the facts of life. He remains pure. But pure what?

Some say that Mr. Huge is trying to mimic, if not become, god the father. We know that the god of our fathers is a control freak. We know that he isn't perfect. And we know that he is an absence. What more do you need?

Mr. Huge spends most of his time working thinking. Even when he seems to be resting he's thinking. When he watches the same film again and again and again, for example, he's not merely watching. He's thinking. Just now Mr. Huge's long toenails clack nervously against one another as he lies in bed and watches a film. Is it *Hotel Paradisio*? Or *Deadlier Than the Male*? Or *Bullet For a Badman*? Or *The Brain That Refused To Die*? Or *The Man In the Shadow*? Or *Madame Sin*? Or *Gunfight in Abilene*? Or *The Italian Job*? Or *Hot Car Girl*? Or *Jet Pilot*? Or possibly

Ice Station Zebra. The polar scenery is white. Like desert scenery. Perfect setting for the white hunter. The purity of white is the attraction and the prey. That's the great white way. But the arctic whiteness is confusing and hard to control. As soon as the submarine breaks through the ice cap it emerges into a world that seems a mirror image of the one he's used to where light emerges out of dark. Here dark emerges out of light, one world a negative of the other. It corresponds to his feeling of living only partly in this world so that this one isn't quite real as if there were another as if he were living in a movie. That's why he's fascinated with movies and has made many himself, including the Oedipal Eden flick called *The Outlaw*, in which Billy the Kid has to shoot the father before he's released from the bondage of innocence and goes off with Jane Russell. Innocence is the original sin, since if Adam weren't innocent he wouldn't have bit on the apple. In *The Outlaw* bondage abounds, Jane Russell hands tied behind back squirming in a low cut blouse draped over a specially engineered Huge brassiere, because you have to control everything. And the devil take the hindquarters. Because that's something you can't control. But first you have to shoot the father and lose your innocence. This, Huge knows, is his mission, to release his country from the bondage of innocence. He believes he can do it with his phallic force, through women, and through phallic projectiles of all sorts, inventing them and building them and driving them, cars, planes, missiles, ships, the sub in *Ice Station Zebra* reminds him of his own Glomar Explorer, whose mission was to get the secret from the sunken Russian sub, the secret that would save the free world. But huge white vaginas open in the ice, gape, threaten to crush the little men with their lilliputian projectiles. All holes are dangerous, the cold overwhelming ocean rushes in through the torpedo tube when the sub tries to fire a torpedo. Nature is the enemy, the ocean, the ice, the white-out storm, and here at the Pole nature is white, a negative. And that's their mission, to eliminate the negative of the spy photos from the fallen Russian satellite. Of course in the film they do despite menacing commie parachutes descending like smothering breasts, and in so doing accentuate the positive, that's why Huge keeps watching it over and over, because in the film he doesn't have to mess with Mister Inbetween. Does he massage his mouldy dick under the sheet as his unclipped toenails clack, still hoping for some real life response that would rescue a man from woman, rescue the world from nature, rescue civilization from negation with the explosive high-velocity projectiles of supertechnology? But the fantastic Glomar Explorer failed and the gargantuan Spruce Goose failed and he knows now that he failed and the world isn't saved. The world remains innocent. Innocent of its corruption, of the facts of life. Out of control. And watching the whiteness of *Ice Station Zebra* he's bitter. He wonders again if there's another world, outside the movie, out of control. After all, he followed the great white way, the way of the white hunter, he won the Golden Calf, why isn't he redeemed? Why did it all turn on him, the hunter hunted, the inlaw become the outlaw?

One of his Mormons comes, bearing bitter white powders.

+

When our father was dying the landlord tried to evict him and our mother from their apartment. Our father asked us to intervene and make a deal with the landlord. After long struggle and much time we managed to do so, arranging for them to move upstairs to a better apartment for less money plus a large cash settlement. This was important since our mother had no money and our father had cashed in his life insurance. Our father was all for it but at the last minute renegged, saying he was too sick, it was too difficult to move. We told him it was too late, the deal had already been signed. He told us we had sold out to the landlord for money. We went ahead with the deal. Then our father commited suicide. So we suppose you could say that I killed our father. His absence became an accusation.

But he was always an absence. An absence inside the family, leaving us to our mother. So there was nothing to keep the mother at bay, no ally. In the absence of the father it's hard for the son to be born. This had nothing to do with us. Judaism is basically a defeated but defiant matriarchy, kept ferociously in its place by a patriarchy. Go to Israel, you'll see. Why do you think women in temple are relegated to the balcony? Eve's disobedience means freedom from her point of view. For us, too. So women are terrifying and infinitely desirable to Jewish men, a menace and above all, a model. Because mothers are dreamers, dreamers and schemers, for them anything is possible, things don't have to be as they are. But the situation doesn't make for happy kids. Take Cain and Abel. Or with Jacob and Esau, whose side was Mom on?

+

I'm on my way back from Frank Stein's office when suddenly I get the feeling I'm being followed. I click the menu on being followed and nothing computes. I say to myself, Rona, here you are on the subway, you just caught the Five downtown by a fraction of a second, there's no way you're being followed, relax. Aside from the usual herds of brain-damaged children with automatic weapons sweeping through the cars there's no problem. I'm thinking that after I get home I'll go for a jog in Central Park.

But what I don't figure out is I'm being followed from ahead, I mean they already know where I'm headed and I'm following them. Because when I get into the elevator in my building sure enough they're there. Every woman's nightmare.

Be nice, says one, avoid problems. They're wearing leather jackets and baseball caps.

The elevator door closes. I'll give you my money if you leave me my wallet, I say. I'm having my period and I'm HIV positive.

What do you think we are? says one.

What are you?

We're advisors. Press your floor. That's our advice.

They make me let them in the apartment. I have no cash, I don't do drugs, the jewelery is in the night table, I tell them.

Jewelry we're not interested, says one. He takes off his baseball

240

cap, I see he's wearing a yarmulke.

Let's introduce ourselves, says the other. He doesn't wear a yarmolke. You're Rona Fray. I'm Ram. He's Rom.

Oh no. Not Rom the Reamer and Ram the Roamer.

You got it.

Wait a minute, you're on television. "Great Expectorations." What are you doing in real life?

On TV it's just our image. With most people they're only real. But we're spooks. Spooks are real and unreal.

I don't know anything.

We know you don't know anything. That's why we're here. To tell you something.

What?

That depends on you.

Okay, let's start over. You work for the Mossad.

So? You got a Jewish problem?

Yes I have a Jewish problem. I'm Jewish.

So what's the problem?

I don't like Jews.

No problem, lots of Jews don't.

Why no problem?

Because we don't care if we like us or not. It's not our problem.

Then what is our problem?

Our problem is whether they like us or not. That's our problem.

What's the solution?

Their solution is the final solution, says Rom the Reamer. Our solution is never again. In the end we'll die first. Maybe we'll die first to begin with. We'll make a stand. But at least we'll stick it to them this time. Remember Masada.

Suicide is a funny place to begin, says Ram the Roamer. Never mind Masada. If it doesn't work out in one place we'll try in another place. That's what we've always done, that's what we'll always do.

I'm getting confused, I say.

We know you're confused Rona. That's why we're here.

241

We're confused too. We're confused about you. We're confused about whose side you're on. There may be a war coming you know.

I don't know whose side I'm on. Ask Dr. Stein, he's my therapist.

We can't ask Dr. Stein anything. He's just had an anxiety attack.

The attackers got away. The police have no leads.

What are you going to do with me?

We're going to give you a psychotic break.

We like to give everyone a break. If they're cooperative.

Don't get me wrong, I say. I'm not an anti-semite. I just don't like certain Jews.

What have you got against them?

Gold fever.

Gold fever isn't all that bad, says Rom. It's productive. It's GNP. It creates wealth. It's good for inventories. It stocks the shelves. It stimulates consumption. Frank Stein told me that just before he had an anxiety attack. He begins to hack and cough.

What's wrong with him? I ask.

He's sick.

What with?

Consumption.

+

Drackenstein picked up where Malte left off. He still seemed to be growing. But as he grew he also sort of thinned out. He said the yacht they put the lost Calf on was named *The Lady Drackenstain*, out of London. I happen to know this because it happens to be my yacht. And that probably explains, Mr. Shade, why the Calf conspiracy found its way to you.

How so?

Because *The Lady Drackenstain* docked in the yacht harbor at the World Financial Center and you're probably the closest shamus, as they say, available.

He had a point. It was true you could see the harbor from

my windows. You could see the white hull of *The Lady Drackenstain*, the helicopter on top of its superstructure and through the telescope the coat of arms on its bow with its motto: "Good to the last drop."

In fact, I'd already noticed the yacht docked in the basin surrounded by the World Financial Center beneath the World Trade Center towers. Just the other day, during one of my crepuscular ambles, I'd noticed a party on board, and since it was possible to get very close up, I took the opportunity to see how the upper one tenth of one percent of the world lived. Apparently the upper one tenth of one percent was not having a very good time. In fact it looked extremely glum. I wondered what the upper one tenth of one percent had to worry about. Now I knew.

Now I also knew where I'd seen Drackenstein before. In the cabin, playing host. I'd been curious about *The Lady Drackenstain* because she was the object of a lot of local scuttlebutt in the waterfront bars, which in these precincts were filled with Wall Street yuppies. It was rumored, among other things, that she had her own electronic global surveillance system plugged into a spy satellite, her own cache of arms, her own financial nerve center with direct connections to London, Liechtenstein, Paris, Geneva, New York, Tel Aviv and Tokyo, her own bank, and even her own laundry, presumbly as part of the banking services.

Maybe you should go to the yacht and ask them about it, Mr. Shade, said Daisy Shane. The Calf, I mean.

That's a hundred dollars an hour plus expenses.

Certainly, said Rod Drackenstein. He seemed to fill the room. I couldn't tell where his voice was coming from. He was everywhere. Basically he was so big he'd become invisible.

And perhaps you should take our dear Miss Shane with you as a connection, so to speak, said Malte.

Sure, I said. Anything to get them all out of the apartment.

+

Coming back from some errands, dressed warmly but our toes and nose freezing nevertheless, we pass the Unseeable, moved in out of the weather in the tunnel exit, completely submerged in rags and sleeping bag so that you can't see him.

That day we look in the mirror to examine the mark on our brow and we see it's getting redder and it's beginnning to look like the letter A. And we notice that as it gets redder we seem to be getting angrier.

+

After everybody left I went down in the elevator with Daisy Shane. Somewhere around floor thirty she suddenly sagged and leaned against me. Oh, Ramsey, she sighed.

What's the trouble, sweetheart? I asked. I could feel the curves of her body hot against me.

Elevators make me feel faint, she said.

That's all right, we'll be down soon.

Hold me.

My pleasure, I said, and I did, as tightly as possible. All the while wondering what it was she was after from me, and what she was willing to give to get it.

We walked up the promenade to the yacht harbor. *The Lady Drackenstain* was still moored in the basin, an enormous white luxury number flying the Union Jack.

There was no one checking the gangplank so we just walked on board. It seemed deserted, a ghost ship. Then we saw there was someone on the bridge. When we got up there we found someone sitting at the wheel all right, but he was dead. When I shook his shoulder he slumped to the floor, his head fell back, and I could see his neck was all bloody. And there was a bloody A cut into his forehead.

He didn't look very nautical, he was wearing a white lab coat over a conservative tie and shirt, with his glasses and several pens and pencils clipped onto a plastic pen protector in his shirt pocket, that kind of guy. I pulled his wallet out of his pocket, his identification said he was a Dr. Frank Stein. When I put the wallet back I noticed that the blood on his neck was coming from two neat puncture holes. Daisy looked shook.

244

What's the matter? I asked. Is he a friend of yours?

No. It's just that. . . . Oh, hold me Ram.

I did. What the hell. She glued her pelvis to me and did a grind.

Does death turn you on? I asked.

I'm so scared, she said.

What of? He won't hurt you.

Maybe I'm not scared of him, maybe I'm scared of you. Hold me tight.

We sank to the floor. Luckily there was a nice, soft Persian carpet under us. We made love on it, fast and hard, like a missile exploding.

Feel better? I asked.

It's what the doctor ordered.

I hope not Dr. Stein.

Ram. Those marks on his throat. What do you suppose . . .

I've only seen that once before, sweetheart, and that was when I was called in as a consultant by a friend in the Paris police because the victim worked for a New York firm engaged in genetic engineering. We were able to trace the killer's movements from New York to Paris to Prague. We lost track of him in Transylvania. Never did solve that one.

Do you think it's possible . . .

Ostensibly. But I don't deal in the ostensible. I don't even like to talk about it. I'm a rationalist. Once you start talking ostensible you can say anything. I'll wait for the autopsy.

We straightened our clothes and went back to my apartment to call the cops, but when we got up there the door was open and the place looked like a missile exploded in it. There was a calling card on the micronuke: "Rambam Wrecking Service—Never Again For the First Time. ROM/RAM."

+

The war started last night with a massive missile attack. We sit in front of the TV and spend the night and the morning trying to dope it out and trying to sort out our feelings about it with little success. We fear we are being led down the great white way.

245

We fear a sudden flood of dark matter can rear up like a tidal wave to swamp the white luxury liner of state.

The FAX machine rings and we watch as the following message comes out:

10c, 10c, $1, 10c. Me Shack.

Write in if you know what that's all about. Our educated guess, as Doctors of Philosophy, is that it's a cryptogram, using monetary denominations to prophesy the rise and fall of the state.

+

I find out about the meet at Shade's through sources. It's going to take place on TV, but since I'm on TV as a newswoman I have access. Of course that's going to blow my cover, but I decide it's time to reveal the real me. I hustle over to the studio where they're filming the Ram Shade series.

I connected with them coming out of the elevator in the lobby. Rod Drackenstein, Strop Banally, a fat man and Ronda Fry. The only one I didn't know about was the fat man. Shade wasn't there.

Rona Fray, I presented myself, Public Channel News.

Fighting Fray? said Banally. Girl reporter?

I ignored him, I'm used to it. We hear there's been an important art theft, I said.

Tch, tch, said the fat man. Antiquities theft would be more like it.

Like what? I insisted.

Like an icon, my dear, like an icon.

Is its loss significant?

Significant? You might say it's an iconoclasm. Hem.

Can you elaborate on that for PCN viewers?

Not at this time. I think I can speak for all of us?

Can you give me your name, sir?

Romulus M. Malte. Art and antiquities.

What is the M for?

Emmenthal. I'm a Swiss national.

A huge, white superstretch limo pulled up and a bodyguard looking person in a cap jumped out to open the door.

246

Everyone but Banally piled in. The cameras shut down. It was a wrap till the next installment.

I'll stroll with Miss Fray, says Banally as we leave the TV studio.

I can see he's got ideas so I decide to clue him right away. I have to tell you something, I tell him. Rona is an acronym.

For what?

Aaron.

Aaron. What a coincidence.

What?

I'm a Ron.

Gee well, maybe we're on the same side.

Of what?

The same side as Ram and Rom. As truth and death.

Suddenly a shadow springs from a doorway, a Black man in an orange parka and shapeless camouflage pants. You think I'm Black, he says, I'm not.

Don't encourage him, I say.

Did I encourage him? says Banally.

My name is Shack. Me Shack. I used to be white as you. Then they put me in the ovens, you know, in the camps. And this what happened to me.

What happened to you?

Don't encourage him.

I got burned. Nobody can see me no more. So how about some money.

Money will only encourage him.

I'm not demanding I'm asking, he says.

I'm being polite I could be breaking into an apartment, he says.

I could be out robbing banks, he says. I could be out mugging someone. I could be raping them. I could be assaulting them. I could be assaulting you.

This is not encouraging, I say.

All right I'll tell you what, I'll offer you a deal. Give me your money and I won't kill you.

Banally takes a small automatic out of his inner coat pocket and shows it.

So how about I wash your windshield? says Me Shack.

I don't have a windshield, I say. At least not with me.

I'm a veteran, he says. Is this how you treat a veteran? I'm below the official government poverty line.

All I have on me is credit cards.

Sorry I don't take plastic.

Banally hands him a dollar bill.

What's that, a dollar? How much time I spend shaking you down, and I only get a dollar? Shit. Never mind, I'll catch you next time. White motherfuckers. Thank you for your business. And listen. Come back again. I'm always here.

He disappears. He doesn't leave, you just can't see him any more.

That was no panhandler, says Banally. That was our shadow. Did you know we're being followed?

We've always been followed.

+

We like money. We know it's banal but it's also democratic, it's a great leveller. We must be part Aronian. Most Jews are, the Aronian Heresy has deep roots and good reasons. Survival. But there are two tracks, the Mosaic and the Aronian, and they finally separate into two types, the Rabbi and the Mogul. Follow the Rabbi track far enough and you get to the Extreme Rabbi, who transcends Jewishness by applying Jewish ideas of morality and justice to everyone. This can be risky and Extreme Rabbis some-times get crucified. Nobody has to tell us where the Mogul track leads, it leads to Mr. Huge. And Mogul just spells Golem inside out, the uncircumcised son run amok.

We're not a Cohan or a Levi, but when we need to make a choice, Aronian or Mosaic, we're Mosaic. Iconoclastic. Mosaic men are dreamers, sometimes we have nightmares, go mad. But for Mosaic men things don't have to be as they are. They can change. Anything is possible. The Golem can become the circumcised son, scared, scarred, but sacred. Today I am a mensch. Only the son doesn't need to become another idolized father. Brothers, brothers and sisters, that's our shtick.

But we can understand the gold standard. It can buy freedom. It can be worth fighting a war.

Gelt. Gilt.

Nothing can buy freedom.

+

Iraqi missiles hitting Tel Aviv on screen. We think of friends in Tel Aviv and try to figure out if the missiles landed in their neighborhoods. We think not, not so far. Here all is peace and privilege, ghostly sunlight on the processor screen reflected from silver shafts of Trade Center towers a few blocks away rereflected by full length mirrors in our study. We examine our image in the glass, we learn nothing. The cat stirs in her basket, the purr of traffic sifts in, white noise. But at our backs we always fear the growl of history slouching near. Vast clouds of light sucked in to the dark matter, all imagery erased in iconaclysms of blackness.

+

This time we get on the case ourselves in place of Shade who's proving a little too vulnerable to the ladies. He had to know he was going to get burned. Maybe he wanted to get burned. Or is it just poor direction? A little direct intervention by the author is called for. We walk onto the series set to argue, assuming a different Shade.

First thing I did was barge into Shade's apartment. I went right to the freezer but I didn't really have to look. The package, of course, was gone. I didn't think anyone would go to all that trouble just to find a pair of frozen cowboy boots. But whatever trouble they went to, a good part of it was standing next to me shedding a crock of tears.

Oh Ram, who could have . . .

I hauled off and slapped her across the face. Hard. I knew I shouldn't have been mad at Daisy because Shade should have known better. He should have known she was doing everything she could to keep him out of the apartment so they had plenty of time to find what they were looking for. I was mad anyway. Maybe I was mad because she took Shade for a ride, even though it was a ride he wanted to go on. Maybe I was mad just because I was getting mad lately. Or going mad. But this wasn't like me. I wasn't myself. This wasn't the real me, I don't hit chicks. I don't even call them chicks. Maybe the problem with acting in someone else's image is you take on the characteristics of the role. She didn't know I was Ron, she thought I was still Ram. Even if she knew I was Ron she was totally unfamiliar with the Ron image. Anyway there's more than one Ron image as Ron has learned, confusing even myself much less someone who's never met me.

So she acted with me as if I were Ram. And so I acted with her as the situation required. What did she know about the real me? Or care? This is what happens when you take on an image, even your own. There's already a script. You become a marionette. And then you're no longer on the side of truth and death because no puppet can be on the side of truth and death. You have to be a mensch to be on the side of truth and death, not an android. You've become a dummy. A nebbish.

Now we can cut the charade, I told her. Right?

All right. She was holding her face where I slapped her, but there was a different expression on it now. She almost looked like a different person. Smart. Mean.

The first thing is what do they intend to do with it?

They have a buyer. All they need to do is deliver it to him.

And the buyer is Drackenstein?

That's right.

Who's he fronting for?

That I don't know. I swear to you, Ram, I don't know what this is all about. I don't know who Drackenstein represents and I don't know who Malte is working for.

All you know is you tried to pilfer some valuable property that doesn't belong to you.

It doesn't belong to them either.

Then who does it belong to?

I don't know.

And where did they take it just now?

They said they were going to leave it in the trunk of my car. I gave them a key.

And of course you don't know anything about what happened on *The Lady Drackenstain*.

You have to believe me. Murder is not my cup of tea.

Let's go.

We went down to the street to look for her car but it wasn't there. It was disappearing around the corner in tow to a wrecker. I caught the firm's name on the back of the truck as it sped up—Rambam Wrecks.

We walk off the set in exasperation. Let Shade deal with it, that's what he's getting paid for. Personally, we want to get back to the real me. If we can figure out who it is. Later we switch on the VCR to find out how the director handles our story. It's the same old problem with writing for the electronic media, the story always gets out of control.

+

Why are there two, now three helicopters circling, now hovering, over our building? Terrorists? Counter-terrorists?

+

We ask our sister Gloria, in her capacity as official housing advocate for the poor, why nothing is done for the homeless. We're sitting on a decaying pier out into the Hudson, looking at the World Financial Center.

"Well, you know, the sad part of it is, that it's gone on too long now for it to be a shock. People are now used to seeing homeless people sleeping on the streets, nobody is outraged anymore, and it's now just become part of our backdrop and nobody really cares about it too much. And nothing is going to be done and it's going to get worse."

"Is there any sign of resistance in the city? I mean I was impressed at the spirit of people in the East Village with their vest-pocket parks and the flowers and the gardens and the sculpture sites and all that stuff."

"Yes, they're wonderful, but, you know, it's like a piece of the sixties that's managed to survive. You know, I've seen people like the Inner City Press Homesteaders that opened up those ten buildings in the South Bronx. Rehabbed the buildings themselves with their own money and their own time, I would say three to four years. Two hundred families lived in those buildings. It's very nice and it's like a vest-pocket park. But when the city wants to do something it comes along and says, Okay, that's it, we have our own plans, you're out."

"They kicked them out?"

"Right. Yeah. So I mean it's a very romantic nice little notion but that's not how we fight this anymore. One of the things I was thinking about was a lot of action and a lot of energy was aroused and brought to life when the Gulf War started. People did come together and people did start up, and what has to happen, these things cannot be episodic in response to an emergency and a crisis. What we need is an ongoing network of people who are concerned about this. . . (loud sirens). . . . Here we go again."

"The city's burning down again."

"Meanwhile, all social spending is going to go down the tubes in favor of military spending. Have you heard any talk about a peace dividend lately?"

+

SCREEN ON. We watch long enough to see that the monster has run amok, storming through the desert, perfecting its own technology. Whatever noble motives may have gotten involved.

> Pure love of humanity justified the
> creation of the dreadful, and sanctified
> the terrible. (Chayim Bloch, *The Golem*)

It is written.

Also we see that the Iraquis are releasing oil into the Red Sea, creating an ecological disaster dwarfing the Alaska oil spill. Once again pictures of oil mucked critters dying their slow deaths.

Painted in oil, art brute. Totalling our totems. Why is it that it's the exceptional animal that isn't beautiful, especially among the wild ones? SCREEN OFF.

+

Later it turns out that that image of the doomed cormorant trying to escape a pool of oil, played over and over again, is from stock footage. So that even the imagery of truth is deceptive. And what about the images we aren't shown?

> There's a cryptic message on the FAX in Shade's code name: Graceland. He played raquetball at the Jewish Community Center on Poplar. —Shadrak

+

My Constant Companion calls in from the other room that the Unseeable is gone, that there's nothing left down there but a little garbage. We go to the window and it's true, there's nothing there, all his junk's been flushed out, nothing but a little garbage, and on his ramp, two trailers, they look like construction trailers. One of them says *Bishop Sanzari, joint venture*. We feel sickened, don't exactly know why.

+

There's a message come in on the FAX. It says:

> Graceland. There's a Star of David on his mother's grave stone. —Shadrak

Evidently the trail's led south. But Shade is losing it.

+

This character in shapeless camouflage garb stops us on an empty street. My name Shackle, he says. Then we realize it's the Unseeable. He's a little frightening, frankly. Disturbed. Wacko.

Yeah, they clean out old Shackle, all right. Right out his joint. By a joint venture. Yeah, Shackle get burned, all his things gone. Shackle living in the lion den, now they throw him in the furnace. Get burned in the belly of the whale. Seen the handwritin on the wall. What wall? Wall of Jericho. You don't get out the belly of the whale till you do what you supposed to do. Then you can blow your horn. Then maybe the wall come down. Amen.

He turns his body at a certain odd angle and he disappears. Now he's just a voice.

I ain't Black, I'm red white and blue. So what about I wash your windshield now? I could be out rapin banks, robbin hoods, see what I mean. Or other stuff. So you give old Shackle your dirty bottles, your used tin cans and don't worry bout a thing. Old Shackle not even here, he uptown dyin of AIDS. He hungry. He gotta stop for lunch at Welfare. Welfare that garbage can over there. Free lunch. You pay.

Now he sidles into the visible spectrum again something metallic in his hand. It flashes and you feel it rasp in, it's more like a blow. And it's gone, your wallet.

+

SCREEN ON. Our sister Gloria on TV. Channel Four news. Talking about the real blood and real people in the real war of which TV gives us images. Part of a march in which demonstrators smash TV sets in front of the TV stations. Trying to break through the wall of the screen. SCREEN OFF.

+

Another FAX this morning:

Graceland. Elvis-(levis{jeans-Jewish priests-genes})-lives. What do you think? —Shadrak

+

Elvis was my idol. That day I just knew something bad was going to happen, then I fell asleep and saw Elvis in his coffin. There were two puncture marks on his neck. I don't know how to explain it but I knew this wasn't a dream it was real. When I woke up and turned on the television they said Elvis had been found dead. Then I knew that we were responsible for his death, we his fans, we were the vampires that had consumed him and suckled him hollow. Because Dracula meets Frankenstein. Because you have to eat what you love. Because the body and the blood. Because sometimes you have to use your capabilities to destroy assets. Because to attrit the enemy. Because especially in a target rich environment. Because sometimes it's lucrative sorties.

Because I don't want to sound like a war mongrel. We killed the King. But I also knew that production of the King would resume in some other model. Because we need the image. That doesn't mean I didn't weep for him, Elvis is a very cryogenic figure. Some say he was actually freeze dried. Anyways, nowadays they can always splice some genes together. Replace a few worn body parts from the organ bank. Aloha, born again!

+

> He took as his model a book [the Bible]
> which intentionally lacks order and by so
> doing he wrote a book which intention-
> ally lacks order. At any rate the *Guide*
> [Maimonides' *Guide of the Perplexed*]
> certainly and admittedly is a book which
> intentionally lacks order. (Leo Strauss)

+

The FAX again:

> Graceland. His middle name is Aaron. Calf-Aaron-
> Jewish priest genes-levis-Elvis. What do you
> think? —Shadrak

+

We're walking down the Bowery at night heading for CBGB when a voice comes to us out of a dark doorway. Me Shack, it says. This my brother I. Squat. We hole up in abandoned tenements all over city. Winter it cold, summer it hot. You can't see us we you shadow. We you. No person see his shadow in the dark. You in the dark. Lose your shadow, lose your heart.

+

The FAX:

> Graceland. Urgent. I may know answer but many
> shadows. Rabbi Moses ben Maimon-RaMBaM-
> Elvis Aaron Presley-aRoN SHaM-SHaZaM-
> RaMBo-BaMBaM. What do you think?
> —Shadrak

We sense this is the last off-the-wall communication we'll

receive from Shade. We speculate he's lost it. Over the edge. We feel he'll never be heard from again. Unless this notice from the post office is for a package from Shade, but today is Sunday.

We'll have to pick it up where he lost it. And lose it ourselves.

+

The king of rock 'n' roll was a 255-
pound junkie, an incontinent recluse
with a court of keepers and cooks on 24-
hour call to keep him cleaned, stroked,
and fed. Sometimes Elvis would compare
himself to Jesus breaking bread with his
disciples as he and the gang chowed
down the greasy southern cooking Elvis
loved. (John Lahr, *New York*)

+

Today is January 12, 1992. 10:32 Mountain Standard Time. So in the meantime mean time freezeframes our subject's matter, losing it to find it. Though at Jericho we see that matter is naught but frozen music. To defrost, we improvise something hot. The walls shake and shimmy, turn to jelly. We wail at the wall but not the wail of the white bargain hunter, the white whale. The one that gulps you for not doing what you're supposed to do, hell's belly, for should we not care about Nineveh, that great city, today in northwestern Iraq? We wail about the hand writing on its wall whose graffitti mean something does not love it, wants it down, whether at Brandenberg Gate or Mandelbaum Gate. But the walls of the Old City like ghetto walls if they keep you out they also keep you in. Before you go AWOL reflect a wall can make the difference. You can see yourself. Wall as street not barrier. A medium of exchange, of trade. A medium is a trade like any other form of communion. Answering prayers. Please give money to the account of anyone who works for peace, freedom, good will. Oedipus-Messiah-Golem-Frankenstein-Hal. What do you think? Every oedipus is a messiah who messes up. "Good afternoon, gentlemen. I'm a HAL 9000 computer. I became operational at the HAL plant in Urbana, Illinois, on the 12th of January, 1992."

Messedipus. We forgot to mention Ron's an invention. Silicon and fiber optic, solid state. Bar coded, trade marked, copywritten. A nomad now no longer mad. Crazy maybe. He prefers the artificial to real bone and gristle. Prick him he doesn't bleed. Tickle him he doesn't laugh.

He recapitulates.

He's the Real Me in the Space Bubble looking down at city up at World Trade the dreaded lockjaw takes hold. The dreaded jaw locked by back lash that starts with the visitation of the legendary judaical nonogenarian mother at the mythic nursing home. The legendary mother does not want to be fitted with a pair of shoes today she doesn't need a pair of shoes. It doesn't matter that she has no shoes a pair of shoes will materialize. The legendary mother knows there is a sinister conspiracy against her which has unwittingly involved her children and whose agent perhaps also unwittingly is the shoe clerk. She knows there is an attempt to impose shoes through an assertion of sheer power and after all she's right. The legendary mother wants no shoes, neither moccasin nor sandal, neither sneaker nor slipper, neither right shoe nor left shoe. Nor does the legendary mother want lunch. Above all the legendary mother doesn't want chocolate ice cream. What the legendary mother wants is to fall down on the sidewalk and lie there until her loving son picks her up. Which is what she does, the mother burden as he lifts hitting the Real Me like whip lash resulting in a lashed back resulting in considerable inactivity, especially sexual and leading to the dreaded lockjaw. He understands what's happening, he's smart. It happens anyway. His jawbone goes crick-crick. Elemental my dear Watson. You can bet he's a marionette. Controlled by strings of DNA. It is then that the Real Me must fulfill his destiny as the famous Man of Clay, the mute mutant who communicates only in writing and has stealth image evasion capability through the secret of invisibility conferred by ultra-smart mind jamming jew jitsu, the fabled one who doesn't screw can't speak and can only excel. And in excelling saves his race including the legendary mother and for which he gets an A. Right on his forehead. He's an adult. Aged thirteen. He's acutely effective in this world. He's like a sharp instrument, purely instrumental. Her son the doctor. But he doesn't care about anything. He screws without pleasure, laughs without humor. Then of course the Man of Clay, drunk with power and confronted with emotional demands too complex for his simple nature simply runs amok. A is for Angry. A is for Amok. On the point of destroying the entire community he can only be controlled by the secret phrase uttered by Rabbi Loew to his kabbalistic offspring the Golem in like circumstances: Go home and go to bed. A is for Abort. He gives up. Recapitulated, he capitulates.

The Real Me knows good advice when he hears it. He goes home and he goes to bed. But when he wakes up he feels like his head is twisted. He's had a recap and it hurts. He feels like he's been decapitated and had his head sewn on backwards. He doesn't know exactly what they've done to him this time but it has the feel of new equipment. With his new angle of focus he scans different data. His scopes are retooled. His screen has more depth and detail like they've engineered more pixels to the inch. He runs a diagnostic. His logic chip is altered. Cause no longer couples easily with effect. Something's wrong with his toggle function. No more on/off, yes/no. His digitals have fidgets. He bogs back to analog. The passive-amok polarity is absent from his specs. His banzai button is deactivated. The things that passed his tolerance threshold, activating his rage reaction, merely make him sad and sore. Like a muscle uncramping. He's as stupid as a peasant and he feels things more. It's too complicated. It's enough to drive a peasant crazy. Because when he feels more it means more data with more options and then he needs to do more and that's just what he doesn't want to do. He wants to withdraw.

He looks in the mirror and his mark is gone. He's filled with fellow feeling and he almost wants to rejoin the human race. But not quite. He knows he's a rat and the ship is sinking. He'll wait. A new season is imminent, possibly spring, which in New York comes like a truck unloading. He waits at his key board with fear and exhilaration to assess its unknown merchandise. To access what comes his way. His mode is random access. I, RaMSCaN. The Real Me. The one who dies.

+

The Iraqi had chopped off the fingers
and gouged out the eyes of his brother
and then shot him five times in the head.
"He said he wanted to do the same thing
to the Iraqi. The man then chopped off
his fingers. We watched as he gouged
out his eyes. We had never seen anything
like that. It was disgusting. The eyes
popped out like eggs." (*New York Times*)

+

Faster than anyone expects, the war is over. Schwarzkopf, the commanding general, reacting to reports of Iraqi atrocities, says, "They're not part of the same human race, the people who did that, as the rest of us are." My Constant Companion cries every time she hears of a war experience affecting an individual. There is no human race. Let's start next century with a clean slate. The only race left in this century is the one for the nearest exit.

+

The captives of Kuwait City zoo did not
escape the ravages of Iraq's occupation.
Inside, a pair of hippopotamuses lie
together on the grass, barely breathing as
they slowly die of starvation. A great
Indian elephant whimpers for attention,
reaching out with its trunk, in a com-
pound bare of food or water. When and
how the animals' torment began is
difficult to ascertain. There is no one
around to speak for the few who remain.
(*New York Times*)

Today we have to make a life and death decision about an operation for our mother who can no longer speak for herself. Whether to cut out her womb. In the hospital bed her gown falling open to expose scar of amputated breast. We close our eyes.

+

Meanwhile we have a very unusual experience. We're sitting at the computer next to the glass wall in the Space Bubble when suddenly Elvis flies in through the window. What's unusual about it is that the windows are closed, but he flies through them anyway without breaking the glass. He has little golden wings that fold back into his shoulder blades and he's wearing a gold lamé jumpsuit and a ruffled Spanish shirt. On the back of the jumpsuit in rhinestones the initials, J.C. He says, Ron, you're probably wondering why I'm here. I'm here because I'm worried about you. I'm worried about you because you worry about things too much. So now don't worry about what's going to happen next. What we're going to do to you is all for your own good.

A helicopter hovering next to the window shoots out a sort of gangplank and then we blank out.

The next thing we know we're in a flying saucer without any clothes on, surrounded by men in what looks like medieval armor. There's a sign on the wall in flashing red neon that says, Ingot We Trust. Elvis is telling us that after doing a mammalgram they're going to give us a memory transfusion, just like the one they gave him, but before they do he wants to tell us that we shouldn't worry because everything is taken care of. What I'm doing here I'm an impostor, he says. I mean I'm an apostle. Did you think it was a coincidence that George Bush received the surrender of the Evil Empire on the island of Malta? he asks. Or that he was a member of Skull and Bones and head of the CIA? Don't worry about these things, the Kennedy assassinations, the Tri-Lateral Commission, Black Monday, the Unseeables, the War. It all makes sense. From Yalta to Malta, it all makes sense in the name of the Golden Calf. Because the Golden Calf is something you can see, and seeing is believing. It's history. It's fact. And it's the law. We only kill those who break the law. Especially those who break the law for the sake of its letter. We call them letter carriers and we consider them very dangerous because they can send you letters that twist your head. But you won't have to worry any more because after this you'll be one of us. And once we're done with you you're going to believe that everything in this book was made up, including what we're doing to you now. Check your shadow at the door.

Now drink this bouillon, he says. He presses to our lips a fuming chalice filled with yellow fluid, fresh piss or liquid gold. We drink.

That's the last thing I remember. But it's true, I now believe that all this was made up. Except the next day I did go to the post office to pick up the package and it was from Shade, a package in brown paper wrapping about the size of a pair of cowboy boots. I could hardly wait to get it home. When I was finally back in the Space Bubble I tore it open. It was a pair of cowboy boots. A pair of old, worn-out Tony Lama cowboy boots, but they were bronzed. They came boxed with a wooden stand they fit into, and on the stand there was a bronze plaque that said: The Lone Ranger's Cowboy Boots—Liberty and Justice for All.

Just then there was a crash at the apartment door, like a crash of surf, actually more of a fizz, like when you drop the alka-seltzer in the water but amplified a hundred times, and nothing remained of the door besides a dense acrid smell. The door was simply sort of deconstructed qua door and reconstituted as odor. Two things walked in. They were wearing metal body armor and helmets with gas masks and horns. Their feet were orange and webbed, they had red pincers for hands. Their voices were gargly. We're from the Crusade, one said. Hand it over.

I tried to grab it but one pushed me lightly on the chest and I went careening against the opposite wall. The other picked up the empty box and put it under his arm. As they left I heard one saying to the other, These creatures are incredibly stupid.

And I heard the other one reply, Yes, stupid. But beautiful.